THE GOOD REMAINS

ALSO BY NANI POWER

Crawling at Night

NANI POWER

THE GOOD REMAINS

Grove Press
New York

Published simultaneously in Canada
Printed in the United States of America

FIRST EDITION

Library of Congress Cataloging-in-Publication Data

Power, Nani.

The good remains / Nani Power.—1st ed.

p. cm.

ISBN 0-8021-1720-1

1. Neonatologists—Fiction.   2. Hospitals—Fiction.   3. Villages—Fiction.

4. Virginia—Fiction.   I. Title

PS3566.O83577 G66 2002

813'.6—dc21   2002027163

Design by Laura Hammond Hough

Grove Press

841 Broadway

New York, NY 10003

02 03 04 05   10 9 8 7 6 5 4 3 2 1

FOR NANCY AND EUGENE O'CONNOR

Dear Punch,—I live in lodgings. I am one of those poor unfortunate helpless beings, called Bachelors, who are dependent for their wants and comfort upon the services of others. If I want the mustard, I have to ring half a dozen times for it; if I am waiting for my shaving water, I have to wander up and down the room for at least a quarter of an hour, with a soaped chin, before it make its appearance.

But this system of delay, this extreme backwardness in attending to one's simplest calls, is invariably shown a thousand times more backward about Christmas time.

I am afraid to tell you what I have endured this Christmas. My persecutions have been such to almost make me wish that Christmas were blotted out of the calendar altogether.

I have never been called in the morning at the proper time. My breakfast has always been served an hour later than usual—and as for dinner, it has been with difficulty that I have been able to procure any at all!

This invasion of one's habits and comforts is most heart-rending; and the only excuse I have been able to receive to my repeated remonstrances has been, 'oh, Sir, you must really make some allowances; pray recollect it is Christmas time.'

Last week I invited some friends to spend the evening with me—but I could give them neither tea, nor hot grog, nor supper, nor anything—because, 'Please, Sir, the servant has gone to the Pantomime—she's always allowed at Christmas time.'

Now, sir, it seems to me that Christmas is, with a certain class of people, a privileged time of the year to commit all sorts of excesses, to evade their usual duties, and to jump altogether out of their customary avocations into others the very opposite of them. For myself, I am extremely glad that Christmas does come but once a year. I know I shall go, next December, to Constantinople, or Jerusalem, or the Minories, or some place where the savage customs I have described do not exist; for I would not endure another Christmas here for any amount of holly, plum pudding, or Christmas boxes in the world.

I have the misfortune to remain, Mr. *Punch*
'An Old Bachelor'

stave one

the people.

love roller coaster, 1

I.

I expect this is the end my kind friends so let it be known:

C.R. is dead. Wounded, locked, and deserted. Though, mind you, no autopsy would be appropriate on these ruddy bones, such hair and epidermal generosity. Lifeless in his office, this posh tomb. Littered war zone of desk, bookcase, taxidermied fox on a mount, hundred-year-old Turkish Belouche rug (burned by a Salem in one corner), and a picture of ex-girlfriend (**Eleanor,** brunette, tan). Add to that debris bourbon, a box of Triscuits, an oily geodome of hacked cheddar cheese upon a pile of papers. The window, with its industrial fillip of poly-blend curtained swag, hints at late afternoon, of darkening clouds pulling across sky. Note his working jaws of worry, the stale odor of failure, and lastly, a portrait on the wall, to which he speaks:

Ah, my good Colonel. Friends, this stately fellow in a velvet chair, stump of leg beside him like a faithful dog, is my esteemed companion and ancestor, Colonel Benjamin "Shrub" Harrison Ash. A physician as well, from the bloody fields of the Civil War.

God save C.R. Bring on the vale of tears.

Call the man in question here, **Dr. Carroll Randolph Ash** (*Hell, you can call me* **C.R.** *That's what my friends say, C.R., you son of a bitch. Yessir*),

Corpse Reviver, Confirmed Rebel, what have you. There's a full glass of Virginia Gentleman Bourbon in his little silver tumbler, he wears a tattered sheepskin vest of his father's (*old Doc Carrie, bought things and never gave them up*), his feet are on the desk, his elegant tanned ankles (*my best part, thoroughbred*) entwined. A famed doctor of neonatology; you may have heard of him. If you are the parents of a too-early-born baby the size of a remote control in this part of Virginia, no doubt you'd know him well, the easy banter of his speech, his white coat slumped on a lanky frame during rounds. You'd regard the man as a form of demigod if your child now played and laughed in the backyard, or a dark shadow in your mind's chifforobe, a reminder of your infant's last days.

A podium-leaning, loafered soldier in the realm of bililights and naso-gastric tubes who invented the cross-venous-nutrient plan (*or CVNP, some call it, I'd be happy to update you, later, to my field, if you like. Fascinating stuff*). A clutter of Plexiglas awards lies on the second walnut shelf in his office, gathering dust.

Fond of history, of antique things.

Old letters, retro wars, specifically the Civil War (*buff, you could say. Love that stuff, just love it*). And the last couple of years he's been drawn and fascinated by the ultimate hobby, the reenactment of battles from the Civil War, though he's never done it, but he longs to (*I'm real fascinated with Ball's Bluff, here in Virginia, probably because we own some land right up to it, to the edge, probably because our own people died on that field*), has subscribed to *Reenactor's Journal*, even bought some period clothes (*I got this, this old jacket, a shirt and such, a belt, just a start, you know*), and really thinks one day he'll join up with those folks and try it out, give it a shot (*I mean I don't know what kind of freaks they might be and all, but it seems like it may be a hoot, you know, out in that canvas tent, feeling like you're really there*).

Don't particularly care for firearms myself. A six-month internship in the ER singed any interest there, the massive rechiseling of flesh by bullets throughout the night, mingled with alcohol and the stale-tobacco stench of trauma-induced nicotinic acid, pretty much offered distaste, despite the fact he'd enjoyed wild turkey hunting as a boy with his father. Yet, thank you, no. (*My great grandpa's shotgun, hand-carved of walnut and brass, lays upstairs. Any of you that cares for that stuff may try it out. I enjoy some good doves, wrapped in bacon.*)

But, he thinks: What's it like to flare nostrils in the hazy attar of gunpowder freshly shot in the air, all sharp and spicy—mixed with human sweat, blood, entrails, crushed grass, amoebic mud—O, he wonders about real life fisted in his face as opposed to the tang of that scrubby iodine brush he uses every day, pale coffee, nurses' deodorant, the goddamned Lysol, that *sweet perfume* on everything, that vanillic whiff of a new baby with a leg like a pigeon's plucked wing, that's the odor in his clothes, his hair, his boxers even, not acrid sweat or burned cornmeal from a cast-iron pot, but this rosy pomander of life, the smell that singularly makes him feel old. That and those candy stripers.

More bourbon.

(*Aah, shoot, what I wouldn't do for some Brunswick stew. Like my mother used to make*). Knocks off his shoes and lays his feet back on the desk. Tosses the empty Triscuit box in a slow lob across the room, missing the trash can and spilling a soft cracker dust.

Damn.

A tentative cause for his demise:

Above his fine head of hair, in room 233G, on the second floor, a woodsy conference room for mucky-mucks, they are meeting, discussing Dr. C.R. Ash with furrowed brows, talking of a certain Baby Hodges, and necrotizing enterocolitis (NEC, in the doctor talk), and the various protocol of feeding, and C.R.'s blatant misconduct and out-and-out irresponsibility. Therefore, unbeknownst to most of the hospital, but not C.R. himself, nor his secretary, they are drawing up excuses to fire the man.

Immediately.

C.R. is impatient. Half sad and half happy, half drunk, half a hard-on thinking of a young candy striper (*her thighs, Shrub, soft as melon meat*). He has written, scratched out a letter on a piece of parchment paper he found in a specialty paper store (*it looked good, like it coulda been Lee's own type of paper, Mosby might've had that type of paper, it works, you coulda, Shrub*), written in pen and ink and sealed it with wax, and the letter says:

Dear Sirs and Madam:
Having received communications from your office and elsewhere, and being desirous of knowing *what* my *rank* really is, have the goodness to enlighten me accordingly and oblige,

Very Respt yrs obt svt
C.R. Ash
Commanding 1st Specl Batt
Ball's Bluff Babies Hospital

C.R. copied this directly from a journal on the battle of Ball's Bluff he was reading. It seemed important-sounding and he liked the jokiness of it and also, C.R. did not give a hoot if those mastodons choked on their own upchuck. He waited, drank, and drew up another letter with the pen and ink:

Dear Sirs and Madams,
Being in arrest awaiting charges I respectfully request that the arrest may be suspended and I may be permitted to serve in some capacity as a candy striper's assistant. I believe the uniform will suit my willowy frame. I am sure you gentlemen will appreciate how important a candy striper is to this fine establishment.

Very Respt yrs obt svt,
Dr. C.R. Ash

It gave him momentary pleasure to imagine those grayed old creatures in the wooded room reading that and saying *What?* and how, fast as buttermilk poured across a linoleum floor in that hot sticky Virginia air, it would spread to everyone in that hospital, full of bleach-washed bloody smocks and hacked limbs and cancerous globs and hypodermic needles and crying children and steamed green beans the color of army fatigues, soon everyone that worked there would say *What?* It was only, though, a flickering pleasure. Like satifying himself in the executive men's room as he heard his longtime friend and comrade, **Dr. Pendleton Compton,** washing his hands while he thought furtively of the patient who turned him on, it was a fleeting thing, over in a second, a brief quiver which left him flattened with regret.

2.

His birdish secretary for sixteen years now with shaking hands because she knows there is something gravely wrong, first, a certain *issue* with a candy striper and now, well, the bourbon, this weird letter, poor Dr. C.R. all bleary, talking to the painting (*You know Betty, don't you, Shrub?*), mumbling about his old dog. She sits outside the room, poised in feline expectancy for the tiniest sign.

Of what to do. Hands in her lap. Her computer screensaver awhirl with cats. She waits.

This is **Betty Owens,** native of the area, faithful aide-de-camp.

She's been a good secretary these sixteen years, out of love, not job responsibility. Fifty, a tiny puckered mountain wren, bones with a skin crust, her figure almost adolescent, wraith in silhouette but for the papery crook starting in the shoulders, up close her eyes, wide and brown, still seem to belong to a smudge-faced imp, she wrests them around the room, flitting, searching for a place to land. Her hair, short brown bob held in place by a single hairband of grosgrain, very simple cotton Talbots clothing and her mother's pearls, a brooch of a cat with pearled eyes given as a gift by a patient, Betty saves things, like lace remnants, rubber bands from the mail, like C.R.'s whole career, she scoots around and puts out fires.

It would be stated, if Betty were doing so, that she is also *the proud owner of three cats, my pride and joys, oh, they are quite unique little personalities, I mother them, I care for them like a mother would, Charlie, Mariah, Dunny.*

Dunny is the rascal, the baby of the lot. He rips up my good chairs, pulls out my needlepoint, they get heavy cream in the evening for their coats. She reads Thackeray, she'd say, and Dickens and Thoreau, though her bedside table reveals Jude Deveraux, and so she consumes those novels se-cret-ly.

C.R. is in a bleary mood, the type of mood liquor brings on, the kind that doesn't care for the moments to come, but focuses in a mopish way on the past. It's getting dark outside his large window in his office in the hospital, the night wintery amidst the background of plush evergreens, and it may snow, it has that crisp stillness in the air. It's a good night for all, working with the usual diligent patter, the green-smocked padding around. Clumps of pastel-draped workers around the various sectionals created for the ad-mittance of patients and bulletin-boarded updates. The ill in the various examining rooms, some silently staring, others entombed in plastic devices. The sweet shudder of the automatic doors swish to the moving feet, the beds, the mourning, the celebrating, the afraid. All lies in normal pace in the elec-trified cacophony of beeps and clicks, the technological backdrop of a hos-pital murmur, yet there exists a promise of frivolity, for tonight, at 7:30, will be the holiday party over in the huge main conference room of the Lord Fauquier Wing, the invite lays propped on many of the hospital's cubicled offices, the holly-patterned card, with the scripted *Good Cheer to All! A Dickens Christmas!* All interns, all fellows, all orderlies, all nurses, all phy-sicians, gravely suture and insert and snip and inject, yet smile in anticipa-tion: a grog, a grope. Holiday parties can be fun.

Tosses more bourbon, talks out loud, his eyes up to Colonel Shrub.

You remember Candy Striper? Hell, you ought to, saw her in here, right? Am I not out of my mind for wanting her or would you've been as strong in those, freaking conditions, a young girl, a sweet thing, blond, and you know I got a thing for blonds, a really big thing for sweet, creamy, buttery blonds with pink cheeks. Oh, shit.

He pauses and Shrub still looks down admiringly.

*   *   *

Shrub, my friend, a cc is a small amount, a very small amount, barely a soupçon, so to speak, a dash, a piffling substance, why, I've just drunk down about a thousand ccs just now of sour mash, yet to these babies, Shrub, a cc is a hell of a lot. You start with a half a cc, see, of breast milk that is, tube-fed of course, just a bleep of milk, and sees how it goes. See if they can handle it. That's the art. Knowing how much and when. Because that Baby Hodges had been on an IV since Saturday, a nine hundred grammer and doing OK, that girl not even named him, that's no good, we're saying, come on, now, give him a name, but her eyes all bleary just staring, so we call him "Tuffy," so Tuffy, see, seems ready for a dash of milk, ready for his supper, so to speak, so I order the dose, one cc, one damn cc, but I don't know, Shrub, I don't know.

Bourbon required.

Back to the one cc, after making this choice I proceeded to instruct Nurse to gavage him, you know, Shrub, we stick a tube down his esophagus to the stomach and hook a syringe on there and just let, you know, let him have the drop, no big deal though I sure as hell wouldn't like that done to me, but you know, Shrub, this is what we do, sir, it's all for the best of the child, and the little ones don't seem to have a gag reflex so, uh, that's that. Then I do a check on the residuals, check out the contents of the stomach by doing a gavage tube suctioning, unfortunately encountered bile and the kid gets all bloated, bad sign, therefore had to decompress the child's stomach activities—

Performed a series of X rays and noted a serious thickening and a few air pockets in the baby's intestinal walls which indicated to me, a serious state, a very bad complication of necrotizing enterocolitis, basically you see, sir, circulation to the intestines is cut off, sorta, and maybe during hypoxia or chronically poor circulation from, say, an open ductus in the heart or something, the normal bacteria goes haywire and just eats on itself, see, and they invade, then they cause gas bubbles that swell up and the whole thing can break up and perforate and cause all kinds of hell in there, a civil war of the personal body, see, Shrub, and in this case, a disastrous case, a bloody one, a Gettysburg. In this case, morbidity, my man.

Now you see, morbidity is the deal around here. Once a month we get together in that big office up on the seventh floor, they got all sorts of catered victuals, paltry ham sandwiches, potato salad, brownies, all that stuff brought in stretched out in Saran Wrap, yeah, I notice that stuff for some reason, anywho, we sit in that room, have a working lunch, munching sandwiches and chitchatting. That would surely annoy the French, wouldn't it? So then, we talk of morbidity, in vague, nonhuman tones. Case #3—Hawkins: Morbidity caused by sepsis, further aggravated by shutdown of vital organs. Twenty-five weeks, 790 grams. We discuss the doctor's actions with Hawkins. Had an aggressive treatment of antibiotic intravenous been followed? (Mr. and Mrs. Hawkins loped in that Saturday, from Warrenton, at 6:10 because of the call of the doctor, they carried a plush purple bunny for Jake, their firstborn, there was a steady calm inevitability in the doctor's voice, a worsening of conditions, a graveness, he explained, they had gone to BuyBuy Baby yesterday and bought a navy blue stroller—*Should we get the green?* they had discussed, *No, I think Mom mentioned she'd be getting that snowsuit in the blue fleece, you know, the one at BabyGap.*) Had an expedient set of bloods been done on the baby as apnea worsened? Naturally, said Steadman, physician on the case, who leaned back in his suede chair, nurses checked the levels and saw the decline, he said in his even factually enunciated voice, we did procedure down to the nth on this one, it was just, as they say, one of those things (*I think a border, well, this one, hon, this one of giraffes would be cute, around the edge of the room, did you manage to get that shelf up, because I need the space for his lamp here, is that the phone? Mike, get the phone, honey*).

During Steadman's monologue on his clinical machinations with this poor infant's situ, I found myself thinking: What was it like in that green Honda Civic driving across the rural road of Route 50 at 1:00 that night for the Hawkinses after Jake coded, or in your jargon, *passed away*, after the nurses disconnected the plugs and wrapped him in the hospital blue blanket as she, Maggie (*I guess a Winnie-the-Pooh theme is good, but, you* know, *the classic Pooh, though, not the Disney*), sat in one of the nursery's white gliders and they handed her the tiny bundle, think of the weight of a roll of toilet paper, think of the length, the width of a small beer bottle, a little grayish head the size of those tiny Christmas tangerines my mother used to love and the poor father, Mike, his hand around the baby (*When does Little League start, anyhow? Is it five or four?*), the screen painted with yellow balloons put up to shield morbidity from the other families holding their baby's squirrel paw hands, speaking in droning, hymn voices. What was it like as they drove home that evening—did music play or was it silent? Did Maggie cry or was she immobilized? Did the stars sweeping across the deep Virginia sky charm as always or was there a steely pain to the shards of light, a cutting flatness now that came from the cosmos?

Would they ever love again?

3.

That was the first thought, Shrub, that brought me to dillydally in the doctor's no-man's-land, sitting there playing with my potato chips on the caterer's plastic plate, Steadman's voice whining on, discussing, as it occurred to me suddenly, this whole family's well-being as casually as if he was ordering french fries at a drive-thru McDonald's, *it was the, uh, usual standards, leading to this case of morbidity, nothing irregular,* I thought beyond the patient's facts, like peering up under your buddy's mother's dress surreptitiously when you dropped your yo-yo, I just had to see, even if it was scary or, I just had to see what I've been missing, I saw the Hawkins pain or tried to feel it, I got beyond the anesthetizing we sometimes think in these moments, or worse, the impulse of *OK, one less chart to think about,* moving on, like that quick sniff a deer gives a dead one in their momentary acknowledgment, *so that's that.* And then, it was shortly thereafter, the candy striper I have been referring to simply as *Candy Striper*—the girl I had been talking to daily and offering fancy Italian chocolates and watching her push the cart and giving her change for the Coke machine and telling her silly jokes when she goes by with a bouquet (*Now is that for me? Why, ain't you romantic*)—fell into a bit of trouble.

* * *

There was a huge rush of personnel one afternoon, the cart of life came whirling by, a few muffled sobs came from the hall. Something was up, son! Code fucking blue, baby! We all came outside our offices and Betty ran into my office to call me up to the OR, *oh, sir,* breathlessly rushed from her mouth, *you are needed at OR stat,* I wiggled on my coat, OK, OK, no problem, wondering why the *hell* she's being so squirrelly for something so usual, hell, I handle premies all day long, but she says, her face sweaty and pink, it's that *girl,* C.R., that girl, the candy striper, she's had *an infant* (even then, I thought with a flash of irritation, call it a *baby,* for Christ's sake, woman), yes, an infant in the bathroom, and it's tiny and that thing can't be more than six months, she's from a fine family, the Hodgeses, up the road there, I can't believe it, I'll need to call her mother, oh, Lord.

Understand, Colonel: That sweet, soft thing, that candy striper, gave birth.

Silence. C.R. stops talking, takes a deep breath. Another swig of bourbon.

4.

Back on that day, Betty's hands flicked around the phone and finally her little creaky voice urged on information and she pressed "1" to automatically dial the number, it was thirty cents extra, but surely this was urgent, and finally the ladylike voice of Cynthia Hodges came through, yes?

Hello?
Uh, Cynthia?
Yes?
It's Betty Owens.
Well, hi, Betty! How are you, dear?
I'm very well thanks, uh. Cynthia?
Yes? Her voice got pale and liquidy because she understood, in the nanosecond feeling appraisal done by women, a *wrong tone,* a deer's bleat, something off, *is there—?*

Cynthia, I need you, dear, to come down to the hospital. Something's up with **Kirsten.**

Oh God. Oh God. Is she dead. Dear Lord!

Oh, no, no, Cynthia, no she's not dead but. But there's a been a situation, a, a,—

5.

That was approximately three months ago.

Yes, C.R. did dutifully run down and smock himself and fall into the OR, where the girl he'd been sharing a light repartee with (*Oh, dear, you're wearing pink, don't you know you set my heart on fire in that color,* as he offered her a chocolate, he gave all people who crossed his path *chocolates*), the girl in question lay still and white, crying softly, the nurse by her side, and C.R. directed the staff to c-pap the child (a-nine-hundred-and-ninety-gram infant), who was consuming 80 percent room oxygen, happily, who avoided intercranial hemorrhaging, who still would need to cross the path of stomach, eye, hearing, and other difficulties, breathing disorders, apnea spells, feeding complications, bradycardia, yet who lay after two hours and difficult state-of-the-art interference in his tiny warm isolette and meanwhile, the girl, the candy striper, sobbed into the nurse's arm, *I didn't know, I didn't know, I thought, I thought, I thought, I was late because of gym or those diet pills, I knew I was fatter I ate cookies too much I couldn't wear my skirts and I thought you had to do it to get a baby I never really did I thought I thought,* and the nurse patted her arm.

Her mother came in, her face a torn strip of pale skin, and then the door closed and C.R. said to Betty, *send some roses up from me, will you,* and Candy Striper then was released with her mom and they went home and after school candy-striping became temporarily inconvenient (Mrs. Feittles-Lopez said, *Let's take a break for a while, shall we,* patting Kirsten's gown-clad knee). She would come to the hospital to visit "Tuffy," as the nurses called him, since she wouldn't name him, the candy striper figured if he grew stronger she would, but it was three weeks later that Tuffy lost weight and apnea grew and his insides flirted with bacteria and his stomach bloated and then C.R. probably made the miscalculation of increasing his feedings instead of discontinuing, the infamous application of the one cc, and Tuffy died at 4:38 P.M. due to severe sepsis and actually on many levels the family seemed almost relieved, it had already come to C.R.'s attention that Tuffy had indeed suffered some brain bleeding and most likely would be incapacitated cerebrally, and Candy Striper didn't feel relief as much as a new leaf open up, a new chapter, her stomach was normal, hormones had leveled, she no longer bled from between her legs, all felt healed and Tuffy was gone, and she came back to candy-striping, the uniform fit snugly and her breasts were bigger and she passed C.R.'s office one evening and he said his same comments (*Springtime just breezed by, aaaaah*) and she lingered, and said, who's that? pointing to the portrait.

That, that was a very fine Civil War surgeon. My cousin, actually. Name of Colonel Shrub, that's who.

What's this?

That, my dear, is a surgical kit from the Civil War, they cut off people's legs with that thing there,

Oh my God! She recoiled from the leather case and stood back.

And of course she'd have a chocolate, and she sat in his leather chair, the girl had a half-woman, half-baby thing going on that was confusing to all, especially C.R., who didn't know whether to flirt or comfort or lecture or ignore her, but the fact she hung around his office on some level irritated him (note the pile of charts he must fill) but also intrigued in the flesh and the mind (*object all you want, but we're made this way, people, God don't make mistakes*), she sat in the chair, spinning, and as he smiled he noted that her postpartum physique still lingered yet her face remained pink and doughy as an infant's, so damn soft as a pillow, dear God, these children have relations at a young age, he thought, who's the scoundrel that managed to get in her pants? Was it a one-time deal or what? Are children as promiscuous as they'd have you believe on 20/20?

Why did Tuffy die, Doctor Ash?

*   *   *

Whoa, that snapped him to, her eyes pooled up, and she whispered it: *Was there some particular thing or was he too small, or is it because I didn't name him?* Tears now. *Can you tell me why?*

And he had started to think about that stuff then, too, you see, that was when the Hawkins baby died and C.R. sat in on the morbidity meeting and thought of that couple and cried driving back home to his graveled estate, he actually cried, and if she had asked him a question like this two months ago he would've said the usual (*crap, I would've said the usual crap, Shrub, you know the levels, the bloods, the sepsis, the rudimentary science answers, the back pats*), but this time he said I don't know, I don't know why anything lives or dies, why any fucking thing does any fucking thing (*bourbon, yes, these are fragile times*), and his eyes looked glossy and sad, and this *girl-woman, woman-girl,* what in hell is she, why's it so confusing? Why? Got up and reached for my hand, I guess I had faltered and seemed the sorry one, and with the audacity of a woman, not a child—closed, closed my door!

It was six o'clock so, yes, most had gone home, but holy shit, a closed door does not look good. Did I care? Does one care? Is propriety worth living for? Or do we just go with the screwing up in the name of, what is it, love, sex? She had switched from girl-woman quickly to all woman, that was easy to do with that look she turned around with, a downward dark glance in my eyes, she went to my CD player as I looked up in a wet-eyed stupor, and put in *Hits from the Seventies* and played "Love Roller Coaster" by the Brothers Johnson, a favorite tune of my hip swinging youth, and looked me in the eye, got behind my desk, this young mother thing, this girl in the short pink and white skirt, and held my hands to her face, that shirt she wore, the pink-striped outfit, like a candy cane, she placed my hands on her face, and as I leaned forward, forward into the airy warmth of this child, I smelled the fresh scent of bloody newborns and rain and I lay against her, and the song played it's crazy course, she moved her hips, my old mouth, with its gray stubble, got inside her lips, my tongue felt joy, boy, I danced inside that girl's mouth, I thought not of Tuffy but of pinkness and bourbon and being young and feeling good and *passion,* and passion, Colonel Shrub, passion is the soul of everything and if you ain't got passion (*and his hands felt around her ass, pulling up her uniform*) then you are indeed dead, toss out adultery, toss out incompetence, toss out loser, toss all your words on me (*in the corner showing her tiny mint green panties, pale as spring grass*), throw them down on me, Shrub, throw the whole goddamn world, I got passion and I'm fucking alive.

Doctor Carroll Randolph Ash

Room 222 Neonatal Intensive Wing

703-568-4500 extension 36

Betty —

I'm thinking Ham to day,
or Brunswick stew,
Call up the Club and see
what's up today.

No SALAD.
NO DAMN TURKEY BREAST.

—— CANCEL MY APPTS IN THE AFTERNOON,
FEELING POORLY.

love roller coaster, 2

I.

Some people do not care to knock on doors.

To some people, doors obscure the good way.

As it was, Dr. Pendleton Compton, chewing a toothpick after his wife Nancy's most excellent eggplant parmigiana, packed in her blue plastic Tupperware, had decided to stroll on by Peds, just at the same time C.R. and the candy striper were drawn to each other and the CD played in his office. A peak moment for C.R., a watershed incident. Pendleton merely sought to check out a few nurses, bid them hello. Quiver them with charm, or some such thing. Waste some time because then six appointments in the afternoon would mean tiny faulty valves in blue infants brought in by shaking mothers, and they would have no eyes for him. Why the hell, why the hell did he pick this vocation, heart mender of the tiny? He simply fell into it, he reminded himself. They said it was *rewarding*. This was the payment, the damaging part, sweet hurt babies laid down on crisp paper-rolled cot for examination by his large hands, that noxious picture on the wall of three bears in pajamas that everyone had to look at while he whirled a grease-soaked transducer across a baby's chest as it wailed, *unh-hunh*, he would say, the mother's eyes darting up to his brow with suspicion, *OK, yes, we'll schedule her for surgery next week.*

* * *

Oh, the pain.

Let me be the man who trudges garbage, who sweeps tunnels, who shoes horses. A man who cobbles the streets! Let me! Any other thing than the cold devil who mouths this bad, bad idea—your baby, my knife.

That, my friend, was the picture of his coming afternoon, six of them lined up anxiously, a half dozen families lined up in the room with the faintly pioneer-themed furniture, amidst piles of *Newsweek* and *National Geographic,* waiting for Pendleton. Thing is, the man was good. He was very good. He sewed little hearts well. He could be the Martha Stewart of heart stitching, he was so crafty with those large puffed-dough hands of his, hovering over the mauve pulp of an infant's chest.

And so, Pendleton ambled by Peds. Somebody save me. Somebody *love* me, my big old self. Can anybody just see through me, my suit, my big-ness, and see how I need something desperately, he thought, yet what he said, leeringly, was, *hey hon.* The nurse smiled awkwardly, shuffled away. Come back, O lovely one. I need your comfort. He ka-lunked a Diet Coke in the big shiny machine, and cracked it open.

He sniffed around Betty Owens' desk, his favorite, but she wasn't there. Empty Dunkin' Donuts cup on the desk with her coral bite on the edge. Meet with the man, he decided, ol' C.R., unload some angst on that mother, and then—

He rashly opened C.R.'s door. Uh, *whoopsie. Lord amercy. Damn.* He should've knocked. It might've been parents or someone in a heart-to-heart. Instead, he came through the door, coughed, and backed out, left. Fled like a Union officer. C.R. and the candy striper, doing nothing really, but it looked un*seemly,* my friend. I know unseemly. Too close and too disheveled. Kissing? And that old song, "Love Roller Coaster." Since when is that hospitally accepted? Hell, we a disco now? He used to jam to that, used to swing the old cooster. Afterward, sailing down in the elevater to his suite to sit for a few minutes before his appointments with sadness, Pendleton felt mad. Until "Love Roller Coaster" came pump-ing at him from C.R.'s CD player, he had become accustomed to the buttery, cinnamon-soaked boredom of his life due to the concept of rela-tive deprivation. Now, the man wondered what his life had become. His old friend, C.R., always getting some. He grew largely pissed off, craved a Snickers.

2.

A Snickers bar offers little consolation for the pain of the soul. It is cold, rough, and wobbly with plasticine innards. It resembles, unsavorably, a turd. Why eat it, he asks himself. He will psychobabble himself: It fills an inner void, you viperish fool. A loving void. A thrill-seeking void. He has inadvertently deadened himself in the name of comfort. Who, where, was the contract he signed with his own blood which said, *you will now cease to have fun*. A man who was a stud-muffin now was a, a plain *muffin*. A chocolate chip one shuffling his puffy can from one padded interior to another. How did the hot love he felt for Miss Nancy, pawing at her shimmying slip against the back shed of her mama's house on a Saturday night, the steam, the wet mouth, how did that promising future boil down to bathrobed nightly news side by side in an antique spool bed? Holy shit.

C.R. and him met when they were young. C.R.'s mother and his did Garden Club. **We boys crawled in dirt in the backyard, snuffing worms. Our mothers talked in kitchens, all the kitchens of the county, all the livelong day. Smell of biscuits high in the summer heat. His daddy made ham. The wax paper around the thing grew cloudier and wrinkled from the ham grease. Smell of hot woodstove, even in summer. The maid's voice as the back door slams, soft, smoky.** All made of an S, it seemed, Pendleton being a kid. Summer. Sex. Smoky. Snakes. Come down to: Snickers. Sad. Sorry, Soppy-assed sucker. Seersucker-wearing. That, too.

Where did I, Pendleton, turn off the road of high roller? In school, I was svelte. Stunning. I cut a rug. I traversed the county in fancy shoes. I wore tweed. I did cotillions and shit. I dazzled young women and they, *they*, smiled back. It was easy to be me. I ate good food, I drank brown liquor, I gained momentum. I was fresh. My C.R., he was my companion. The insults we lay on each other's young backs, in jest. We caroused. We drove. I enjoyed the man.

Was it marriage?

Would I still be me if I had stayed detached?

No boys, no Nancy, no French toast. No back of her neck. No slippers. No magazines in my bathroom in a rack she painted. No her holding me. No feet against mine, cold from the floor, under the covers. No curtains that cost two thousand dollars, that's for damn sure. This dude, though, the best friend of Pendleton's, in the arms of a young fluff of a girl. Same as high school. Not fair.

Pendleton, alone, a Snickers bar.

3.

Before Pendleton barged in, though, already the nurses had been sniffing around outside. A Closed Door, their own portable romance novel to snicker and croon about—who's the lucky one this time and all—and already the mastodons at that time perusing the Tuffy Hodges case found it odd and poor judgment and downright absurd, that when the infant showed such clear signs of gastrological disaster via his X rays, Dr. C.R. Ash requested the cc feeding, and thus they called in the board for further analysis, wondering if C.R. was off the deep end or something, too bad C.R. hadn't had a warning of the artillery setting up around him, or, perhaps he knew but didn't care, some of us chip away at life with a tiny hammer, piece by piece, some of us, though, sit still and then dynamite the whole damn thing.

C.R. continues to drink his bourbon this fine day in his office. The expiration of his soul has been described, yet the man's own gullet accepts this bitter juice willfully. It tastes rather unpleasant and he's had too much. He doesn't even really *like* liquor. But down it pours. He needs to be free and loose. It's the unlawfulness, the damage it represents. Liquor dehydrates the brain, rots the liver. He's seen it in the tissue.

I'm going to get some biscuits, Shrub, some fine buttered biscuits maybe with some good ham. There does exist a decent ham. My father used to cure it, he'd smoke the haunches outside in the woodhouse—

Dr. Ash?
Yes, Betty?

Are you all right, Dr. Ash?

I am fine and dandy, Betty hon, I am good. Sit down, Betty, sit—

Oh, Dr.—

C.R., goddammit, C.R.! Don't be so formal! Here, here, woman, on the couch, have a finger or two—

I don't really drink too much, Dr. Ash, and I just came—

Humor me, Betty. Help your old boss. For a bit, till I get my reserves back. One cube or two? Branch water or plain-Jane?

Uh, uh, one cube, a tad of water I suppose, honestly, I really don't thin—

—As I was telling my honorable Shrub here, my daddy would smoke hams up in the summer, cover them in pepper and soak them in the winter for two whole days, Betty, two days, and bake them with cloves and pepper he applied with a thumb in even circles. You like ham, Betty?

I, I've enjoyed boiled ham, on occasion. My sister, Pam, gets a honey ham at Thanks—

—*Honey ham! Honey ham!* Goddammity hell, Betty, You haven't lived! You've been lied to, fooled, swindled! Honey ham is a hunk of foul, sweet fat! That *shit* ham, pardon my language in front of a lady, is simply a piece of candy. You want a giant, pink piece of candy for meat or you want something real. Something *real*. Listen, Betty, there are certain good foods, certain. Betty, take a list—

Beg your pardon?

A memo, woman.

I see, uh, OK.

One: Virginia ham and biscuits, with butter. But—*ter*, to quote old Pendleton. But-*ttteerr*—

Virginia ham—

That's right. And biscuits all out of buttermilk, crispy on the edges. Yessir! You know, like they ate on the field, those boys out on Ball's Bluff. Sitting around the fire. They basically ate ham fat day in, day out. Stuck on a biscuit. I want to get back to my roots, hear. My roots are not *nachos*, woman. I am not from *pesto* or, or *bagels*. I am from ham, is what I'm saying. My people ate some good ham.

OK. I don't care for nachos, either, find them—

—*Two*, Brunswick stew with lima beans. Hell, with squirrel meat. Why not. Fresh squirrel from the Ashland hills. Lord knows we got enough of them.

Unh-hunh.

Three, a good tomato sandwich on white bread, with mayo. With salt and pepper. Lots of it!

OK.

Four. Four. Bourbon.

A food?

Bourbon is underrated, my dear. This is the good stuff. We don't know what we have. Liquid gold, it is. My poor Shrub had to drink Everclear mixed with creosote on his last live day, imagine that. Those poor boys. So, bourbon—

But, Doctor, a food?

A food, yes ma'am! Nourishment! Put this list up somewhere, like, like in the lounge, put it there and let them memorize it, let them whatever.

Are you *sure*, Dr. C.R.? Are—

Betty?

Yes, Dr. Ash?

I believe I'm going to get out of here.

Beg pardon, Dr. Ash.—

It's C.R., thank you Betty, and I said (he reaches up and grabs the painting, the surgical kit, puts his chocolates under his arm, his bourbon under his armpit) I gotta go. I'm leaving, I'm—

Oh, Dr. Ash, you'll get through this—

I don't care. Betty. I don't care.

Dr. Ash—

Oh, Betty, you've been great, take these chocolates, don't worry, I'll talk to them about you, set you up,

Dr. Ash (she says sobbing), Dr. Ash!

Betty, hon.

Dr. Ash.

He kisses her cheek, puts on a rumpled Stetson hat, the evening is setting in, and as the mastodons chomp their bits, discussing C.R., reviewing his excellent records, his body of work, his curriculum vitae, his morbidities, Pendleton coughs (he rehearses in his mind, *there is, gentlemen, a certain gossip, rumor, what have you, that there may be a improper relationship between Ash and a, uh, uh, candy striper girl*, what do you think of that? Goddamn bastard! But he holds back. It is his best old friend, after all. He feels subdued, he feels jealous, sad) and C.R. gets in his Jeep, snow starting to fall, the month of December always a favorite, it's Christmas, and when someone's in trouble, they think of the past, they visit the times things worked, snow whirling past the guard's face at the hospital gates, he could be thinking of the candy striper, who came out of his office *very* noticed that evening, it added to the embarrassment, to the notion he could be a human being, but he's not thinking of her, he's thinking of *Christmas parties*. Aren't there any? Where's a good party?

4.

Nowadays, he thinks, what *is* a party? A boring rehash of medical procedures, sparkled by the tinkle of ice wedded to liquor and a hunk of some prefrozen Kraft-made tidbit, resembling a wild product in a chemical sense. He would stand and laugh, maneuver the elbow of the lady he'd escorted over to another group of doctors whose asses he kicked in racquetball, or golf. Move to the next cluster. A joke, an amusing anecdote. A snippet of fake crab. Bourbon. Next group. Move on. Where was the sizzle of fun, the dazzle of old? Who knew.

There are certain things a young C.R. Ash looked forward to, and one was the occasion of a holiday party:

Meaning a Christmas party and even as a youngster, this was C.R.'s very favorite thing, the invitation coming in the mail, a dark green trim border a giveaway, or a gold wreath on the edge, the printed address of the hosts, Mr. and Mrs. Pendleton Charles Compton, etc., then his mother would take her bony hand and poke it into a bulletin board in the kitchen and draw a neat circle around the date, scribble *Compton*, and then about a week ahead, when all the parties started snowballing into one heightened season of car doors opening and slamming in frosted air, bundled people in coats, wafting perfume, patent leather shoes crunching in snow, crunch, crunch, crunch, knock, knock—Wellll! Come on in! Come on, Carrie! Helen! Wreaths on door and jingling bells, and smells, and, being twenty at this time, in his stiff bowtie and slicked-back hair, this being the Comptons, there was usually a ham, punch, and various warmed seafood canapes, C.R. being twenty had quickly drunk two potent family recipe eggnogs at the bar manned by his friend Pendleton (their son, the infamous Pendleton Compton, young, still trim in grass green jacket, with plaid bowtie, helping out his family) and eaten some crab dip, Beck Compton's famous creation (one pound of jumbo lump Maryland blue crab, chopped onion, a garlic clove mashed up, paprika, celery salt, mayonnaise, cream cheese, and Monterey Jack, heated for thirty minutes, served with water wafers, actually this was her maid Agnes's recipe, who made it from *Redbook* December 1939, who now made it for Beck's cocktail parties, and Beck called it her own). So C.R. ate some of that. He talked to George Custis Billings (*You sorry ass sucker, George, did I hear you going to Yale, boy? Are you abandoning our good Virginia tradition? I thought you'd got better sense*), then Mrs. Debutts (*Why, C.R., hon, how are you? How's it down at the university? Unh-hunh. I know your poor mother misses you. Pendleton, dear, I'll have a daiquiri, thank you, now you don't be a stranger, C.R.*), then Doctor Macgregor "Doc Mackie" Page (*You got to go on my rounds sometime, C.R., that'll show you something, university and all, but it's a fascinating thing, is. I got a case of gangrene, yesterday, what do you think of that? Gangrene!*). Doc Mackie and his father hunted hounds together. The man's hands trembled around his highball. Liver spots. He heard his mother's voice in the other room, *oh, grand!*

Lord, he was bored.

He heard carol singing.

Hey, Pendleton. Let's get out of here. Down to town. I don't know. Hell. The diner. A bar. Unh-hunh, just a coat. I'll tell Mother. Out front in five.

5.

They stood out oddly, one sandy-haired boy in a tweed coat, and a louder, larger boy with a shock of black hair and a plaid bowtie walking into the bar Joe's on the edge of their small town, on December 21st, when most people they knew in town were at Christmas parties, drinking eggnog or gnawing on ham, and they walked in to the tinny beat of disco, saw two couples grinding on the floor, it was actually a black bar, they'd never been before, it was kind of forbidden, so everyone's eyes flashed on the couple for a moment, but then flitted away as they approached the bar and ordered whiskey, another song came on and two girls came in, one with an Afro and black-lined eyes, she wore a pair of pale blue bell-bottoms and a sequined top, and she got up and danced by herself to a song as the boys stared and then she reached out and grabbed the hand of C.R., he was pulled out to the floor and did his best, his loose-limbed best to dance with the beautiful girl, whereas he jerked and stumbled and made her laugh, he then realized the girl was **Verona,** the daughter of his mother's maid, Muriel, whom she had proudly sent to Virginia Commonwealth to study and whom he'd seen in flashes back in his boyhood, they'd played and climbed the tree when he was younger, and some days she helped her mother in the kitchen, but as she grew older he only saw her face briefly in cars that pulled up to the driveway or occasionally at the IGA, he'd tip his hat and they'd say hello, this night, though, they danced together for a long time, and later in a car on a back road, as he made love to her by the same song he'd heard first in the bar, he enjoyed her immensely, the sight of her dark skin naked in his car hugely exciting, in the snow-glow, as he opened the door for air, he was burning up and sweaty and they spilled out naked in the snow, he and this girl, as the disco song, popular that year, came on, she was powdery-smelling and soft and he remembered her running around his house while Muriel cleaned, when she was seven, in this car, though, she said *turn up that song,* he reached over to the controls, he remembers it vividly, the song turned up louder, actually a song by the Brothers Johnson called: Love Roller Coaster.

pendleton compton +
betty owens, 1

I.

Miss Betty sat crying at her desk. She tried to hide it when a nurse would walk by, *oh, these allergies are such a nuisance, such a nuisance,* but after a while she had to admit, no one seemed the least bit interested. Why, she could probably code right on this very desk and the nurses would merely trollop by, unawares, unless of course Dr. C.R. was in the area, then it was a different picture, oh, yessiree bob. Then they got, *sniff,* all kinds of friendly, didn't they. She smelled a strong aftershave, looked up.

Well, howdy dee doo, loveliness.

Stood Pendleton Compton. After C.R. left his office, portrait in hand, he is rung for, called, visited again by his old statuesque friend. It was C.R. who was the best man at Pendleton's wedding, watching their lovely child-hood friend, Nancy Carruthers, walk up the aisle on Pendleton's beefy arm, a pretty little brown-eyed blond, a girl whose hair had been white all her childhood, a girl he kissed on a hammock for a couple of hours when he was fourteen, a girl whom C.R. had liked but Pendelton had carved away. It was C.R. who wanted to be a doctor first, and Pendelton followed.

At this moment he had breezed in, tweeded, for a *short word with the man,* but Betty doesn't say he's *gone* gone. Betty says he stepped out for a while, he wasn't feeling well so he went home to rest it out. A bit of the flu, perhaps. Pendleton notices the portrait is gone. Why, where'd that go? Oh, it, it needed a repair in the frame. I see, he says, well, tell C.R. not to worry about a thing. We always been tight. He's a good man. All's well. Hell, it's Christmas nearly. Tell him to call tonight. OK, Betty? Tell him I'll chat with him at this here func-*shone*. He followed that with a quick little wink.

Pendleton Compton liked to add a little risqué fillip to certain words by lengthening the end syllable with a certain toadish extension, for example, when waddling up to the country club white-jacketed bartender, he might say if there is a woman revolving with her white wine, I'll just take a shot of your best bour-*bone*. Miss Bett-*aaaaaaay* was another favorite distortion she often heard boomed up the hall in her direction. This was all a symptom of the fact that Pendleton had been, in his youth, a *southern man on the move*, before *embonpoint* occurred, flooding the waist zone with an obstacled mass, before his belt hung roundly and he'd have to yank the sucker up a few times an hour, hefting it brusquely up his middle. Before he distinctly could not reach to tie shoes or pick up things too well. Had to trick the old belly and sidle around the edge of it when a pencil dropped. He didn't like to be seen when that happened. Combine this with his pickled and fleshy face, two soggy eyes. He had good hair, though. Couldn't keep it down. A thatch of unruliness. Great fountains of greasy Vitalis poured through these locks. Thick, streaked hair, which stood up, tufted and massive, when he pulled off his surgical cap, a hair erection.

Pendleton attends a club, the Fairfax Club, across from the courthouse. There are old-fashioned bartenders named Johnny and Major, who serve nuts and tinkling glasses of liquor. Simple food is the norm at this place, sans beurre blanc or blackened this-and-that. Oysters baked in casserole is a favorite. The rolls are homemade by a woman named Sarah in the kitchen. Wednesday is a favorite for the roast of beef and on Tueday one needs to arrive early for the famed Brunswick stew. The club exists in its own little bubble of time, a honed, selected relic of the warmth of southern childhoods. The chairs in the dining room are worn, cobbled leather, and although the new golf club in the area sports freshly decorated Prussian blue velvet banquettes, the old Fairfax Club remains threadbare and solid, fragrant with old smells and aflutter with white-jacketed waiters. Johnny, now in his seventies, a little elfin man with thick glasses, knew Mr. Carrie, as they called him, and made sure to bring him rye whiskey neat on a small linen napkin as he came to his seat and *Mrs. Ash,* his lovely wife, Johnny would say, *I understand it's getting warmer out there* and she'd flash a big pink-lipped smile, crinkling in her dark brown wrinkles, *let's hope so, Johnny.* So Johnny stands at the bar, looking into the street, and sees Pendleton walking up. He bites a small roll, which Sarah snuck him in from the kitchen, his purplish arthritic hands clasped around it stiffly. Sarah sits at a chair in the back, making those rolls or chicken salad. She'll tease Johnny, *get on with your fool self,* as he tries to poke the soft rolls on a baking sheet. Sarah is the sister of Muriel, the Ashes' maid, and she lives by herself down in a small house with chickens by Battlefield Hills and gets a ride each day to the Fairfax Club from Major these last twenty-two years. Her own eggs supply the egg salad in the crockery bowl in the walk-in, made fresh daily. In her years, Sarah has seen the club stay unchanged, same old screen door in the summer, hot heat wetting her dress, same old rolls. Some changes, as in her paycheck has gone up each year. The chickens cook up different, softer and yellower. There are now men of color in the dining room, eating with white men, that's changed.

Pendleton arrives, a slight hip tossle as the belt gets yanked up, before he pulls the door. They know Pendleton there. Johnny says, *oh, here he comes, here comes Maker's Mark double with a twist,* and the other bartender will start to make it, both spotting Pendleton's belt twist at the door, *unh-hunh, better get out the extra.* He has discussed heart valves over chicken breast supreme with colleagues, he has thrown up in the dark blue-striped bathroom, resting his head on the cool metal stall, wondering *what the fuck is wrong with me?* and has dried his face and gone out and had another bourbone, laughing with Johnny, who notices his pallor, yet laughs back in a joke of unity.

Betty offers Pendleton a coffee.

Well, oh no, things to do. Things to do. He smiles. How *you* doing, Betty? he says quietly. He touches her hand.

I'm fine, she lies. How are *you*?

I kind of, kind of, *miss* you, you know, he says, leaning down low, his breath hot and coffee-stained, I still don't know what to make of that, that *time* . . .

There had been this staff birthday party for Pendleton, and he hunkered over Betty's personal space, gripping in his hand the sad little card signed by all the people which later he would store on the floor of his car, not quite able to throw it away. He had given the card the quick once-over again and noticed how some of the nurses said, Hoping you have many, many more! in fancy cursives and how Betty wrote, You hang in there, big guy! and how some of the doctors gave an obligingly hard-pushed hiero-glyphic of a signature, and the thing made him uncomfortable, so while he talked to her he used it to scratch his head.

That was a Tuesday night, and she did an unusual thing, she'd had a full glass of punch and they had talked for nearly an hour by the NICU of things like cat trees and yard sales. He smelled like a lime aftershave, one of those Bermudian ones, like rotten lime skin and cloves all mushed up. Fact of the matter was, he'd always liked Betty and her neat little suits, manicured bony hands. His wife, childhood sweetheart Nancy Compton, was a great favorite in the community with her "Christmas in April" leader-ship, and Pendleton loved her quite a bit (yes, he loved her as in he loved coming home to the house, all festooned with greenery and his son Scott home from UVA and they were eating chili Nancy had made and trim-ming the tree, the terrier barked at his calves as he walked in, it smelled heavenly in the house, like cinnamon, and Nancy looked up rosy-cheeked and Scott got up, all leggy and tall, Hey, Dad! and that was what he felt when he thought of loving Nancy, that kind of family warmth. Is that love? or comfort? or nostalgia? or what?).

And, as Pendleton grew in girth, so did his wife, tiny white-haired Nancy became large red-skinned Nancy, her hair darkened to the shade of light iced tea. The acrobatics of their intimate nights over the years, the frantic fumbling on the bathroom ledge or kitchen table in the first years, migrated to the big bed upstairs, reduced to the awkward battling of two large masses, legs getting cramps, stomachs uncomfortably wedged, the whole became an embarassment to himself, imbued with a sense of shame, there came the distinct feeling he was doing some form of perversion to his wife as he shrouded her in his great stomach wiggling desperately around to find the entrance (for he couldn't see his own member, sad to say), and his wife's thighs hurt spread like so, and what was a fevered gymnastics became a pitiful reminder of something lost, so he found, well, *he found he often thought of other women*. Often. Found he'd taken to renting an occasional video in a hotel room while at conferences (OK, every damn time, he runs in that room like a freaking schoolboy) and then found himself oddly interested in Betty, from a fantasy point of view. Not interested in wrecking his life or anything. Likes that tree trimming, likes the Easter ham, likes Nancy in a quilted zip-up lounge robe making French toast Christmas morn, likes her damn Beanie Babies on the back window of her car. He does! He loves it!

But Betty, at the birthday party, was laughing at the fact that Pendleton made his own cat trees as a hobby, meanwhile Pendleton was fascinated by her angularity, this spritish and bony woman, who he imagines could scud on his stomach during lovemaking like a love-crazed banshee demon. Pendleton could just lie back and watch that shit. Talking bour-*bone*, my friend. Talking, punch sped up the craze. (He'd had two. It was a cherry, Shrub. It was sweet, yet deceptively strong.) Betty looked good. Goddamn, if she didn't look good. Miss Bett-*aaaaaay*.

Unaware of his ascending lust, Betty said, Well, I'd better go, so late.

What, what? Oh, come on, girl. Having so much, such good time here. Aren't we? I enjoyed, enjoyed, I, uh, talking with you, he said, in his loud/soft drunken way, I mean I sure, sure did. Can I, can I drive ya home, Betty? Before he knew it he had offered because he knew her car was in the shop, she was going to get a ride from Carol, Peds nurse down the hill, she said, Oh, Dr. Pendleton, I think—

I insist! I insist! Damn you, it's my birthday! It's my birthday and Nancy, Nancy isn't even home, she's with her sister in Arkansas who's sick. So I'm all alone, he said while his mouth appeared all twisted and distorted, and as a hunk of his mighty hair fell on his reddened face and he blew it up out of the way, laughing and grabbing her arm, come on, come on.

Pulling down Route 15, toward her house, she suddenly said, It's up on the hill, see, with those little Christmas lights on the bushes.

I know perfectly *well* where you live, Miss Bett-ay. You live near my man. You live up on the side of the battle, THE battle, in my mind, of the war of northern aggression, ha! Or civil, whatever. I practically spent my youth on those hills, girl. I know them like I know my feet, you know. I seen you there, cutting bushes and stuff. I can see you pretty near well from their porch.

Oh, mercy. I didn't realize that.

I didn't say you were naked or nothing.

Doctor!

Oh, woman, relax.

Then he says to her, Now what you think, think of that party? Eh? You eat any of that Vietnamese shit food they brought in, eh? You eat those meat rolls? I bet they put dog meat in, oh, *Jesus*—

Not looking, he'd taken a turn and the car slipped in the ditch.

Well, that's real fine, he said.

We aren't far, anyhow. I can walk.

Now that's pert stupid of me.

Oh, come on.

And Betty and he had to get out out, she wearing her sensible little rubbers on her shoes and he in his glossy loafers all slimed with oozing pale brown mud, *goddammit,* he said in a suddenly sharp voice like a whip crack, *Goddamn, my shoes are all dirty,* he looked up at her beside the car, they planned to walk up to her house, call Triple A, and she stood there, her hair frosted and gleaming in the moonlight, her face bones sharpened and cut glacine—

Reckon I ought to kiss you or something.

She looked down and a silly hum came out of her mouth, he stood like a man taking a pee, legs spread, and his hammish hands came down to her chin and held her steady, and he kissed her, light little smoochie things, like a five year old might do to his mother, Oh, Betty, he breathed out, hell, he said, he fell against her, but then he pulled back and her face was close and smiling, all lined like a woman older than Nancy and he felt strangely ashamed. Suppose, suppose I ought to get you back up and get you warm now, shouldn't I. And so they trudged, funereally, though he almost fell a couple of times, and when they get to the door, he pushed it open after she clicked the lock and for those minutes, a strange thing happened, she was the proprietress of the moment, not Nancy, despite his marriage of many years, that right-then of the snow and the dark and the night, a feeling of confession and kindness overtook him, *maybe I ought to get back home now,* he said, coming in her house, *I don't know what I'm doing,* the half-drunk clutching for a last spasm toward more inebriation, *maybe, maybe I ought to have a beer, you got a beer, anywheres,* but suddenly he felt dizzy and nauseous and everything got a bit smoky around the edges, his baby brain went *oh* and in a corner of his doctor brain he thought *myocardial infarction?*

In—tra

Cra—a—a—nial

Hem—m—o—rrrrhage . . . ?

Those words went whooshing down the vortex of blood rushing like the white water of the swollen Rapidan River, his eyelids trembled, he drooled.

(Gravy, that's what he loves about Nancy, woman makes the best damn gravy, some kind of secret recipe, nothing like her chicken with gravy on a frosty November eve, he and her stuffing the arteries with that kind of love, hee ho, ha, ha, stuffing the arteries with fat and glop and from a professional point of view it's almost murder, oh, oh, and now, what's this, my child in his pajamaed feet running down the stairs, he must be a baby still, it's Christmas morn 1980! Good Lord, I feel lighter by thirty pounds and Betty is in not her quilted zip-up lounger but cute PJs, she's still got long blond hair, before the sensible bob they talked her into, she's laughing and thinner and I'm a young man! I must be dying! I'm a young fuck again. Oh, shit! It's my mother! Oh, Daddy!)

Pendleton, Pendleton, she said over and over, bathing his coarse oatmeal skin with a little squinched-up damp paper towel, *Dr. Pendleton, you all right?* There was puke on the floor and he fell and crashed down a magazine stand, whimpering *Mama,* and threw up on her Berber rug and on the corner of her new *People* magazine and the cat licked it, she went to call 911 but he whispered and got up, his eyes bulged, Holy son of a bitch, I saw my *mother*. I saw her right there by your, your, whatsit, armoire thing, standing clear as light. Holy shit. Hoooooly *shit*. Don't call no one, just get, get me some water please. Pheeew. Whooo, *shit*.

Betty got him water, he sat half naked and pale watching an old rerun of M*A*S*H while she hand-washed the shirt in Woolite and ironed it, got rid of the puke, he sat there watching that show, still trembling from the experience and sweaty and shirtless, his tummy bulging over his belt, his mind all numb from endorphins and tried to remain logical, Did I, did I, *die*? He hated the fact that his question of death is interwoven with a flash of interest in the plot of this M*A*S*H episode, he hated thinking of his own mortality while hoping to see that asshole Frank get put in his place, he knew he should go to the hospital, but the blood levels were too damaging careerwise and embarrassing in general, and he doesn't want to die in a hospital, if he's going to go, then, dammit, he wants to just, boom, die! maybe at home, maybe with Nancy in his big bed, and with his dog, Luther. He's seen so many poor fucks die on a steel table and it won't be me, no way, he thought. Betty came back with the shirt and he said, I think, I think, Betty, I think I might've just *died* there for a moment, and she sat down and said, What? I beg your pardon? and he said, I feel real bad I pushed myself on you, I'd like to apologize for that, *oh, shush*, and I'd appreciate if we could keep this, thing, between us, I just want to go on, see. And she said, Oh, Lord, Dr. Compton, I think—*Pendleton, for shit's sake*—Uh, well, then, Pendleton, I-I think I got to call up ER, you know and just, check you out. *Hell no, no way, I'm a doctor. My pressure's fine now,* he lied. *I'll do my own check, how about that.* He kissed her face. Well, she said, OK. She walked him down to the car and she got in the seat while he waited on the curb and her skinny arms draped across the wheel, she revved the car back and forth and it flew mud everywhere, red wet Virginia mud, full of Union and Confederate fourteen-year-olds' calcified remains and blood, ground arrowheads, deer droppings, crushed leaves, contaminants and pesticides, the historical stew of the last hundred years, and then when the car was safe on the dry gravel she got out and he held her arm,

What the hell happened to me? he said in boyish wonder, Did I *die* for a minute?

She frowned and kissed his forehead, You take care. You go in and see someone. But he shook his head. Can't do it. He waved, got in, and she watched him speed off and then, though she owned him no more, she did own that moment, a moment he thought of often, by the Coke machine waiting as a Sprite came ka-lunking down, *did I die?* or as he stood peeing in the doctor's urinal *I died!* or as he lay in the dark next to Nancy *I died. I saw my mother. Looking all pissed off. Darn amazing.*

2.

When C.R. left, Betty was in a quandary. She ended up standing awkwardly by his desk, like a sentinel, her hands roiling together feverishly, looking at the blank space where the portrait had been. It was dark outside, the offices were closing, and she feared for C.R. Then when Pendleton came in, he leaned down in her face and said, *I still don't know what to make of that time,*

Well, she said. It *was* weird. You ill?

He looks up at her, his eyes always soft and calf-eyed like a fourteen year old's since the incident, What's that, hon?

I said, You ill or something? Because. I'd check it out. Get it checked out. Call up Dr. Howell or. I don't know. I don't know—

—Shssh. I'm fine and dandy. Where's the man?

That's just it. I think he's falling apart, I think you ought to help me. And where *is* he? He'll be fine, everything's OK—

No, it isn't OK, she whispers, despite the fact half the hospital's gone, I just feel it, he's off something terrible, he left here all liquored up, with his picture and his things like he's never coming back, I want to go talk to him, you and me, you're his friend,

I used to be, we used to be real tight. He was my best friend all my life. Used to be we'd play racquetball and hang, but lately—

It's just, it's just, something, some feeling.

Problem is, supposed to go to a cocktail thing right, he looks at his broad gold watch, just right about now, Nancy'll be waiting, and then we got to *vamoose* and get our butts up here. Back here, to the party, shit, woman—

I'm worried! her face twists up, I've worked for him for sixteen years!

You can call me on my cell, well, try around—

Oh, Lord.

Hey, he holds her face, I can tell you everything's fine. Nothing bad can happen. Now I'll tell you, that time, that time, changed me, I'll tell you,

Something's not right! she sniffed,

You call me at seven, I'm serious, then I'll make an appearance and I'll, I'll call him at home, unless he comes. Hell, he'll *come*—

Oh, *Pendleton*.

Hey. Call me.

He left, and as she packed up to leave herself, she took pictures from her desk and put them in her bag and then she went, hunkered over, a wee found-ling of desperation and stiff anger, a lavishly sad gait of mincing steps, of livid bewilderment, oh, the Betty inside a person—unused, unfooled.

verona + diane, 1

I.

The holiday party, the one so lightly mentioned, so casually tossed around in the banter about the hospital, had become the torture, the ball and chain, the annihilation of two would-be amateur caterers in town: **Verona Howard** (yes, the very same one of the sequined top and bell-bottoms, now matured, now wearing large preshrunk jeans and a sweatshirt) and **Diane Redmond** (whose son, **Todd,** was mentioned earlier in regard to the candy striper; more on him later).

As for a holiday party, if you attend them, as most people have on occasion, I doubt you give it a thought, much less than momentary, maybe whether you'll attend or not or what you'll wear, there are expectations naturally, that it'll be well-decorated, warm, pleasant-smelling, that food will appeal, that liquor will flow, no waiting in lines, hopefully, but this is all an assumption in the back of your mind, you're not directly eye-to-eye with the sweat, the toil, the tears behind it all, the people slaving around you who might've had other hopes (*I am an engineer*, thinks the waiter from Pakistan who shows you a tray of deviled quail eggs with cod roe, *I was trained for other work, but my green card is upheld*). You may walk in, receive a cold vessel of fluids from the bartender (*Name's Ted, just trying to get back on my feet, I do pottery*), you pluck a smoked salmon roulade from the waitress (*You try and make ends meet with two kids, you just try*, says Evelyn, she lives in Loudoun House, works at Piedmont Sheetmetal dur-

ing the days and her mother watches J.D. and Caitlin), you might snag a
Spinach, Portobello, and Asiago Rustic Tartlet from another (*Jason, I just
am trying to figure out, you know, what I want, but college doesn't seem to be
part of the, you know, picture, I don't know. I don't know*). Then you leave,
get in your car. You leave your plastic in a trash can by the door or hand it
to a waitress. She gets your coat. You're out of there. What many hands
touched and sculpted and baked and filled and tossed lies in your stomach
with some kind of love attached to it, some meaning, some measure of kind
repartee, you digest it, you acknowledge it, it goes through you, it becomes
you. I don't blame you the disregard, if a person assumes the world the
burden is great. I beg you kindness, that is all. Awareness. Attention.

The holiday party, the one so lightly mentioned, so casually tossed
around in the banter about the hospital, had become the torture, the ball
and chain, the annihilation of two would-be amateur caterers in town. This
is worth repeating.

The catering manager, the function organizer, the main chef, the menu
director, Verona, had met with Mrs. Grigsby, head office manager, at the
hospital. The truth of the matter is, Verona and Diane had never had this
grand of a *gig* before, merely catering from each other's suburban island-clad
kitchen (Verona had the green granite, Diane had chosen a Mediteranean
Turkish gray imitiation that came with a video which showed her how to
sand out any stains her son Todd might have caused with pizza). They had
only catered a few small picnics and office lunches with the new company
they formed by printing cards on the computer, Thymes of the Essence, in
an italianate font, on parchmentlike paper:

Thymes of the Essence
Catered events and functions
We do it all!
Formal or casual
Diane and Verona, owners
703-776-8989
703-776-3467

And so, when **Bob "The Mayor,"** Diane's husband, had mentioned to Mrs. Grigsby, the hospital's top office manager, during a dentist visit that his wife's catering business was *taking off, they've got all kinds of stuff going, big functions, corporate stuff and all,* she took one of their cards and gave those girls a call and Verona had to furiously cram her kids in front of a video of *The Muppets Christmas Carol* with promises of Oreos if they were quiet, while Mrs. Grigsby was on hold, and then she put on her most authoritive voice, *well, hello! yes, of course, we do all types of functions.* (She'd quickly deduced that all caterers use that word, *function,* excessively, along with *event, occasion, proposal,* as well as the odd, architectural *hors d'oeuvres display* and, of course, *linens* and *service personnel.* She had found these terms in a catering brochure from Washington and had underlined them several times and committed them to memory.) She also toyed in her mind with the concept of adding an e to the end of every word, Olde Englishe style, and how one would pronounce that. But she stuffed that thought away and addressed the issue at hand.

What *exaaaac*-tly did you have in mind, Mrs. Grigsby?

Verona extended her vowels, in the relaxed way salespeople do. She thought about calling Mrs. Grigsby by her first name, Frances, incessantly at the end of every sentence the way the Toyota salesman did with her, but didn't want to push things. Mrs. Grigsby was older than her. She had manners.

Well, said Mrs. Grigsby, just our annual holiday party. About five hundred people. We usually like to do it up, you know. Last year we had a "Winter Wonderland" over at the Sheraton. And we heard you all were real good, so I thought I'd give you a call.

Yes. I see. (Jeez! Wait till I tell Diane! Those kids better be quiet!) Umm, sure. We have a lot, oh Lord, a *lot* of experience in these type of functions, holiday occasions. Oh, yes. Definitely.

Well, what I mean is, could you do some sort of theme thing?

Oh, of course, of course, why, one, one, of our most interesting, fun, holiday ideas is, is (she could hear from the other room her kids' video, *bah humbug!* and she could hear Kermit the Frog as Cratchit, *why, Mr. Scrooge, have a merry, merry—bah humbug!!) is,* is the *Christmas Carol.* Yes, it's a popular, highly popular theme, Mrs. Grigsby. Olde England. Very, very charming.

Well. That sounds interesting. Really does. Maybe we can have a meeting and we'll look at some menus or something. Can you give me some idea of the type of decor you've done for that theme? It sounds like such a cute idea. It really does. I'm a Christmas nut, myself.

Of course! Of course! Well, well (peering around the corner, noting Kermit the Frog talking to Michael Caine as Scrooge, seeing the Muppet set), we do, uh, snow. Lots of snow! And Scrooge and Marley's office serves, you know, grog, and there's turkey—

Ohhkaay (she was a little hesitant. On some level. But open).

So, in a later meeting, Mrs. Grigsby went with the Dickens theme (ever popular. Always a hit, she said, we really do it up) and they discussed decor: One thing we like to do, real nice, is use lots of fake snow and set up cottages for each station, you got your grog station, see, and Tiny Tim's Sweet Shop, and Mrs. Cratchit's saddle of roast beef, and so on, isn't that cute? See, our waiters wear knickers and all, you'll notice we do the street signs and everything, and our banquet manager will be dressed up like Scrooge, it's real cute.

As for menus, we like to blend modern and Old English, now we have some real delicious items here for tasting, sun-dried tomato and sausage brioche, I call this *ye olde sausage-in- a-pocket*, and here's mini hot dogs we call *Dickens Doggies,* with our signature strawberry-mustard sauce. Unh-hunh, people love it. They really do. It's a very popular, very popular, um, *concept* that we promote. We really believe in the whole package, what have you, with themes and all. And Dickens, people love the *Christmas Carol.*

To Be Passed:
Cheddar Scones with Ye Olde Ham
Smoked Irish Salmon, with Dickens Dill Sauce, on Pumpernickel

Now, these, these, salmon items are ve—ry popular. People. Just. Lo-o-o-ve them. They do. Now, even old Scrooge would say, bah *yum*bug, now, wouldn't he, Diane! Wouldn't he? (Diane dished out her standard canned giggle, yes, he would,Verona! Oh, heeeheehee!) Oh, this is delicious. Totally delicious. Mmmm. These are our stationary islands. Decorated in the thematic way, Cratchit's house, etc. Fun. Lots of fun.

Scrooge and Marley's Office:
Ye Olde Roast of Beefe with Horseradish Sauce and
Mini Yorkshire Pudding
Gold chocolate "coins" strewn for local urchins

Pen and Ink, and parchment, for props

We have fun with it. We really do. Sanji and Mario dress up as Scrooge and Marley, they've been with us for years, real nice guys, they do a great little Scrooge-and-Marley routine, in their knickers and scarves, oh, big hit. Big hit.

Tiny Tim's Sweet Shop:
Mincemeat Tartlets, with Chantilly
Ye Olde English Plum Pudding with Hard Sauce
London Twelfth-cakes

The two women had spent many hours at the computer together, scanning menus, recipes, and snowflake designs, brainstorming, watching the Muppet movie for extra details. That's where the gold coins strewn on tables came in, a Muppet touch.

Mrs. Grigsby, now, this is a really special thing:

Ye Olde Steamship Round of Beef, served with Horseradish Gelee
Sage Roasted Whole Turkey with Oyster Stuffing and
Cranberry Chutney, bestrooned with Marzipan Holly and Berries
The Ghost of Christmas Pasta (Baked Ziti with four cheeses)

And to quote Mr. Dickens himself here, *Poultry, brawn, and great joints of meat! sausages, mince-pies! barrels of oysters! juicy oranges! red-hot chestnuts! cherry-cheeked apples! seething bowls of punch that made the chamber dim with their delicious steam!* Ah, but a feast was a feast in those days of 1843, when Stove Top stuffing didn't exist to fill a water-injected turkey, nor were there the insults of a "tofurkey" or, even though it's kind of good, an entire dish made from frozen green beans, canned mushroom soup, and crispy tinned fried onions, who thought of that! No one sprayed an atomizer wrapped in a plaid ribbon, labeled *Old Bayberry Christmas*, in the air for atmosphere! And wreaths were made of greens harvested from the woods, there weren't all these pseudo-wreaths from Kmart for every season, made of fake tulips or harvest leaves. A Christmas feast consisted of a Great Boiled and a Great Roast, and a lovely broiled goose. And glogg, punch, shrub, Purl and Bishop filled the bellies of many. Pheasants dripping with ambergris! Roasted perch! Brawn and mustard! Mince pie! Sowen cake! The people danced, whipped endlessly in great circles of spinning, shining cloth, flapping and reeling. What it must've smelled like in those days. A heavy tangy musk must've hung in the air as pillowous as clouds, given the lack of personal hygiene and bathing, then the pungency of the various aromatic oils used to cover such odors, though poorer servants and such couldn't afford such oils, so humankind reeked in a distinctive hunkerous way, a man smelled heavy and dank, a woman sharp and feline, children of milk and sweat and chicken drumsticks held in their greasy hands, candles flickered and burned sheep's fat which added to the sour animal fat whiff in the air and cloves hung heavy and fruitaceous from seasoning and perfume, punch bowls steamed for they were served hot and central heating devices didn't exist so heat was rare in all corners, there existed a blazing fire which sputtered and brought forth woody smoke which clung and gave a bruinish tang to hair and clothes, like when camping, so that when a hot punch came into the room in the arms of a young girl, filling her face with wafting citrus and strong alcoholic drafts, the air was heavy and passionate, the air you breathed, full of steam, and smoke and sweat, joyous and hearty.

*   *   *

Mrs. Grigsby thought their ideas were *real cute. You two got some imaginations working that's for sure.* She signed on, giving them a deposit of two thousand dollars. Diane and Verona marked their calendars.

2.

The holiday party, the one so lightly mentioned, so casually tossed around in the banter about the hospital, had become the torture, the ball and chain, the annihilation of two would-be amateur caterers in town.

They sped through Costco two days before the party with their lists in hands, grabbing hams and huge cardboard boxes of Cokes and plastic bags of peppers and hefty five-pound bags of grated cheese and skipped the premade quiches, though Verona insisted (*They taste great, Di. You want to kill yourself making that pastry?*), but Diane persevered, she would make them from scratch, from butter! They would melt in the mouth! Verona agreed, reluctantly. Diane would not skimp on anything, even honey mustard would have to be mixed with Dijon and local Virginian honey in an earthenware jar late at night on Diane's granite, as the floor of her new suburban pseudo-mansion lay strewn with browned carrot skins and onion shards and bits of meat and crunchy balls of peppercorn, she mixed the honey mustard, gleefully scratching that out on the list:

~~honey mustard, one quart~~

Strawberry-mustard sauce
Horseradish gelee, 2 quarts
Hard sauce, 2 quarts
Dickens Dill Sauce, 3 quarts

Oh, did it ever end? The endless mixing and pouring, while she fretted over her teenage son's whereabouts. Where? Where? Ah, and she lost the biscuit cutter in the shape of a snowflake so that, hands full of biscuit mix, she'd dug through the drawers, time ticking way, *hon, what about dinner?* her husband impatiently asked, *oh, oh, God, just grab a pizza, will you,* so he paraded through as she desperately set out hams with a glaze on every available counter space, injecting cloves in neat, linear patterns, and he tried to fumble and get a pan for the frozen pizza, but as he did, he knocked into the counter, and horror! a ham slid to the floor, leaving a long, gleaming line of coppery glaze across the white linoleum tile, *oh, crap! honey! please, watch out!* So Bob "The Mayor" hustled out and she picked up the ham in her arms like a chunky one year old, washed it off until it was pale again and reglazed it, then, then, it was 11:00 at night, her hair was greasy and sweaty against her brow, catering has a way of soaking the beauty right out of a person, maybe the constant animal oils and grease coarsen the skin, or the heat reddens the neck and cheeks to a turkey-cobbled sandiness, the hair strained and tightened back until patches of baldness appear at the hairline, and most of all the endless loading and unloading packages and boxes, walking and walking and walking up stairs with box after box, in the service elevator which always smells like moldy vegetables, your shoes which pinch and burn, hellacious, hellacious, hellacious!

God save her, it was then 12:00, and she burned a rack of biscuits. The fatigue was oppressive. She remembered working for a caterer in D.C., to learn, back last year, and she remembers the spiffy little pastry chef, a woman in her forties from Down South somewhere, so she had a twangified accent and she made everything, that woman, every mille-feuille, every tea biscuit, every puff pastry rectangle, every damn bucket of ganache, that woman stood over the table with her feather-light, cool hands, reddened and papery, and stirred and mixed and spread until one day she was just crying, quietly sniffling over the endless white bowl of flour. So, Chiu, a flamenco-speed Thai chef of a woman, came over to her, hugged her to her waist, for Chiu was small and rotund and Beth, the pastry chef, was tall and thin. And Chiu said, *why you cry, why you cry?* and Beth said, *oh, oh, Chiu* (now she said that like this, like *Shoooo-eeew*), *I'm just so darn tired. I'm just tired, Shoooo-eew,* and then she said, *Shoooo-eew, why are you crying? Why you crying, Shoooo-eew?* And Chiu said, *I cry 'cause you cry!* and they all laughed and went back to work, back to the toil, back to the flame, back to the clock.

3.

The list went on! And on! It was 1:00 A.M. the NIGHT BEFORE THE
PARTY and she was worn to threadbare fatigue so exhaustive her eyes
burned and her feet pinged with little kernels of sharp pain, *who says slav-
ery is gone!* she howled out loud, and she cursed Bob for his mortgage business which was in a low slump and she had to do this stuff, and Verona
was right! She should've bought the damn mini quiches instead of baking
all two thousand of them as she had done in the morning, two thousand
herbed chevre and Gruyère tartlets, two thousand "Tiny Tim Cheese
Tarts," that's six hundred eggs, people, that's six hundred eggs she and
Verona had cracked by hand, you must estimate that, when making a
quiche for yourself, this procedure takes a mere two seconds, but for them
it took TWO HOURS, two hours just to crack the damn eggs (I told you
we should've gotten Teenie to do prep! I told you, said Verona, all sweat-
faced and smudged, flour caking on her dark skin. At ten dollars an hour?
Hunh? You want to make money on this, retorted Diane) and then she
knew she was wrong, then at 1:00 A.M. she'd have taken all the prep in the
world, she'd gladly have thrown away the entire profit just to have relief!
Relief, relief, relief!

Oh, at that moment the list lay voluminous and the refrigerator, the
Sub-Zero, bought specifically because it could hold the industrial amounts
of proposed catering items, lay full of ingredients still wrapped in their plastic awaiting the laying on of hands, vacuum-wrapped whole sides of beef,
stewing in purple juice awaiting the placement of garlic cloves and crushed
peppercorn (she had started the crushing in a tea towel earlier, thus half
the corns fell on the floor and now crunched unpleasantly under her Dr.
Scholl's sandals), huge chunks of lemony-hued Asiago with poundage tags
awaited grating to be mixed with "local naked mountain morels" in an Olde
Time Mushroom Pie, the mushrooms lying ridged and conular in their
simple farmers' market box, exiting their prime musk with each easing of
the fridge door, a scent of reminder and tragedy, oh, the work, the toil that
lay ahead, the forcemeat, the trifles, the fondant, the morsels, the viands,
the victuals that lay in wait. Dear agony!

4.

She found one wrinkled stale Camel encased in a crumpled pack in her old coat pocket from last year, it took a while to find, she had to tear through the cardboard box of winter things in the attic upstairs, and she smoked it hungrily, making her dizzy by the porch outside and the nasty staleness filled her mouth, she spat out the shrivels of tobacco, spotting by the shed the rented van, with the magnet sign, THYMES OF THE ESSENCE. She stamped out the cigarette and searched for her cordless phone amongst the boxes on the front table, and when she found it, she rang up Verona, though it was now 1:45 A.M., she thought Verona should be up, after all, Verona had the crushing list of Linzer stars and gingerbread men, not to mention the vast amounts of twelfth-cakes, the mincemeat tartlets, and the plum pudding, which required a full day of steaming, and by the third ring Verona answered peppily, hello?

I quit, said Diane. I'm done.

Whoo, OK. You finished? OK, OK, Diane, 'cause I still have a *ton* to do. I got George working here, too.

No, I quit. Done. I'm not doing this shit. I'm *through.*

Whoa now. Come on—

I can't take it!

Hey, settle down. George! She says, she says she's *quitting*—

I'm. Outta here!

Now, Diane! Diane!

Fuck this shit!

Diane!

5.

Verona and George drove out in the frosted night in their silver minivan, speeding through the dark, overly decorated manses of their development to Diane's colonial one on the other side, on Primrose Lane and even coming up the road, they could see Diane's crumpled silhouette on the porch, shaking with tears as their doors slammed while her husband in his robe patted her back, murmuring *it's OK, hon, it's OK.* He looked up

to them with a sleep-bent worried look, like, what the fuck is going on!
It's only food, hon, he kept saying, a weird way to comfort, but he liked
it, *it's only food.*

Verona came over to them. All eyes were on her, waiting.

She tried the camp counselor approach, in control, fearless, OK, come
on, baby. We're gonna do this thing. Stand back, Bob. Baby, stand. Stand.
Un-unh, no wimping out, get up. Get up now.

So Diane stood up, her face runny and blasé. Yeah, well, she said.

So what you want to do here.

Nothing.

You gonna wimp out here?

Yeah.

You're gonna let twelve hundred puff pastry shells ruin our careers?

Well. Uh. *No.*

A few *hours* of work?

Uh.

What I'm asking you is, you gonna screw it up for me?

Silence. They all stood around.

I mean, I drive here at three o'clock in the goddamn A.M., and I'm not
gonna give up this shit.

Yeah, well.

No, Jack, I'm not.

Unh-hunh.

Damn straight. People, put on your aprons. We're finishing. Come on.

And then, Bob, Diane's husband, starts inexplicably sobbing in a tiny
tissue wrenched up from his plaid bathrobe. **Bob,** or **"The Mayor,"** as he
was affectionately termed by his friends, had always been gentle and considerate. "Hon-bun," as she often called him. (About once a month, would
put down his magazine as they watched TV and gently touch her knee over
the tentlike shape of the quilt, *can The Mayor pay his respects?* he'd say with
a weak smile and downward-pulled eyebrows, pitiful, and they would resume slowly the ritual as banal as their morning act of Metamucil and
orange juice, stirred three times. Last week, it was during *Seinfeld* and Diane

had to suppress a laugh at one particularly funny joke.) So Bob "The Mayor" starts whining and sniffling and managed to get out, *I, I, I, just feel so damn, damn guilty watching her slave, Verona. I think it's a terrible idea, a bad idea this catering, just a really bad thing.* And Verona said, as they came in the strewn kitchen of flour and butter and monstrously dirty pans, it's not any worse than life's ever been, Bob, hell, what if you all were ditchdiggers or working in one of those tunnels at this hour or a coal miner or a hooker out in the street dragging your sorry ass, it could be worse, my friend, than baking a few goddamn *muffins*, and I *will* take some scotch if you have some, yes, I will.

So it was Bob "The Mayor," mortgage executive at Ball's Bluff Banking, who gave the roasted steamship the cracked pepper and the garlic in all the right places and made the horseradish gelee and he actually was proud of that, proud the gelatin melted in water and cream and salt and horseradish became a gelee, that was a fancy term he'd heard about in books and stuff but not something he thought he'd ever make, in fact, he plans as he makes it to do it again, to make horseradish gelee at every church supper that he would attend and envisions it becoming the town's favorite, Oh, goody, people will say, it's The Mayor's famous gelee. He might even be able to make it in bulk, sell it at the annual bake sale. It was a lot more fun than the "Re-fi Hell" his life had been lately, or the curse of golf, and George, Verona's husband, had fancied himself a meat man, a real barbeque king, but Verona has him stuffing pâté into tiny puffs and he snags a few and he deems finger food an OK deal, and then he whipped up hard sauce, butter and bourbon and cream and sugar and finds that rather nifty, too, though it starts to curdle and Diane runs in and saves it by adding a tiny smidgen of hot water which he found so magical it even bordered on witchcraft. All four of them in the kitchen, busy in their alchemical pursuits, changing eggs into cakes, water into sauce, butter into bread, meat into pâté, then light comes up over the Blue Ridge Mountains just as Diane makes coffee, just in time as all four of them finish, their aprons blood-smeared, chocolate-smeared, egg-smeared, coffee in hand, they watch the sun come up and *in just an hour,* says Verona, checking her digital sports watch, *we'll need to move our butts. Get on over to the hospital. Set this bugger up.*

Whoo boy, says The Mayor, I'm on, rubbing his hands together.

You on? says Verona. You on *what*?

I-I mean, he says, his face purplish. I mean, I'm ready. For action.

Well, this isn't exactly action, son. We don't expect no action. This is a party. And you can come.

Th-that's what I meant, The Mayor says.

OK, then. Just clarifying.

The holiday party, the one so lightly mentioned, so casually tossed around in the banter about the hospital, had become the torture, the ball and chain, the annihilation of two would-be amateur caterers in town. The van was filled with boxes. Wearily, they drove on.

Don't forget ice. Leave room in the back for ice.

love roller coaster, child

4 summer adventures of kirsten, candy striper

adventure #1

Getting up one day, July 23rd, bright summer fun day. Her ballerina clock spun and chanted *Good morning, Good morning,* then her mother at the door—Kirsten dear? It's breakfast—she proceeded to her bathroom with Hollywood lights in her fuzzy nightgown of ducks, her feet stuffed into giant puffy slippers of ratty pink fur, to brush her bright gleaming teeth with a sonic toothbrush, then to her closet, eschewing all teenage finery, all her newly purchased halters, jeans, sundresses, opting instead for a crisp starched candy-striper suit of pink striped pinafore and white blouse. Applied deodorant (actually smells like "Teen Spirit"; small factoid: Kurt Cobain named the famous song not for some esoteric concept of teenage essence, but after the pastel-colored deodorant, marketed for teenagers, of that name). Snapped on white opaque panty hose.

Shoes were to be similarly white and nurselike, so her mother ordered a pair from a uniform catalogue because it was worth $39.98 to have Kirsten helping others and now Kirsten wore them down to breakfast, consisting of a Nutri-Grain bar and a Coke, she watched approximately seven minutes of *Today*, then she walked outside to her VW Jetta, petted Mr. Puffin, carefully backed up her Jetta to avoid the scampering, drooling dog, and accelerated out of parking lot, turned right, noticed pimple in rearview mirror, popped said offensive blemish at the following stoplight, felt a cascade, a wave of tremulous chemical activity (or *endocrinological mischief*) caused by

65

a dusty-haired adolescent man-boy (**Todd Redmond,** son of Diane, the caterer) in a Ford Expedition, color of forest green, who acknowledged Kirsten with a simple raising of the first digit on the left hand draping the wheel, the same hand which, shortly, would pull at her new halter, bought with her mother on a sunny Friday afternoon, in a striped pattern of greens and blues ("Perfect for the beach, Kirsten or, the pool, or-"; "Mom, OK"), would pull at the new halter on a back road by a construction site (future name of Fox Manor), full of piles of Virginia's red dirt, still loaders and articulated dump trucks (cherry picker, backhoe loader, concrete mixer, track excavator—Todd Redmond's mind holds a virtual encyclopedic disc of knowledge concerning these vehicles, left over, no actually still quite rampant, from a childhood fascination with these gems of machinery), would pull at the halter as he and Kirsten slobber tongues, their third date after the field party, he will have picked her up at eight in order to see a movie, but instead, liquor and coke in a plastic cup (VA. TECH inscibed on the side) were shared, there was a certain vehicular looping around a restaurant's parking lot (*cruising Pizza Hut*), a certain ceremonial ritual before driving to Fox Manor rubble, then the pulling-off of the halter bought for $6.99 at Old Navy by her mother, resulting in her breasts exposed in moonlight, trickling from the sunroof of a Chevy Blazer, he stared for a second, then his hands were on them quickly, thus she lay back and didn't hear the honking, then they both stood up, lights were flashed in their face, she dressed quickly back in the halter top, both were told to *drive on, now, kids,* he dropped her off, she rubbed against her stuffed bunny, she thought of what to wear tomorrow, Todd was far from her last sleepy thoughts, approximate time 10:32.

adventure #2

The lifeguard at her pool, a freckled sandy blond, slightly gawky, too skinny calves, which crossed as he sat up on the lifeguard chair like a giant flesh X, engaged in *endocrinological mischief* with Kirsten at a pool party at her best friend's (Amy Perelli) hyper-colonial manse at a cul-de-sac in Strawberry Hills, as bland and microbrewed as all the development tracts surrounding the small historic village, giant clumps of camel and chamois shades with smooth blackboard driveways. Teenagers were in the basement listening to rap music of that time, dancing on the off-white Berber carpet, trailing in the side door from the pool, Kirsten was chatting with the lifeguard named Ryan, dripping chlorinated pool water on the rug, he suggested they grab a Coke and sit on the side hill and talk, they brought a Godzilla towel and sat down, he lit a small stub of cannabis material (some kids call it *chronic*, in suitable current lingo), very quickly kissed her with his meaty, corn chip mouth, she kissed back, they were making out and he had slipped his hand under her tankini when three adolescent girls (Julie, Meg, and Kitty) came around and giggled. They stood up abruptly. Julie stated that she was leaving, sorry to "interrupt," and since Kirsten had arrived with her, she might wish to join her. End of adventure #2.

adventure #3

Todd Redmond called at 8:42 P.M. She was watching TV and the sound of the phone produced definite *endocrinological mischief* and chills along the curve of her buttocks. Her mother answered and further signs of E.M. broke out (chills, tachychardia) as her mother's words indicated that indeed the call was for Kirsten, and as she answered she heard the cool breathy voice of Todd:

Hey.

Hey.

What's going on?

Not much.

You wanna hang—

Oh, well—

I can meet you—

—my folks

—*Fuck* that—

—Well—

Say you need girl stuff or something, like go to CVS.

Unh-hunh.

Come o—o—n, Kirst.

She waited a reasonable amount of time, watched the end of her show. Anybody need anything? she said casually. I got to go to CVS. *No, hon. Thanks. Drive safe.*

They met at the CVS. She, Kirsten, suggested they go to the Battlegrounds. (Her plan is to make out for a half an hour or so, and go home. She likes to teeter on the edge of passion and then run away.) Todd deferred, said it was kind of boring there, I don't know, just is, embarassed that in reality the park is scary to him, he heard it was haunted. When he went there a year ago with his friend Sammy, the woods were dark and thickish, and Sammy told him lots of boys were killed there and their spirits ranged the forest and they were looking for fresh blood, they ripped your guts out and so on, said Sammy, getting all frenzied, and Todd said, Yeah, right, hey, I got to get back, I have to do stuff for my mom. He, of course, didn't admit Sammy had freaked him out. He didn't want to go back to that creepy park. Too many "The Hook" stories of kissing teenagers in cars getting clawed up combined with the Sammy story had made it imperative he stay away. He suggested to Kirsten, instead, a construction site, a comfort zone for him. She got in his car and Todd parked next to a front-end loader and a cherry picker, on Route 626 by LAKEVIEW, *offering scenic waterviews in the heart of Loudoun County.* He drank a Coke and Southern Comfort blend that she shared (provided by the fact that both parents are out of the house, his mother at a shower she catered, his father on a golf weekend, Todd is at home by himself. Mother Diane locks the liquor cabinet and the wine cellar due to an unfortunate occurrence last spring where her daughter, Candace, had a sleepover party, whereupon boys entered throught the french doors and the children, seeking quick intoxication, managed to consume husband Bob The Mayor's prize 1946 *Saint- Emilion Bordeaux,* bought at his company auction for a cool $1,000, especially irritating as they mixed it with sugar. The locked cabinets are no problem to Todd, who has mastered the crude lock with a hair pin.)

After the teenagers imbibe the concoction, Kirsten and Todd proceed to kiss (to Kirsten, Todd always has and always will smell of an overly sweet dryer softener, and taste of Sprite, lemony and wet), Kirsten is eager for activity but has learned the protocol requires her to turn over all initiative powers to Todd, and she has her plan of stopping in half an hour or so, yet Todd has removed her sweatshirt, removed his T-shirt (while they listen to Blink 182), she actually removes her bra, meanwhile they are tongue-kissing, he pulls at her pants, clothes are off in a few more minutes, she is starting to panic, she has lost control of the situation, she means to get up and stop this acceleration, things are going too fast, yet some part of her can't stop, she lies down beside the steering wheel, there is quite a bit of flesh grinding, *Now,* she says to herself, *stop now,* but then Todd suddenly pulls back and plunges, roughly, into Kirsten, she reacts and leans up quickly, *Owww!* he is thrown back into the glove compartment, *Owww, shit!* End of adventure #3.

A Candy Striper's Duties

Being a candy striper, one is exposed to all sorts of people, there are the patients, the doctors, the administration, the social workers and one must learn to be courteous, kind, and cheerful. A candy striper, after all, is performing an important duty in society, volunteering to aid in the speedy recovery of patients. We are grateful for your time and ask that you obey certain rules.

1. Please keep your uniform neat, and pressed.

2. We ask for your punctuality at all times.

3. Please do not fraternize with any of the staff or patients beyond your volunteer hours.

Sincerely,
Mrs. Feittles-Lopez
Director of Junior Candy Stripe Program

There is no adventure #4. Adventure #3 promptly sealed the deal, thank you, albeit unromantic and clumsy, it stilled managed to cleave DNA to DNA and matter to subject, and after that night, when she returned slightly confused, thwarted, still aroused, a loose and liquidy feeling in her tummy, she brushed her teeth, and unbeknownst to her, a stirring in her deepest regions, there popped a tiny rice grain speck of life, a spiraling dot grow-ing in that flat, tan abdomen of Kirsten's, she brushed her teeth with Pepsodent extra brightening power, she put on her pink Hello Kitty PJs, curled up around her old ripped doggie, Brownie. So then she slept, Kirsten, slightly sad, school tomorrow, then candy-striping, homework.

Todd at that time had fallen into watching an old Danny Kaye movie on the classic movie channel. He had gotten sucked into the story. He ate potato chips, tried not to think of Kirsten, because when he did, his whole being buckled in a whippet of heat, from his reddening face down to his groin.

She was sleeping and didn't dream of him as cells split inside her, tis-sues formed, a tiny spinning in her center.

free bird
1, 2, & 3

C.R. goes home

On the occasion when your woman has left you.
When it's almost Christmas.
When you probably have no job.
When you've fallen in love with a sixteen year old earlier in the
week.
When babies have died.
When snow is so beautiful falling on your face you want to tell
the world with bourbon-laced words—

I.

All said about passion and all, it still hurts to come home to a place where a person who supposedly loved you, has left. Where the lights are off and you feel around the wall for the switch. Where a sunken chill lies in the rooms because no blood has stirred warmth through the air. Where his old dog named Djinn finally died a day ago, too, so he doesn't scratch up on C.R.'s knees the way he used to or bark sharply (in fact, the last years of Djinn were defined by the poor bony hide dragging himself from one ratty dog cushion to the other by the fireplace, filling the air with that heated burlap old-dog smell as he sashayed across the wood floor, scratching his nails, *s-cc-rr, s—cc—rr,* settling in his circular creaky swirl, heaving a swoosh of fragrant dog sigh, two brown wet eyes blinking and closing. Yet, C.R. was grateful for even that from the dog, for Djinn was the last of his family, the last one left).

There are no kind smells of meat cooking or coffee or even dog exhalation, there is only bland darkness, another kind of death, not a mass of struggling horses and men, ripped and bleeding like Gettysburg, but a barren emptiness.

Now you know he and this Eleanor woman weren't married: C.R. could never figure out how to do that. When he was younger there was just too much stuff going on, there were late nights at work, there were conferences, meetings, speeches, lectures, field studies, and he fit in occasional women as sidelines, and there were plenty, and this suited him just fine: blond nurses, an occasional Realtor, a horsy photographer, a divorcée, there was a pleasant casualness to it all he liked, and if they didn't, he very limberly swerved out of the way, kept it *lite*, harmless, fun. For example, seeing a nurse named Shelly, a slightly plump girl with wavy hair like a heavy camp blanket and big titties, which were nice under a shirt but in bed were a bit pale and stretched-looking around the areolas, loose and out of control, they kind of fell against him as they embraced, soft and pillowy, basically they were in the way, but that wasn't like some huge problem. She would get up flouncing those buoyant things, he'd be shaving, a towel around his middle, his body always suggested compact leanness which was very appealing, and just a week earlier he'd said, passing her by the stained, beige coffee machine, *I've got a reception tonight at Leniere's if you'd like to go, just thought we could have some fun*, of course, they'd been flirting back and forth, she was new from Dallas and yes, she'd heard the rumors, Oh, he's nice but danger, danger, a big old flirt, they said, but her relationship with Steve, the computer management guy, was over since he was getting married to a woman he'd met in his office and most nights were spent alone watching *Friends* with portable sushi, or going to Spanky Shenanigans where she met contractors and plumbers and cops, so she'd said yes, she had found him very charming in the shabby tweed coat and his long, gangling legs and the constant smile and his messy hair, he'd picked her up in his '65 Ford truck, admired her lovely angora sweater ($24.99 at Marshalls), pinched her leg, jokes, a few bourbons, chitchats at the party, then they'd left and gone to his house. Then there had to be the first move. One of them would do it, a casual touch, then kissing (C.R. had a deep and probing tongue, a soft curved mouth that opened warmly), and in this romantic sense of himself, C.R. imagined he had *the man-woman thing* down, he knew, or he thought he knew, what women liked, he enjoyed foreplay and in this particular case, on their first night after Leniere's, they started on the couch listening to John Coltrane, he had lit a fire and was telling Shelly a funny story about a doctor they both knew, Alvarez, and she laughed a snorty little puffy thing, and then there was The Moment, so he said, *oh, well*, and he reached over and brushed her hair to the side, she smiled a little smile and said, *oh,* so he and she both tilted forward, and their lips grazed and then there was the parting of dry skin leading to wet insides, their tongues kind of helixed in a moist reverie. And then there was the awkward thing, which C.R. didn't even realize was part of his standard mating pattern, he knocked her teeth with his, or slightly bit her tongue, or slipped in his seat a bit, precipitating a retraction from both, and a muffled giggle or two, which would unleash the built-up tension at this point and allow them to begin anew with fevered passion, so with Shelly he knocked her teeth (and this was all complete limbic methodology, a slight faltering pattern C.R. wasn't aware of: If he had been a physician of this neuroseismology, he might have advanced theories in this direction, but since it was part of him, that ganglion lay fiercely wild and separate from his neocortex, like two lost continents with different languages and customs, ones that mistrusted each other and led wholly separate lives). So, the release valve of laughter, and then a surge of hormonal impetus and he became feverishly busy, the tongue a swashbuckling whippet in her mouth, the soft angora sweater pulled statickly from her downy hair, the pink-as-an-anemone lace bra palpated and gnawed and undone and the great slippery bosoms wet and firming under his tongue, her skirt splayed forth up over the hips, her soft, manicured hand trifling with the thick veins of corduroy on his crotch, the elastic around her pale lilac underpants snagged around her hips as he rolled them down entwined in his large, knucklish hands—

(At this point, you can signal the beginning chords of "Free Bird" by Lynyrd Skynyrd, young C.R.'s favorite song, the ecclesiastical organ, the whiny guitar chords, C.R. coming home from the hospital has found this CD as he stands now, swaying slightly from all the Triscuits and bourbon earlier, he sways in front of the stereo console and finds in the back their *Greatest Hits,* bought by himself at the local Wal-Mart, along with his old favorite teen songs, his Led Zeppelin, his Aerosmith, his beloved Bad Company, but most of all Lynyrd Skynyrd, his "Free Bird," his anthem of pimpledom, drunk with Wild Turkey and Coke, pouring out of Chevy Novas or Mom's borrowed Country

Squire wood-trimmed station wagon, a gaggle of girls' legs and Thai stick smoke and "Free Bird" blaring—when you reach that *return moment,* when, like C.R., you've tired of cocktail parties with Harry Connick, Jr. and retro martinis, tired of swing music back in again (and tiresome dance lessons) or feeble attempts at Pearl Jam or, like housewives imagining themselves up to date in white Ford Explorers listening to pitiful freeze-dried whiners like Matchbox 20, when jazz, that noble rioting, becomes *Kenny G,* when rock becomes Muzak ("Purple Haze" by 1,001 Strings), when punk rock becomes yellow spray paint for hair bought at the CVS, and maybe the closest he's come to knowing new music was back on an eight-track, he found himself in Wal-Mart, sent by Eleanor to pick up a new dog bed for Djinn, and walked by the music section, saw the rap section and didn't know any of the names, and then saw *Lynyrd Skynyrd's Greatest Hits,* and suddenly all pumped up, he bought it, and all the others, now this was what he liked! He'd forgotten! It was joyful rediscovery! and when he brought it back, Eleanor! Hell, listen to this! the first chords brought not this familiar feeling he hoped for, the giddy joyful feeling "Free Bird" used to bring, signaling nights of drunken, sloppy, stoned driving and fucking and yelling at cars and cruising around Pizza Hut and beating up other boys, blood mashed into his knuckles, instead it brought this funereal sadness to the room, Eleanor in her jeans making a Bloody Mary, her ass flat and Realtoresque, the hunt prints on the wall, a burgundy leather couch in front of a fire, a brass fire set, a Butler wood coffee table, Stouffer's lasagne in the oven, what happened to sucking a smelly bong with four others crammed in the back of a Bronco, what happened to *turn that fucker up,* what happened to warping his hand in the soft underwear of a high school girl—?)

There lies moist-mouthed Shelly, in anticipation:

Her underwear springs from her arched-up behind like a boomerang and ricochets to the corner of the room, and then pursues the zippers and the buttons and the crumpling of sweaters and shirts and twisting around and fumbling, always like this the first time with a new person, learning their size and accommodations and feel, he lies against her, kissing her ear, moving in the usual up and down, and around, she strokes the pale golden hairs on his ass, and now:

His hands woven in her hair, he is always present, always says *you're so fucking wonderful* and he means it, C.R. makes love, and the woman is the most joyous, most lovely thing he has ever had the good grace to enjoy and he will say that full-heartedly, *you feel like something unreal,* the voice shaking with emotion, there is water in his eyes, and he loves her with the generous heaving of a kind of happiness he wants to share, his body is fully present, it is the whorling splash of champagne in the mouth, stars in the black Virginia sky, divine intervention, tangerine and honeyed kisses, the end of the world couldn't be more cataclysmic, *dance with me, sugar,* limeade in a hammock, dancing girls, *oh, you, you,* lightning, bonfires in October, Goddamn,

GODDAMN, GODDAMN
Sweet.
Jesus.

Over. Hot skin, quivering heartbeats, tangled bodies, the fire needs another log, the CD's stopped, makeup smeared. There begins the kind smile of detachment, the good decent towels of *move on,* the freshly ground coffee of *it's been nice, but.* There's always good, decent politeness. There are doors and phones, too. And C.R. just manages swiftly, as wind, to move on in the kindest way, almost inadvertently. Eleanor, maybe because he's in his forties now, stays around for a while, they dine, they laugh. Movies and such. But marriage?

Why?

2.

Why, exactly?

That's what Eleanor thought two months ago when the problems started. She said to C.R., when she had so delicately broached the subject of marriage in an artful schoolteacherish way, the way some make math fun, like instead of numbers, let's count Hershey's kisses! Wheee! and then suddenly they were doing multiplication tables. In this manner she said, Oh, guess what, Kerry and Lisa are getting married. Very simple. Very oh-by-the-way. The subject broached. She waited a bit. Stirred two Bloody Marys she was making at the bar with her expert recipe, two spoons of horseradish and Beefamato, and celery and all that. Kind of like an atomic gazpacho, she liked to say. C.R. said, unfortunately, *holy shit! That old fool.* Didn't sound very promising, so Eleanor added a bit of sugar to her voice, Now what do you have against marriage, hunh? Just going to be some old geezer by yourself? as she draped herself next to him on the couch holding both drinks, I mean, it's not the end of the world, darling. She did have the right to call him darling and angel and baby, she had earned those. He used those words, too, and they sounded so sweet coming from his leathery voice, they had been together now six months, his longest relationship in a while, the fact is, he very much *liked* Eleanor. She was an attractive woman (longish dark hair against her shoulders, a thirtysomething trim and sinewy runner body, though lacking an ass unfortunately, tanned skin, perky green eyes), a very suitable humor for C.R., a familiar type of woman, not overly sexy or soft, not soft at all, kind of hard in a real estate lecturey way and plaid pants and grainy forearms, kind of like his *mother,* no nonsense, hard legs in loafers, she was even a Garden Club member, going to luncheons frequently and returning with canvas bags of free gifts).

Well, he said stretching out his long legs against the threadbare Belouche rug his father had picked up from Persia in the thirties, I'm sure it's fine for some, just not everyone, certainly not old losers like myself, and besides, it's *crazy.*

OK. An impasse. She rethought. And what if you want to have kids?

Oh, Eleanor, he smiled, can you imagine me as a Daddy? Come on. It'd be illegal. Obscene. I can barely take care of my own sorry old ass.

He knew where this was going, he'd been down this road before, fact is, it scared the shit out of him, and sipping the Bloody Mary, he felt full-fledged sadness seeping through as nausea, he didn't really want Eleanor right here, right now, he had just put in the new *Lynyrd Skynyrd's Greatest*

Hits, played "Free Bird" as she shook the Beefamato, and how damn sad it made him. Her Realtor's ass! His goddamn Butler table from his mother! He had a punch bowl in a cabinet from his mother! What was that for? And he had shoe trees made of polished cedar his father gave him years back and handmade tweed coats and Eleanor talking of marriage! He would be what so many women loved to say a "commitment-phobe," as if so many choices lay ahead but he couldn't commit, he could commit, fucking A! He'd committed to life, to living in Virginia, to working at the hospital, to saving babies' lives, it wasn't commitment, it was the fact that she didn't all that grab him. Eleanor just didn't make him crazy. He wanted to love her insanely. He didn't. He was absurdly idealistic in this matter. Marriage would be some form of death. He was sickened by her now, her motherly pose. She droned on. He was getting edgy. The Bloody Mary was loosening him up and he felt mean and reckless, and how many times did he have to talk about marriage, the dreaded subject. *What* is the damn deal with this thing. Can't people just *hang* without a future involved. Can't we just enjoy the moment? So many thought themselves clever, as if he'd never thought of it. Why, here's an idea.

Never, is what I mean. And Eleanor, I want to be real straight. He looked at her and his eyes, which often looked hooded, lifted up.

I could never do that. That's not me. I don't want to mislead you. I'm just, no way, *not* the marrying kind, that bullshit crap, that slow death, that awful, awful—

Oh, sssh, she said. You old bear. She smiled and made him smile.

Why *ruin* things—(the old cliché)

Why do we have to be like everyone else? she said (another cliché).

Oh, that's it. She said *we.* She meant them, getting married. Now that's that. She'll be prodding forevermore, slowly carving away. He would never hesitate if it were the woman he wished to marry, he would be bold, as he was in all things, he would stake out her house, implant himself, consume her, confiscate her, he wouldn't, over Bloody Marys, Stouffer's lasagne, and Realtor chitchat (*showed the McCauley house today to two yupsters from Herndon, ugh*), he wouldn't over those circumstances slowly come around to the idea, like deciding to purchase property in North

Carolina or something, and the glaring fact she was so distastefully plodding forward, so stolidly biding her time, burned his heart. She got up because the timer went off for the lasagne (Is it a crime to actually cook a meal? he thought then. Maybe I'll take it up as a hobby and make some Boudin Blanc or some Pork Vindaloo or something, day in and day out with hospital turkey sandwiches and Stouffer's or Reubens at his club or Triscuits and cheese, what happened to the days of home-baked rolls and such?), his dog Djinn limped over for a sniff and a headrub in C.R.'s lap, he loved Djinn, the old scamp, he rubbed her ears, Djinn stood gravely while Eleanor semimoved in, there were a few suits of hers in the closet, she'd slowly infiltrated his drawers with a few *essentials*, she placed a bowl of some kind of citric potpourri on his toilets, and bought pot holders with grapevine motifs, so he wouldn't have to grab a towel for that, and brought her good pans and knives in case she decided to cook (OK, so she made a stir-fry the other day, but it was fat-free, she used spray Pam and it was half raw and sauceless, kind of a tumble of cooked salad), and glacine-sighted Djinn took in the woman, unmoved.

The lasagne ready, she brought it to the table and they ate it with their Bloody Marys and already there was a feltlike quiet to their dinner, like the old couples at the Denny's in town, they ate the familiar rubbery layers of pasta and he kept trying to switch subjects, bring it back to where they were, discussing a movie he wanted to see, and she glazed over on that, fork in midair, You know what's funny, she said, Kenny said he'd never marry either, remember that?

Oh, C.R.'s spirits sunk.

There had been a perfectly nice, sweet woman named Spiffy Edwards last year, who decorated for the horsy set, lots of fun, they went to auctions together, and she started this banter also, and that was that, C.R. faded away in a quick, compulsory manner, and she ended up marrying a divorced doctor he knew named Seay, an endocrinologist, and he would run into them at parties and Seay was uneasy now around him, suspicious and kind of overly friendly. And there were lots, actually, that would start the marriage bit and so C.R. was patently and irritatingly used to it.

Worse still, there was the inevitable lull after dinner, the plates washed tidily by them both and the counters wiped down, another log in the fire, she'd picked a CD, because he'd stay away from that place now, the Lynyrd Skynyrd plunging an icy dagger in his old heart, she'd picked Ella Fitzgerald and settled down next to him on the couch and they'd have to make love, he hold forth and fake the emotion required, for at this point, he almost disliked Eleanor, and all her plans that he felt duped and led along by, he would have to lie there afterward and feel horrible streaks of a barreling need for newness and she'd murmur stuff, and each day would fall forward into a stiff mockery of their life before, and he'd feel like a pursued animal. This had all happened before, so as the mating rituals began (she started kissing his neck), he pulled away sharply, his heart was pounding, *Eleanor,* he began,

Yes, darling? (Oh, oh, make it a little easier, he thought.)

I'm never, and God I don't mean to be unkind, I'm never going to marry you or anyone, in fact—

And her eyes were pooling now, those sharp Talbots eyes, and he sat up straight.

In fact, this whole thing feels, feels just kind of *wrong* or off and my heart's just not in it. I'm sorry.

She didn't say anything or argue. She bolted up and there was a scramble of things as she sniffled and pushed Djinn aside, *oh, C.R.!* she yelled at one point, he resisted the urge to go to her and smooth it all over, although he desperately wanted to, but why add another six months on the painful death of their relationship? She paused before she slammed the door, looking at C.R. and the dog, and said, *I'll get my things later oh screw you. You are so dumb, C.R. So dumb. I always hated that stupid dog.* He didn't answer.

So for a while he awoke and dressed to the silent disapproval of those few suits in the closet she hadn't picked up yet, they stayed stiff and pressed under folds of sheer dry cleaner plastic, swaying gently like jellyfish as he would roughly grab a jacket, and the potpourri lay undisturbed, wafting its arid odor of sickly interment, her knives lay in his drawers and her pots stayed in the drying rack permanently, their copper bottoms the reminder of Eleanor's anger as she sped out the door, he left them there, wondering what the lull meant, why she didn't get them, did she lie in hiding waiting for the gravel's crunch of his sorrowful arrival at her house?

A few weeks went by and then there was the candy striper moment and C.R. had been in some reckless frame of mind to go along with the young girl, no Eleanor, Tuffy dead, the girl in his office, and now C.R. arrived at his cold home, jobless, a sixteen-year-old girl's phone number (her private line) crumpled on Hello Kitty stationery in his left pocket and Eleanor's things were magically gone now, the closet's left side empty, the pans and knives gone, the essentials, even the potpourri.

His extra house key flung on the Butler coffee table, no note, nothing.

Back to C.R. now, swaying from the bourbon, he finds the "Free Bird" CD and plays it, gripping the edge of the fireplace, now the music doesn't sound like seventeen anymore nor like a slow death, it is actually snowing now outside in the tiny and fine way it does when it means business, at this point C.R. feels slightly festive, and wishes he could go and chop down a Christmas tree, right here, right now.

Instead, he feels the crumpled paper of the candy striper in his pocket, and then asks himself:

Am I that type of old loser now?

3.

Attempting to dial her number, he says to himself, I suppose that *is* what type of loser I am now, but *jail* somehow stops him dead in his tracks, what a chill. No girl's thighs are worth that. What starts to cross his mind is how much he misses that dog. He sits on his couch reading *Time* magazine and misses that dog curled up next to him, he's propped up Shrub on the mantel, he has his bourbon and his Triscuits and his chocolates from work, and as he sits down missing the dog, the phone rings and it's Pendleton's voice rough and brown-sugary on the message machine, *C.R.? C.R.? Give me a call will ya? I'm at my office, I need to discuss something with you* and there are lots of messages he realizes, the light is blinking frantically, he wonders what Betty told them, but strangely, he feels his whole career is probably down the tubes, all the years, but how could Pendleton, his best friend, his childhood buddy, fire him, his years of dedication to the hospital? For a mishandling leading to NEC, in a world of guesses and near misses for babies that years ago died within seconds? Or miraculously lay in shoe boxes, drinking the breast milk dribbled from an eyedropper, and somehow survived? *Am I supposed to be some fucking God, now, Shrub?* he said to his beloved portrait, Because try as I may, I can't guarantee life, you know.

C.R. got the portrait of Colonel Shrub from his daddy, who claimed him as their relative on his side. He spoke of how he had their house built of stone and wood for his family, and how he, too, mended the local town through their illnesses.

Though Lord knows it was primitive, his father would say. They hadn't much, son. Just a few tools and poultices and such. They were big on poultices, son. Mustard ones, onion ones, horseradish. Hell, they'd chop any old thing and smear it on themselves if it meant a cure, you know? Flu could take you right quick and surely it did. All the time. Children just *go*, overnight, whole families. Just up and gone. I wouldn't've wanted to be old Shrub, may he rest in peace. Almost lost all he won, then he died out in his own field by the river. Although he was close to home, that was good, I suppose. Was it? I don't know. I don't know.

And his father used to tell him tales of Colonel and surgeon Doctor "Shrub," his kindness, how many men he saved on the field, his wild outfit with the red sash, and to C.R. he became some kind of God, and in fact as a child he prayed to the portrait, Dear General, Please let my dog get better when his childhood dog, Lefty, lay stiff from a copperhead bite and C.R. was eight and he begged that portrait to get the dog better and strangely enough that dog recovered and lived five more years, until it was run over by a tractor. So even though that was many years ago, he couldn't break the habit of talking to the portrait when alone, and truly, in some sense he considered that portrait one of his best friends. His father told him more about the man, how he had eight children and lost all but one, two to influenza within two weeks of each other, young Wil-

83

liam, age three, and baby Maria, three months, how Teddy, who was dearly his beloved boy, was knocked from a horse and died ten days later and how one, Cannie, was stillborn, another, Joseph, died from pertussis, the fields of childhood were strewn with the littered bodies of tiny children back then to whom disease lay waste.

It was December when Colonel Shrub lost Teddy and Maria Hampton his wife lay in bed in some bleary reverie of madness, already she had lost five of her children, already any futile attempt she had made to secure them to safety had been dissolved, she lay with cloths on her head and felt mad and delirious, not knowing a fever had set in, she made her nurse bring baby Richard and Elizabeth into her room where she would not permit them to play or sing or speak and they began to whine, the girl brought them batter bread to eat and they ate it by the fire and watched their mother's odd glasslike eyeballs stare at them and allow them no recess, it was years back, a time of simple joy in December, time to eat an orange and sing, they sang fully in those days. Colonel Shrub hadn't spoken to Maria in weeks and the jolting, stabbing pain in his leg grew worse, the doctor gave him ether and bourbon and he lay him on a wooden table and he felt a bolt of lightning shoot hot through his bone when the doctor sawed off what was left of it, he lay back and saw the roof of his own eyes and heard his voice bark out deep and womanish in the dark night and his ears rang, he was ashamed later, he yelled and he heard voices hushing in circles around him and the doctors yelling, and the iced smell in his nose of the ether and he went somewhere else, to his home for a while and saw the driveway, saw the trees. Every flower in bloom. This was not his house forever. This land would go on, unperturbed. Other people would inhabit it with their own good lives clogged with grief and joy. Then, smashed back to the wood table and his flailing arms. God sakes, Colonel, the doctor screamed. Lay still! Every move jolting the pain up through his groin, the candles burned and smelled of fat, his five children were dead but there was this anchored rod of resolve that would see the end of the war, that would get him back to Maria Hampton, to the last of his children, the waters were foul, and Colonel Shrub groaned distressingly, Lord have mercy on me, he muttered, amongst his men lice-infested, eating mules & dogs & dead horses, gathered round fires between the savage brutality of combat, whilst a deadly rain of shot bespeckled with blood, hummed and pinged thru the air, midst this spectacle Colonel Shrub felt this sickly sharp agony and thundering from his voice came the bellowing, jagged cry he had forced down, My children, my life, my leg, all agonies torn forward, at this time, as they hacked down through the gangrenous flesh, through the purple interior of his bone, his small child, the next to last, at that moment grew faint and silent, curling up by the fire, coughing, the mother popped up at the sound, she could hear gunshots in the distance, her husband was gone and maimed, but that particular weak cough of a child bolted her upright and surged another current of adrenaline through her tiny-boned frame, *ohhhh, William baby boy,* she whispered and the child looked down all bleary, Colonel Shrub bellowed then at that moment as his leg was cut through, Maria Hampton screamed for Tillie, the nurse—

C.R. stands in front of the portrait, his hands on the rough, painted surface. What part of me is you, sir? What part of me contains your valor?

C.R. feels distraught, gets up, puts on his long, tattered camel hair coat and big Sherpa hat, snow boots, and prepares to set out, finds his gloves in the back of the closet, and thinks: Ought to at least put a bone on Djinn's grave, ought, ought to put a wreath on the door, ought to get a tree, ought to burn this place down with me in it. What am I doing.

All a jumbled rat-tail of thoughts.

So he goes out, the door releases a pretty wave of whirling flakes caught in the rays of light from the above hall light. Is there anything more lovely? he thinks. The snow has fallen on the trees and grass and smoothly glows in the twilight.

snapshots of the land,

1 – 7

Now and always:

Outside, the vast fields. The ragged pines, cedars. Shrub fields. Cool springs sunk in the valley of rocks. Huge warts of rock, white quartz. Sucked-in valleys. You get to know the land from walking, from feeling it with your gait. From the femur and hamstring bend. When you hunted, you traipsed, sat, thought. The air became subtle and showed the day.

2.

One day ago:

At early morn C.R. awoke in his big drafty house called Ashland up on the hill by Ball's Bluff, he awoke and something was wrong. The hour, evidenced by the faint light, was about five. He never used an alarm clock. Just the quick wet tongue of the dog, old Djinn. Yet, the man lay there in this dark bed, a half-indigo light against the yellowing paisley wallpaper of the thirties, and knew something was different. His face was dry as sand. No hot blast of rancorous dog joy. Rising up, panic, to his dog's round form at the end, and one hand, no, one *glance*, for C.R. being a physician knows all too well the loss of life by eye, yes, one brief glance portends the conclusion of this episode. Indeed, the dog was dead. A cold coat and an improper texture of artificiality greeted his hand. His old dog, Djinn, had finally died. So now is either the beginning or the end, depending on how you view it, up on the edge of his land. We can start everything here in the blue light of dawn as C.R. in his bathrobe digs a grave for this dog, steam chopping out of his mouth, and lowers the animal in that hole, wrapped in an afghan his mother made, that is where the story starts, on this old land with the stiff, cottony red coat of the dog, covered in wave after wave of brown dirt glistening with frozen crystal, we start here with the fact that now, after many generations of children, dog, mother, father, servant, friends, horse, cousins, grandfather, uncle, niece, all the rich stew of familial presence, in this house of Ashland at the present, with the loss of this old Labrador, Djinn, a beloved dog, C.R. is the only one left to walk this land.

3.

Twenty-eight years ago:

The Potomac River lay dark and liquid brown, glossy as wet blood. In the morning, from a corner of the land, it glowed like sulphur. In the evening, it hovered with steam.

Find the stuff, said C.R., a teenaged version of the man, lanky and bold-muscled.

Pendleton lay out, smoking.

This here's the spot. Aha.

The boys moved over in the squashed grass, C.R. casually pulling through the weeds in jeans.

I might find a bone. If I find a bone of some old soldier I'm going to make a necklace of it.

Creepy, said a girl.

You're in all, shit, all *mud,* my boy, says his man, Pendleton.

Whoops, uh-oh, my shoe. *Sick.* Covered with it. That's my dad's shoe, too.

He'll be happy.

I'll hose it off, is what I'll do.

He'll smell that river on them.

I'll perfume them, how about that. I'll use your stinking cologne.

C.R., come over here, a redheaded girl named Tammy said. I'm lonely.

He passed her a bottle of Southern Comfort Pendleton had brought.

This is the prettiest spot. Where's your house from here.

We're south, it's to the north.

Over *there*?

Yeah.

It's getting dark.

Let's walk over on the bluff.

No! There's ghosts.

Come *on*. Whoooooooo.

I'll go, said Pendleton, to impress a dark-haired girl named Emily.

I will, too, she said, being sweet on Pendleton.

Come on, Tammy.

You'll have to hold my hand hard.

I will.

They walked on through the cedared woods, snapping underfoot.

There's the graves.

I say we have a *séance*.

Like you know what a *séance* is, friend.

I can figure it out, though. Conjure up ghosts. Come *on*, Confederate boys, load your muskets, let's see what you look like.

Pendleton and Emily sat by a grave. He kissed her mouth and she lay against him.

I am ttHe GGGGhost off Colllonelllll SSSShrub!!!! said C.R., running around the headstones, Give me MY LEG!

Stop it! screamed Tammy. Stop it!

I WANT MY LEG DAMN YOU, you cute thing. Boy. YOU ARE PRETTY FINE AND GIVE ME MY LE—

Aaaaaaaaaaaaaaah! AHH! I'm not kidding!

I COME FOR TAMMY. *Shoot*, girl! You just grab my leg?

No, I did *not*. Aaahhh! C.R. I wish we'd get, go, out of here, I'm leaving!

Hell, something *did* grab my leg. Let's go. Jesus! Let's go to my house, then. Hey, butthead, come on, you all.

You all go on, said the sleepy voice of Pendleton.

4.

Thirty-eight years ago:

Young C.R., hair, hat-stiffened and color of brass. Standing out in the flat winter air by the thicket of evergreens by the edge of Ball's Bluff. Clippy sound of birds loosened on the wind. His breath, uneven, sending out steam, thinking, Where'd he die, exactly. Where did Shrub actually die. Was it here?

C.R. sat next to the edge of the woods, on lichen-covered felled log. Grass was greener near this spot and a person could've come up through the woods like they say he did and be shot and be dead in this very spot dead dead right here, wondering, like how many eyes looked up here branches crisscrossing the sky like so many spiders' poky legs and saw that for their final look not fireworks or pretty candles or anything. Probably hearing boom boom of cannons or maybe nothing just the sound of blood running out of you maybe like the sound of creek here and seeing clouds in shapes. A young C.R. thought these fast worries, scraping at a log with a little stick. The bark came off soft and chewy while he sunk back toward the leaves, crunched up, looking around the dawn of this edge of woods, a cold rifle in his other hand (lent to him by his father):

Does it hurt. When you die.

How's it feel to have a cannon flung at you.

Or being stabbed. He wanted to stab himself once with a knife. Almost did. To find out what it feels like. Then he thought he might die so he didn't.

Add that to being bored, being hungry. Being bored and wanting to go back to bed. Also, not knowing how he can shoot the animal if he sees one. Why, anyway. His father doesn't seem to entertain this idea, young C.R. becomes scared of this idea, ricocheting into thoughts of causing death, blending into, fearing death. His own. Realizant of the fact many died in this field, so he was told. Legs were chopped off and etcetera worse, gross things he tries not to think of.

Then:

Corner of his eye, he missed the tom that cracked by, fast on its feathers.

I sent him up your way, his dad said later by the fire in a can out back where he burned extra brush, I sent him up but you were daydreaming or something. I myself liked to have nailed that mister.

I was thinking.

Well, hunh. That's good.

About that Colonel dying and stuff out here.

I told you that. Minnie ball. Don't throw stuff in the fire please.

No, I mean. What he feels like. How it feels and stuff. Does it hurt badly and stuff.

Well, I've seen my share of people dying. It doesn't seem bad. That's all I know. There was Mrs. Yates last week. Mrs. Viola Yates, you know who I'm talking about? That lady teaches piano? Nice lady. She says, she says to me, I say, Well, hello, Mrs. Yates and she just says, Guess where I'm going? Well, I don't know, I said, but then she just falls over. Just like that. Over on the edge, you know, edge of the bed, stone dead. That was right *weird*. I've heard all kinds of stuff, and it all I guess seems OK to me, son. Hard to explain. If you keep throwing those damn things in the fire, I'll smack you.

5.

Forty years ago:

The engine was on, humming. The radio played an old tune.

His mother in the pickup truck, her bandannaed head out the window, smoking. Carrie, there's a perfect tree here, right here in front of our truck, she said. No, no, his father said. Sorry, sweetie but that one's missing a whole side from over here. Well *pick* one then, for Christ's sake, I'm really freezing out here, where's C.R.?

I think he's on the other side.

I thought he went up by that grove, Carrie. That's a good spot for trees.

His dad's voice boomed out across the snow:

Where *are* you son.

I got one, his young voice said.

You sure? Where are you?

I'm on a grave.

Do *not* stand on those graves, son. Get *off* there C.R. this instant.

I am I am, the boy's voice came in choppy waves, closer and closer, until he stood next to his father, out of breath. Who died here. Anyway. But that *was*. A good tree. Daddy.

Catch your breath, son. You know the man in the picture?

The Colonel?

He died here, that's who.

Why did he die?

Some men were fighting wars here.

Was there blood?

Surely.

Lots of blood.

A whole ocean of blood.

Yuck.

Doctors see a lot of blood. You get used to it.

He was a doctor too?

He was. A fine doctor. He saved a lot of lives. We have letters.

He sewed up people who were chopped up and shot up.

In a sense.

I said, I said, I'm *really* ready to go back boys. I'm awfully cold.

Your poor mother is freezing, son.

We don't have a tree.

This will do. It's weak on the side but looks all right.

Can I do the saw?

I prefer not, son. When you're ten you can.

I can do it.

I said no, and I mean it. OK. Understood?

Yeah.

You were practically born out here, you know. You were almost born in these trees.

I was?

You started to come along here because your mother fell, just over there. We were getting a tree, just like today. It was damn cold. Muriel was with us. I was scared to death.

Was that why I was born so little?

I brought your mother into the study, in front of the fire and Muriel went to make tea and I went to wash my hands and call Dr. Ferguson, and your mother yelled.

Yeah?

And I come running and she was holding you, you little skinned squirrel, you.

Was I crying?

Thankfully yes, thankfully, you were in front of a fire. We wrapped you up quick. You were squalling out little peeps, waaahh, like a mouse or something. We fed you her milk with an eyedropper. You were so tiny, son. God, it's a miracle you're here, it is.

That shoe box part.

Well, we kept you in there. Got the chicken incubator and put the box in it. Though your mother stayed right by all night, all day holding you. Muriel would take turns. They all'd sing to you. I'd sit by you, too. We took turns, the three of us. We didn't put you in the hospital. There were some scary moments, I thought you might have sepsis.

What's that?

Infection and stuff. But you pulled through.

I want to be a doctor when I grow up. I want to help babies.

That'd be nice.

What if I had died?

Well, we'd be sad.

I'd be sadder.

God sakes, have you gotten anything yet? Just chop something down any old tree boys, yelled Helen from the car.

Well. I guess we'd. Hey. Look out there. Look, son.

What's that?

That's a eight-point buck is what it is.

Whoa.

Carrie! Do you hear me hon? (bleating of car horn, bleahhh, bleahhh!!)
Shuh, woman. Hot damn. There he goes.

6.

Forty-six years ago:

Ashland, surrounded by field and vale and evergreens. Carrie and Helen
Ash lay out across the snow, flashlights in hand, seeking an appropriate
evergreen to go in the front hall. Muriel waited in the car. She didn't care
to get cold. No sir. It was a *truck*, actually. Carrie's new truck, bought last
year, to go with his recent marriage to Miss Helen Abigail Stirling, whom
he'd known since he was fourteen. The wedding pictures lay in silver on the
piano. She was a lovely girl, now pregnant with his child. She moved through
the snow carefully in a tweed coat, saying Carrie, where are you and Muriel
could hear his dark answer through the vale, I think I found a good, good
one here now. They had just moved into his family's home. His mother still
lived in the back wing and Muriel took care of her. That old lady lived for
the radio. Muriel thought the roast might burn if they didn't hurry. She said
this loud to the answer of muffled voices. She said, your supper's going to
burn up if you don't hurry! And I don't want to hear about how dried up it
is. She heard a tiny screech throught the woods. Oh, Lord! is what she heard.
How's that, hon? she heard his response. Hon? Hon? and then there was:
Help me, Carrie. I've fallen. And Muriel got out of the car, fast, pushing
through the snow. Muriel! he yelled. Muriel! I'm here, man! she yelled back.
Helen! Where are you? I'm here, over by the well, far left.

Carrie saw her form, dark and huddled in the field, Oh, darling, he yelled,
running.

I fell on my stomach, oh, God, and it hurts terribly and I feel something,
something wet coming out of me, she said plainly.

Let me get you up—

Owww! Oh, Carrie.

Steady here.

Muriel came huffing up through the path, Oh, my girl!

Get the other side, would you, Muriel.

Something wet here. Oh, mercy, said Muriel.

They struggled and got her to the warm truck.

I just did something on the seat, Carrie.

Hold on, his face, though, was so grim. Keep your legs together, sweetheart.

Together?

Hold on, and do that, and I'm going to back up and get out of here.

It hurts me.

Lord! She's only six monthes along.

Muriel, calm down. We can handle this.

Careful of those loose bumps, Carrie, (*Oh, God, help my baby*).

Her head lay out the window. She always remembered the misty rain landing on her brow that night, even years later.

7.

Right now:

C.R.'s eyes open out onto his snow-covered hills, now. His eyes could be your eyes. Over to his right, Ball's Bluff Battlegrounds, all darkened and black-treed in the shady snow. Over to the left, their family's land long sold and developed, big trucks came and smashed and uprooted all the evergreens he traipsed through when he was young, where he was almost born when his mother fell on her stomach, where he took girls to kiss, where he and Pendleton and that fool Curtis White would smoke something or drink sitting on the pine needles, where he built forts and dug for cannons, pulled up the trees and they lived for a while with an ocean of great red dirt, raw and iron in the air as sewer pipes were pushed into the ground for all these little cardboard houses they put up, Battlefield Hills, where his secretary lived, Ms. Betty Owens, and the Raylins bought into when they sold their old stone house from the back hills. He pulls the eyes of his along all that land he misses, which his father sold because it cost too much to keep Ashland, with the taxes and Mother in the manor now, so they sold all that land and lived locked and deserted in the midst of a type of construction mall. Like their house became the Gap. As if soon people would start knocking on the door asking to see the garden, asking if they had a woodstove and how *authentic* it all is. A bit of local color. A good day-jaunt from some other suburb. Maybe, you could kindly tell an old-timey tale or hand out ham biscuits or something. Gone were the sweeping hills to the left. His eyes shut and so do yours, warm, brown-as-fur eyelids and here's a moment, a brief one, of peace. How are you different from him, anyway. Who is anybody beyond this two-hole specter.

Envelop the flesh of a man. He is tall but his legs lay loose and sprawled underneath his heavy coat, weighted and leaden.

We are on the vale.

He wears a sheepskin vest, you feel it, your hands are large and feel papery and moist in the grooves of his palm, turn up to the sky, the mouth opens, whispers,

Dear God,

I don't you know pray much I should more often I hope you'll forgive my rusty words but I ask you for some guidance here what shall I do I really haven't felt much direction lately and all, but now,

now

I would ask you kind sir should I do something here because I mean well dear Lord I do but it appears I make huge mistakes and I am so terrible sorry for that if you would assist me show me a direction,

who am I trying to fool,

I am consulting you at a dark hour and where was I before,

But you know in your deep wisdom how I have underneath it all felt about you and I do believe I need to learn some things but Lord right now

I am a tad

confused.

(This is an odd place to pray, the doorstep, but his father once prayed there too, exact position, years back:

Good sweet Lord, save my wife, save my child, help me, help me, I *beseech thee,*

Muriel, help me here with her arm, oh my God.)

As did a young Colonel Shrub, a child's loose form in his arm, a horse snorting and buckled in the front yard, *Lord, no, not another, not another.*

Snow dusting outside that window in spirals, this foreign presence, this man who is not you, who will never be you, except somewhere in the eyes.

tuffy hodges, 1

I.

True, the snow began to pour and C.R. stood there on the outskirts of the world but as he did, he felt deflated and pulled back into the house, stood in the hall, once again the piece of paper with Kirsten's curling handwriting came to mind and C.R. had had enough drinks to now think that would be the perfect solution to the bout of loneliness he was experiencing.

There was the first day she worked in the hospital back in July, when C.R. was commandeering the lives of five twenty-six-weekers and one tiny twenty-four-week child, bald and crumpled, by the name of Daphne, who was just going to make it, though bluish with infection already and pumped timefully with antibiotics, he had just skimmed by the isolette and kneaded the father's stiff shoulder through his wilted seersucker, Mr. Roberts was his name and his wife, Mrs. Roberts (June and Bill, active members of the Vineland Baptist Church, their fifth child), then C.R. skimmed by the lounge for his fourth cup of coffee, saw the troupe of candy stripers, saw Kirsten and gave her a little wink, *hello there*, he said, *doing good deeds, are you?* The group giggled and Kirsten looked down shyly, her hands grapsed together, *I believe you are a new one, aren't you*, he said, and she looked up and smiled, *well, we welcome you here, and Lord knows you're needed, ain't that right, Mrs. Feittles-Lopez*, he said to the director, *definitely, definitely needed around here*, and then he just graciously nodded his head a few times and sped away, there were reports looming and a lecture on macro-causality and

counterinflammatory cytokine levels in NEC that was looming for tomorrow, but suffice it to say, he was momentarily impressed to think briefly
how pretty young things are, that girl was a doll, all dimpled and blond
and young, like some kind of overgrown baby, is it possible, he thought
passing a cart of bloods led by a pimply intern, is it possible I ever had one
of those?

He walked down the hall, long femurs bounding. A secretary handed
him a jar of peach preserves, *why, thank you, Martie, that's my favorite fruit.
That's real smart of you. You're gonna get some kind of favoritism or something
now.* She giggled. The truth was, there were very few women at General
that didn't harbor some type of infantile crush or preference or hankering
for C.R., and he didn't even know it. He was unaware, he felt blanketed
by a certain taken-for-granted female kindness, maybe, he even thought
on a perception level, a level-of-comforting zone, women will be on my
side when I walk into a room, I can expect pretty women to notice me or
if not, I am assured I can charm the best of them, but he did not know,
though he would've been pleased, of the swell of female desire that lurked
in his presence.

In his usual daily manner, he offered chocolates to those pink-clad girls
as they went by, *hey, stop in here now, I got a sweet for you girls.* They would
politely take a few, thus weekly memorandum to Betty always included
1 lg. tub Peruginas or Godiva 5 lb. Plus, pick up shirts from drycleaner,
medium starch, *that is a pretty girl,* roast beef sandwich from the Fairfax
Club with extra bread and butter pickles, *I mean, real pretty, like some kind
of flower or something, eyelashes and all,* 2 boxes of Triscuits, no frigging low-
fat! *What a damn angel.*

2.

She started talking.

She went from the shy looking-at-her-hands type to pausing while she
got a chocolate and looking at the man. He wasn't particularly handsome
but he was sweet and lanky and his eyes sparkled, he looked at a person for
a good long time, and thus Kirsten the Candy Striper, like everyone, begun
to think she had discovered him and his charms. That he was a hidden

jewel. She would pause, so you been a doctor long? Well, he laughed, don't want you to think I'm some kind of dinosaur or something. Longer than I'd like to admit, put it that way. Pretty long time.

Is it fun?

Fun? Well, I, I, well, *fun's* not exactly the word, ha, ha, I had in mind, maybe. *Interesting,* I suppose you could say.

Oh. She paused by the door, sighed, studied the lintel for a second. He coughed, *what the hell is she up to?* Then, she walked away. Back to reading letters and washing baby blankets and playing with the sick toddlers in Room C.

Thinking back, he did notice her looking different, but not in a bad way. She seemed to be bursting out of her uniform and he figured she had grown. She stopped by regularly at his office and one day, reaching for the chocolate across his desk she passed his arm with her small pink hand, just brushed it and he coughed in an electric jolting way and she jumped back slightly, oh, she said and he just smiled dumbly, he joked to ease the tension, *you making a move on me, girl?*

Kirsten laughed. Yes. Yes, I am. And she did it again. C.R. blushed. Hadn't blushed in years. He said, looking out over her head to the hall for snoops, *let's not get out of hand, here, hon.* She felt funny, sickish, and needy. Lately, she felt goopy between her legs and burning horniness and tenderness at the same time, and most of all, this hormonal *softness,* a need to be gently, gently held, and then fiercely screwed, she was mixed up and pukey and weird. She attributed it to teenagerhood, she avoided the boys who would lope up to her locker and converse in monosyllables, and the dances because she was just too tired all the time, her mother said *you're having a growth spurt,* but she eyed Kirsten in the sweatpants at home and worried she was gaining weight, how to broach the subject gracefully to her about calories and healthy reducing without her spiraling into anorexia or something? In the bath Kirsten's breasts bobbed hard and impossibly firm, as if surgically enhanced, her nipples hard and purplish and thick, ropy veins now popping out through the skin, and she gasped and worried about diseases and such, and her friend told her she'd gone up two bra sizes this year, so Kirsten felt calm, yet part of her felt her body was morphing and merging into something else, so she looked at C.R. with a certain hormonal boldness and took his hand to her mouth and kissed it, quickly, with sharp, wet heat and he gasped. Then she walked out. C.R. just sat there, his erection burning through his pants. He noticed her differently and she felt this loose reckless dizziness and he tried to avoid her, he really did, but somehow he always ended up by the candy striper room, clutching his rounds clipboard and looking pink in the face or strolling by a bit too fast, scratching his head and the next week when she came by his office, her face puffy he noticed, as she reached down to the chocolate she placed his hand on her hot, feverish breast through the pinafore. *Goddamm it, child,* he said, half amused, half horrified. *You looking for me to lose my job, this is insane.* But it was obvious from the glazed look in her eyes that Kirsten was either feverish or crazy or something, he tried to talk to her softly, *you are a beautiful, beautiful girl, I cannot deny that, hon, but,* and he was horrified to see the tears burst forth from her eyes, and her muffled grunts and he instinctively reached over to her and she fell in his arms, she felt sickly and sad, he handed her a tissue, by now a nurse's aide looked in the door as she walked by, attentive to the strange occurrings, and C.R. stiffened up and said *hon, you want to take the day off, or should I* and she looked up at him and walked away, as he lay back in his chair, his heart beating.

It was that same afternoon all the flurry took place and C.R. looks back and of course, she was pregnant, hardly showing in the front, must've carried in the back, he remembers Argila White, who worked for his mother when he was a teenager, no one could tell she was carrying, she mopped and swept to the last day, her skirt only eased a button and his mother had said, *that girl got a baby on her back,* and, lo, so did Kirsten, she held the baby toward the back of her spine. He feels oddly responsible, the girl coming to him in his office so frequently, all the strange happenings, the hand kiss and such, was she asking for some help, was she seeking him out? How could I have missed the obvious signs? And it breaks his heart to see her puffy and pale in her hospital bed, all confused and damaged, *girl says she didn't know, goddamn,* a nurse's aide huskily breathes out as he looks in, *imagine that doctor, if you will, the girl say she didn't know no baby growing inside. Damn.*

How did she not know, he thinks. How the heck can that happen. Was she some kind of a slut at her school (he thinks of his first girl, Marsha Raylin, with her greedy black moist eyes, who climbed on him behind the back of a fence when he was merely thirteen, she lived down the road to the tenant farmers, her father did all the electrical work on their house, *come on, you, come you, don't funnin with me*, she said, she was older and huskier, with big meaty thighs, and she unzipped him down by the fence, just got on him on the grass, and even his friend Pendleton watched in awe as the girl gyrated and laughed, unh-hunh! she said, unh-hunh, unh-hunh, unh-hunh!! then she paused and the front of his pants were wet and she got up, pulled her grimy underwear back on, *how you like that, hunh, rich boy, how you like that?* she said, laughing as she wet her mouth with her Fresca).

3.

Barbeque. I would like some barbeque. Mashed up with coleslaw on a bun, like they make up at that store off Route 50. All drippy and sweet.

C.R. doesn't eat much, grabs stuff, pilfers, whatever makes its way across his desk or the nurses' station, most times just skips breakfast. It's all a matter of time, not interest. The man longs to wake slow, sauté some eggs delicate-like in butter from the farm, fresh corn bread, eaten outside. Like to fry a fresh trout in a cast-iron pan and sleep in a tent, thus the interest in Civil War reenacting, not that C.R. has a clue how offal-charged, how desperate, cold, and wet his beloved Shrub was in his last days, how the cornmeal sack had wetted and molded and they still had to eat out of it, gnawed down with a the last hunk of bacon fat, and at the end, during the rain, the night before Ball's Bluff, how the food was gone, how the men dug roots out of the wet mud and rinsed them and ate them, bitter and gritty and all, just with the light of the moon to illuminate, Colonel Shrub thinking, When I get back to my home, we'll eat a fine meal, a good chicken, limas from the garden! The man didn't know it was his last night. Very few know that information. And they can't be called lucky.

Eleanor had tried to fix the lack of breakfast in C.R.'s life with sensible low-fat cuisine which was a huge turnoff to him, *I've scrambled up some yummy egg whites, hon,* which he accepted and then fed to Djinn who then consequently threw up fifteen minutes later on the Belouche rug, *shit, Eleanor, the dog's done puked!* he said, stepping in it with his felt slipper, but he saw the obvious contents of the scrambled egg whites, *I got it! I'll get it, hon,* he yelled out in his booming voice, how little the woman knew of the romance of the stomach, how she could've fed the man crisp scrapple and gooey eggs and popovers on an enamel speckle plate in his back garden and what a long way that would've gone to fixing his soul, but the lack of imagination in some women, the shortsighted *Redbook–House and Garden–*Martha Stewart way of thinking.

So, most times, when hunger hits him full force like a pounding throb, he tends to go with meat, high fat, high protein, quick fix. Ham, of course, a big favorite. A hot dog. Bacon and how. A steak at the Fairfax Club. Potato barely scraped. No dessert.

Thinking about the candy striper has made him hungry and slow and tired and the drunkenness this evening is ebbing and he feels just damn hungry. The snow outside is thick, it's pleasantly lavender-hued across the lawn, thick and hilly now (must be up to half a foot) and does he want to trudge out the truck and drive through that for some barbeque? He's figuring it would be a bitch to get to that store and find it closed but there's a 7-Eleven about fifteen miles away, he could go for that, he's got his coat on still, he swigs some more bourbon, the bottle is almost gone, he opens the door as the snow flurries in and the path is pure and white and there, there in the middle of the snow, there in *the bleak midwinter,* lies the tiny baby, "Tuffy" Hodges, the infant of the candy striper, swaddled in a hospital blue blanket, peaceful and meek and appearing to sleep, and in C.R.'s lauded appraisal, his color is good, somewhere between 86 and 87 percent oxometer reading, free of sepsis and all other nasty discolorations.

4.

He'd called that baby's death. He remembers it clearly, nurse Margaret Talverez looked up at him with her grim eyebrows and he'd spat out, time of death 6:03 P.M., cause of death, sepsis caused by NEC. Remembers the baby lying, stomach bloated in the isolette and the nurse lifting it out, swaddling the poor thing, thinking a sad, flat feeling, yet indescribably a feeling of relief. For Kirsten Candy Striper. Feeling, as they swabbed out his isolette with alcohol and placed fresh bedding, placing Tuffy in an isolette on wheels for a trip to the morgue, feeling a disquiet, a singular feeling akin to guilt. He quickly drove his attention to the child to the left of Tuffy, Baby Moranis. He'll need an increase on fat intake today, he said. OK, nurse replied. And switch that IV, too, been three days, right? Unh-hunh. OK, do that and I'll check with you later. He remembers then calling the Hodges and Kirsten, having them come in and view the baby, remembers their tears and the mother's unmistakable relief. It all happened, so what the *hell hell hell* is this?

He opens the door and the wind howls coldly through his coat and the snow falls down and it doesn't land on the baby, he walks to him, stands over him, and the child reaches out for him, and C.R. reaches down, gets on his knees, and picks up the child. He lifts the small package up and holds it to his chest, he holds the baby and hears the soft mews of its little cry, what is happening to me now, he mumbles, and as he holds the child and wonders, outdoor sensor lights flip on, illuminating the crystallic world around him, showing up the heavy snow and shining on C.R., on his knees, he is grizzled and white and looks a million years old, the child in his arms.

tuffy hodges, 2

I.

Why the hell would he see Tuffy lying on a snowy path? C.R. thinks, as
he holds the child and the child seems so full of pinkness and life and
he knows he's either a full-fledged drunk in the throes of delirium tre-
mens or his mind has gone around the loony bend much like his mother's
did, it's a fear he secretly harbors and one that is not misguided, a subtle
thread of mental fragility weaves through his family sinuously, being
that as it may, the child, if even a figment of his imagination, is lovely
to behold again and as he does, his heart feels sad that Tuffy didn't
survive, but what, he says in frost-coated words out loud, could I have
really done?

Thinking harder, sitting down with a solid little fall, still holding the
small child, he places his mouth to the baby's cheek and kisses it, and it
is warm and smells sweet and C.R. says, I'm sorry! I'm so completely
goddamned sorry, his tears are wetting the baby's standard hospital cap,
he must be freezing! This is way more cold than any premie can take, he
gets scared, *I won't lose him again,* because so much of paternal love involves responsibility, and in this instance he is no other than the father,
not in a DNA sense, but in a protective sense, nobody else knows this child
exists, it is he and the child alone in the world. but wait:

There are issues to contemplate.

2.

The night is fully dark now, powdery, still. He has covered the child with his jacket and gloves and C.R. is cold and his face is half frozen, he reaches for a glove in his pocket and encounters the crumpled memento of Kirsten, her scrawled number, Holy fucking hell, what's happened to me, he moans, what the hell have I done to myself.

He's rocking, the baby mews occasionally and he prays: I'm so so sorry I have misused the gift of my life. (He remembers church as a giant bore. He remembers sleeping. He remembers fumbling with the darn books, taking too long to find the hymn page, then too long to find the stanza they were on. Remembers his father's sidelong hawkish brow glaring his way, remembers his mother's gloved hand pinching his knee hard, and he straightened up, he never wanted to make his mother sad or mad, because he loved loved loved loved his mother something intense, like this burn-ing shaft of lightning power, there were days, while she rested in her room on the third floor, and Muriel had told him to stay out, he would sneak a few stairs up until miraculously he got to her door, and saw her, lying on her bed on the chenille cover, reading a book or writing letters, she'd say, Well, hi! as if she hadn't told Muriel to keep him downstairs, she'd read him *Little Lord Fauntleroy* or tell him a story, those were good days when he was young.)

Father, he said, I have mortally sinned, the last word a mere whisper, the pine trees sounded louder in the slight snowy wind. (There was the time Bertha, Muriel's mother, died. He remembered it, she was in the kitchen with his mother and her brother, Uncle Bert. And C.R. was in the mudroom and, oh, it was right before bedtime and he was watching TV, in his fireman PJs, drinking a glass of milk. He was watching *The Beverly Hillbillies*, as a matter of fact, when Mother closed the louvered doors of the mudroom and said, Don't *come* in here. Do *not*. I'll tell you why later, but Bertha is feeling poorly. Stay in here. He looked through the slats of the door. He saw Bertha lying on the floor of the kitchen, his uncle kiss-ing her! His uncle was kissing Bertha! Now that was strange and his mother was calling on the phone and she had a teary sensation to her voice that made him feel very sad and he opened the door and his mother's face flew up in his direction, I told you! Dammit! Stay in there! More of a shriek now than a request, so he slammed that door back, but still looked. You could see up Bertha's dress. She wore those pink-tan heavy stockings he saw always hanging on the rack up in her attic room, up to her knees, the rest of her was dark and shadowy and it looked like she wore big white underwear. He saw Bertha's underwear. When he'd tell his cousin Johnny about that, they'd laugh. Uncle was still kissing Bertha and she looked weird, she was sleeping. In a few minutes those guys came running in, with the bed they carried. They kissed her, too. They took her out on that thing and she was hard to lift. Her skin looked strange, paler. That was a color he'd never seen then, though God knows he does now. A flat olive drab. The gray you'd see on dry rocks. Was that the day the colors in life began to change, he wondered, was that the introduction to the flattened life he led now? The hues of lifelessness that surrounded him in his job, the color-lessness, the lack of oxygen, of blood, of life lay strewn about him on a daily basis, how he yearned for that which glowed, which beamed pink or red or brown! Mother was crying. Uncle, too. Daddy was off on a call other-wise he could've done something. Get Carrie, Mama had yelled, quick, Bert, call Carrie! But who knew where he was, helping a family maybe on 50 who had the flu or a fellow up on the hill with emphysema. Could take hours to track him down in the truck. She had died, they said, when they pulled back the door on my face suddenly. She was gone. I told Mother I would be a doctor, then I could fix her. That gave me some attention from her. Did I mention I loved her.)

By the time he finishes thinking this, the baby is gone. The baby in his arms, that frail premie, has departed as silently as it came before, and what lies there in its stead, half covered in snow, is a newspaper, there is only the sound of the gentle buzzing of snow, or how else can you de-scribe it, the delicate crystals falling down and brushing in the wind, quietly whispering.

daddy

I.

Son?

The sound is only a whisper, but it engages C.R. enough to open his eyes a bit, a full minute or two as he started to fall asleep in the downy snow,

Son? What, what *the hell* are you doing?

Daddy?

I've seen it all now, he says, poking him with the reedy end of his cane, I've seen it all, you lying here, *in the snow* holding a newspaper, *talking* to a newspaper, by golly, I swear to God—

Where'd you come from?

From up, he points with his large knuckled claw, up on here, son—pointing to the glowing main house of Ashland—I hear a noise and I come on down, get up son, please—more poking.

His father stands silhouetted above him, in his slippers, his cane, his face dark, the wisps of his white hair on his head lifting in the slight breeze and the snow falling on his head.

You'll catch pneumonia, Daddy.

I have no intention of leaving till you do.

You have some kind of stock in sheepskin, Daddy?

An old joke, his slippers, his vest, his chair, all lined in sheepskin.

Comfortable, that's all.

Daddy.

Son, tell you what. Give me the paper. We'll go in. He reaches his hand down, grasps C.R.'s knee, his hand cold and aquine.

I suppose so.

Some *good, hot*—he lifts his son by the arm.

Daddy, you'll fall.

—*toddy*'ll fix you up, he heaves him. There, brush yourself off. Let's go.

Something weird's happening here.

And that would be, son.

I'm seeing things.

Life's a mystery, son.

I'm off my rocker. Like Mother.

She, she was a good woman, I'd mind you to talk with respect of her.

I loved her.

I'm aware of that.

They reach the front door, and C.R. pushes it open and warmth hits him, and the house is snug and the fire burns still. His father skittles to the kitchen,

Now. Some hot toddy coming right up. You want a lot of lemon or a little?

As usual.

Then, that would mean a lot. That'll make it right sour, if you ask me. Extra bourbon, too?

No, a, just a touch please, I've overdone tonight.

I see that.

Don't think I'm. You know. *Cut out* for this, this profession anymore—

Rough moments come along—again C.R. marvels at his father's bony hands, squeezing a lemon   there are moments that test you, C.R.

I'll say. I don't like being a harbinger of gloom, you know.

I wouldn't call it *that*, I'd call it more an angel of mercy.

Oh, I'm no angel. I get in the way. I mess up.

Now, sit here, son, and he hands him the drink, let's talk here a bit. Every man, every profession has a weak moment. Think about it. You've the *duty*. Of helping others.

Daddy, when you were a doctor, did you, did you—

Yes.

How do you even know what I'm saying?

I know what you're saying. And it was an act of mercy, son.

Confound it. He leaned into the hot warmth of his drink, let me get a grip here. I'm losing it.

His father drinks his toddy, looking at him, his blue eyes hooded by the top lid's flesh and droopy in a most elegant way.

I am so comforted by you, Daddy. I want to ask you some stuff.

Well, all right. Just don't tire me out. Where're the Triscuits?

Same as always.

Got some cheese?

I do, some nurse gave me a cheese ball, I think, in the icebox.

That nut thing? Oh, well.

Exactly. Oh, well.

Why do people continue to make, these, things, he says stabbing at the cheese ball, scraping off the nuts.

I believe she said it was *port-flavored*.

Good Lord, flavored this, flavored that. I could do with some of Muriel's blue cheese stuff.

Oh, so could I.

Remember her tomatoes? Oh, Lordy.

Tried to make some the other day. Came out too sweet.

Use bacon grease?

Indeed I did. Think I added too much brown sugar.

You know, she cooked everything in grease. Every damn thing. That's why it tasted so good.

I'd give an arm right now for a slice of damson pie, a whole arm up.

I like those limas, son. She made some kind of butter sauce or something. It was thick.

You eat over there, Daddy?

Over where, son?

You're dead, Daddy. No offense or anything, sir. Just. You are.

I beg your pardon?

Oh, come on. It's been five years since I found you in the hall. What exactly happened, anyway? Did you trip on the rug? I was mighty sad.

Oh, I'm not dead.

Yeah?

I'm here, ain't I? Eating Triscuits. Dead men don't eat Triscuits.

Oh, this is some dream. I'm probably hallucinating. I probably passed out in the snow and I'm near froze to death now. I'll see a, you know, the old tunnel of light or something. The cornball deal. That's OK, I suppose. Shit. This toddy's good though. Hey, sir!

I'm no dream, son.

Hey, what was that, that, that time, you know? Right before you die, I go in your room and see Muriel in there with you, Dad, what the hell, hell, hell was *that*? She was in your bed, her little old arm across your chest in those PJs when I went to get your hot water bottle, what the fuck?

Afggh! his father coughed. Agghh!

Daddy?

I remember when you were born. Yes I do. You came fast as lightning, shot out, there in front of the fireplace, almost fell on a rug. 'Deed I do. Damnedest thing I ever saw in all those years bringing out babies, I said, I said, get 'em Muriel!! Helen was just, just lying back screaming, I said, get my son, Muriel! We, we, were getting the tree, you know, over on the Bluff. Getting a Christmas tree. Poor darling fell down. You come out fast afterwards. We got her inside, and bing, bang, out you go.

I had things to do.

Ardgh!! Hoo boy!!

Stop coughing so much, Daddy. Stop talking.

Arrgh! Damn this cough, I says Muriel, that boy'll be a rocketeer or something, called you speedy for a while there, ahem. Speedy. Then we all calm down. Call you Carroll, like me, after your great-great-grandpa from Ireland and Helen goes with Randolph after her side, Muriel comes up with C.R., says Carroll doesn't sound right on a baby. Doesn't sound right.

Remember my question?

Christmas's my favorite, you know that, son? It's a lame excuse for decoration in here now, no "boughs of green'ry in th' air"—

Ah, the wasp-y ignore, the skirt aside—

De—ck the ha—lls wi—th boughs—oooof ho—o—llly!!!!! Fallalala-lalalalllaaa. Argfh! Aghghhhh! Helen! Oh Helen! It's Christmastime! Time of jolly!

I'm cutting you off toddies, sir.

Wear the red velvet, my love!

Oh, that dress of Mother's! I loved her in that.

You wore matching red velvet britches and jacket Muriel made. Little brass buttons. I wore my, that, that.

Dinner jacket.

That's the ticket.

Daddy, you know Free Bird?

Free what? What's that? His old eyes, obsidian and blinking.

Free Bird, a song?

Oh, some rock stuff. No. No.

Free Bird, it's a good ol' song.

Now, Stardust, that's a song. That's a song, my friend, his voice wispy and smoky in the kitchen. He hums. He gets up and does a twirl. There you go, Helen. Yessir!

I walked in to get a water bottle, it was about, *oh*, about, about twelve midnight, I had a headache, this was six? Six? Years ago, after Mama was in the place over there for a while, when we found her wandering in the garden, out of it and all, said she could fall, sir, so we, we put her up at that place, I'm wondering why *did* I. Do that. To my poor mother. You don't want to send your family in those places. I *know* those places. It hurts me to even think. That's, that's a travesty, sir.

She, she was the shining star of her day, yes she was, that dress. That damn dress. It was satin with roses, in the fashion of the day. She had a grace.

Why did we put her up there, Daddy, after all, I am a physician, you are, too, couldn't we handle her? You told me, you said, they can handle her better, you said. How about the smell of bleach in your nose in that place, like a fog of lies in the air, like, like an antiseptic erasement of your life. Maybe it's the bleach. It hurts your nose. It's sharp. My own mother. Is there, is there a tendency for us to, to *avoid* what is ugly? Did it work for us when she was young and nice and useful and then when she, she faltered, did we find her too much trouble? I'm beginning to think I take the easy route, Father. I'm beginning to think, why can I not accept the challenge? Why was Muriel in your damn bed, sir?

She was talking in that group, and that damn Jack Conrad tries to cut in, ha! Oh, yesssiree. He did. Thought he had the fine Harvard moves. I don't think anyone up north can compete with the university, I just don't—

That Muriel, she wore a nightgown. Permit me, Daddy. Permit me, but was this a sex thing? God's sake, with Muriel? Oh, Jesus.

Don't take the Lord's name in vain, son. I could *freeze up your young blood*.

You know she went right after you, don't you? Where is she, in the next room? Is she about to come in, fix up some limas for us? She went, that's right, infarction in her home, her son called me, only two months after you. And she was fit and sprightly, too, until then. I do miss her, goddammit. I miss you all.

One more toddy coming up! Hoo boy!

His father stands in front of the icebox, wiggling in his large, voluminous khakis,

I see bacon. I can do the old standby! Yessir!

We don't have tomatoes, of course. Out of season.

I'm talking corn chowder, son. I know you got potatoes, frozen corn.

I do.

Milk?

I'm sure.

More than a cc, perhaps?

2.

Silence. The wind continues to howl and the snow is piling up in the windows, slices of white against the pane. And the fires are dying out and C.R. lays his head on the counter and his brain feels weighted and cast-off and dull.

Oh, I see, Daddy.

Oh, you do, hunh?

Yes, you're my conscience coming out in reckoning form or the Lord sending me some message, that's why, that's why. I see. Now you'll escort me to the flaming gates of hell, right, and before, before I'll probably pass that candy striper naked on a bed, or some such. *Torture*.

One cc.

I know.

You're not *sick* of your profession.

Indeed I am. What's it all *for*? I'm, I'm damn confused.

What was your *intention*?

I don't know.

Does a chowder get, how much bacon exactly? Four piece sound right?

She just so pitiful, you know. And the baby no hope. No hope what with the brain bleed levels, real bad, level four. We called him Tuffy.

Oh. Tuffy.

Yeah, I. I ordered the cc feeding. Even the dumb-ass night nurse knew it was wrong. She repeated my order. I said yeah, one cc. Not a half even. A full cc. You got it, I said. She gave that twisted-ass look. She *knew*. She can burn my butt. Probably will.

About two potatoes?

So he's gone, Tuffy. Damn! I saw him outside! I did! Was he with you? Do you have him, Daddy?

Where's the damn corn?

He's gone. They were relieved. I don't think anyone wasn't. He was too far gone. God sakes. Oh, goddamn. Oh, *goddamn*. Did I do that, did I do that, for myself? Jesus, Daddy, did I off that poor babe just so I could get at that young girl? Just to free me up? The easy route, the easy route. Am I so, so godless, that I'd do even that?

Who's the father?

Some pipsqueak high schooler, I suppose. Or, I don't know. I don't know.

I'm no expert in neonate stuff, son. I can't recall stuff. Seems I see just a shadow of myself being a doctor in my youth. I don't remember technique. I remember just, just, a few things. Odd things. When we fed 'em, we fed 'em. We didn't trifle over ccs or whatever. We fed 'em. A mother can't measure ccs in her breast.

You didn't trifle with NEC, too much either. Milk feeds it. It's the bane of premies, Daddy.

Even a cc.

A cc's a bathtub-load for an eight hundred grammer. A bombardment.

I see.

It starts up that NEC and then forget it. Bacteria, sepsis, what have you.

I see.

Unh-hunh. You see. Is Tuffy over there?

Ahhh, she smelled of camellias in that satin dress, swaying to Stardust. Candles burning in the halls, silver gleaming. Somewhere in the yard you could hear the boys singing, Silent Night. There's cookies, Bertha's ham biscuits. A night. A night of *joy*.

I'd tell you stuff if I was dead.

I ain't dead, son.

Then I am.

And you most assuredly ain't.

Is Tuffy there? Does he forgive me?

Rung through the garden with lanterns, those carrolers, singing tra—la—lalllaaaa. Yes, I will have more nog, Miss Elsie, yes, indeedie. Right fashionable frock, and suits you well. Ohhhh! Falalalalalalaaaaa! Ha, you enjoy my baritone! You flirt! Now Helen might get jealous, here, Miss Elsie. Even if you are her mother. It's obvious where she got her beauty, hello, Mr. Dean! Yes, I'm busy, busy at the university, indeed. I do—

Daddy?

His father walks off, waltzes off, to the hall, singing in his bare hoarseness.

Maria May, you pretty devil, I'm going to ask you for a dance and throw my fiancée in a tizzy. Sil—ent ni—ght! Holy night! I see the ham gleaming in the candlelight and the laughter through the house. All the silver shining, shining! All is delight! All is *wonderment*!

Don't go, Daddy. Because I'll follow you!

No you won't! Oh, no, he calls from the study, no, you won't! Not if you *ever did your dear father love*.

Daddy! Take me with you, Daddy.

Miss Margaret! Miss, sweet sweet, Helen, radiant jewel. Caught me off guard. I would have a piece of coconut candy. Yes. Thank you, my dear.

Daddy.

C.R. runs to the study, he is alone now, the fire, once crackling and golden, stirs to a dusty last wisp of smoke.

mother + daddy

I.

Corn chowder in a mug, corn chowder made by a spirit no less, C.R. traipses through Ashland, through the dusty rooms, over to the basement bedroom/apartment which he used to call home all his younger years, up until his daddy's death and Muriel's death last year, when he saw fit to move up in the house, move upstairs and take over the guest wing, which he had always coveted and which lay largely unused, with the exception of visitations by his cousins from Richmond or earlier on, his grandmother and her Mexican maid, Ervita. Sitting on the small double bed with his plaid comforter, perusing the small room he grew up in, the one small apartment with the convenient side door to the garage, so he could sneak in his lady friends, and he certainly did, parades of them came through the doors in all sizes and colors, and lay naked on this worn plaid comforter, through his years at Fauquier High, to UVA, to his final intern days at the Ball's Bluff Babies Hospital, he lay in this small bed, the shuffling of his family above. It was only one time his mother made the terrible mistake of coming down to the basement with a mug of coffee for C.R. one day, and to her horror discovered him astride a young student nurse, name forgotten, but he does remember her long red hair and her reddened cheeks and his mother's almost laughable little clucked *whoops!* and he saw the splash of coffee on the stair in her haste to retreat, thank God she never mentioned it, though it be a cold day in hell before she'd ever try that again, and his father, slightly enamored with his wife's prudishness, liked to tease occasionally, as the three sat eating lamb chops on a Friday evening,

Mother, working his great gray stubbled jaw, Mother, take note, today is Friday and son is going out on a *date,* therefore—

C.R. smiled down at the table as he saw his mother's eyes shoot up to his father—

—Therefore, I bet he'd love it, just love some fine coffee in the morn—

Carrie. Honestly.

She'd leave the table in a toss of her napkin, throwing it on the chair, clanging some pots around in the kitchen, mumbling to Muriel, something or another, while C.R. and his father laughed, C.R. would say I think Mother near about had a heart attack that day, and Father would say, You may wish to hang a sign or something, C.R., hang a tie on the knob or something because I'd hate to come in early and see your sorry ass on a fine Saturday morning, indeed I would, pass the mashed potatoes would you son, now son, has Armstrong (his attending physician), has Armstrong got you on the orange wing yet? Because I want you pay particular attention there to the families, son. The family is the key, son. The key.

Yes sir, I will. Though he thought, (Jeez, you are out past the brackets, old man. That might've been so in those cowpoke years but I don't intend to do door-to-door, see).

I'm inferring, son, from the familiar furrow of your brow, that you may have some other ideas, would you care to share them, son?

Now years of harsh discipline with a young stick, either by the father or Muriel who certainly was able in that department, had given C.R. the infrared ability to sense displeasure in the adult figure, as well as to placate it, and one glance at the hard, coffee bean eyes of his father said he may have trod in this area, though there was also the wave of knowledge that he was an adult now, could very well kick his dad's ass, though that was about the most unlikely situation that would ever occur, so he spoke up, though nervously:

Well, Father, no disrespect or anything, but family practice hereabouts is, is, uh, quite different from the world of neonatology, which is quite high-tech, and more *modern.*

Unh-hunh, I see. I see.

(Oh, crap, displeasure on the face! He could see it!)

When did the beatings stop? Did it occur when the bulge of a preado-lescent muscle occurred imperceptibly under the polo shirt of a young C.R.? And the father, Carrie Ash, took that in silently and calculated the odds of his retribution? Or did C.R. simply begin to adhere more to his daddy's will? Regardless, it faded and became more a memory than the daily pinch afforded by the whack of his hand across his brow or the snippet of a branch, as quick and sharp as the willow branch brought back while circling the pond with his local urchin friends as they fished the edges for bluegills, that subtle sting in the cheek which left one feeling foolish and tearful,

Is that so, his father said menacingly.

Nowadays, as the beatings faded, the impertinence grew, and C.R. began to disregard his warning signals,

Yes, so. Called, moving on, old-timer. Technology.

Unh-hunh. Well, we did all right. Not too many complaining.

Can't complain when you're dead.

Pass, the uh, preserves, will you, son, *well*, we did the best we could. Ever heard of birthing a child with your *hands*? Instead of any old comput-erized gizmo. Give that a whirl. Actually just using your hands.

Hunh. Where you get one of those contraptions? Pfizer make one?

2.

The mother, Helen, was the softener between the two, the charm, the velvet-clad river that smoothed all the testosterone down, coming in with her C.R. adoration, brushing his hair back as she discussed the day, *if you have any dry cleaning Muriel's going to town,* her once pearlescent youth in velvet now the family tan, hard ankle jutting from her lime green skirt, en route to Garden Club meetings, straw purse in hand or assisting Muriel set the table with china for the historical society or fingering chintz in the study, Mrs. Ash fell about in her duties, her questions about the or-derliness of her day's activities (*Gentlemen, I thought we'd have a cold supper tonight, how's that work out, boys?*), which is how the family existed for so many years, harmonious daily laughter in the wide-planked colonial house of blooming daylilies and green grass, easy chatter between the three.

The defining mood of the adults (and they all were around C.R.'s house at every minute, cousins, aunts, every which way, Mr. Sawyer and Cousin Carter and Aunt Lillian and Uncle so-and-so, all ages) during that time was talk, incessant gabbing, sitting around on perched chairs on the lawn, talking of this and that. *What'll you drink, Powell? Name your poison, my good man.*

Weaving through the conversation was cynicism, irony with a touch of boredom thrown in. Laughter, downright hoots and snickers. Joking and mockery were always allowed. Sentimentalism, artifice were frowned upon. Perfection was a funny story with lots of imitative accents, that made the place crack with a wave of burst laughter from everyone, but especially his mother. In those days, her laughter burst forth, sailed above them all. This was her domain. C.R. lived for it, sat briefly on the lawn, hot and buggy, and watched her talk to the people, her glass wet and frosted, saw the laughter, her teeth wide and white, neck thrown back, just for that moment, then he'd scamper off, shirtless, to find a snake, to wade in the sludge of the pond, to traipse the house, the house of mudroom, first level, children's area, next level, the kitchen, which Muriel owned, C.R. wasn't even allowed to look in. Up the stairs, one passed the parlor, which every Virginian seemed to have. Untouchable, silvery satin love seats, twin porcelain doggies by the fireplace. And then, winding up the stairs, past various rooms—the bedroom with the odd copper "bed warmer" that you filled with coals and slipped in between the covers, the rose-covered bedrooms, past those was his parents' room, their large white bed, where she often rested in afternoons.

On Thursdays she went to Mr. Roberto to have her hair done and in his younger days, blond ringlets and sailor suit days, she'd bring him along, sit him down to the adoration and poke-fingering of all those crispy-curled women and their crumpled tissue paper asses and the sea of hair mounding on the tile, they drove in his mother's big boat of a car, sailing along at eighty miles an hour in a pale air-conditioned velveteen oasis of Muzak and her occasional conversation, C.R.'s knees had grown hard from scrabbling around finding lost pencils on the hard, screw-covered industrial floor of his daddy's truck, shivering as cold air always leaked in, stopping to say hello to this one and that, but en route to Roberto he luxuriated in comfort with his mother, Mr. Roberto would scream with delight when she would enter, rushing, comb in hand to kiss kiss kiss her face in a flurry and he always made the appropriate fuss over C.R., although she was the star, and C.R.'d watch, in awe, as he pulled lick after lick of hair through that white baldy cap and smother it with blue stuff that turned a frothy silver and smelled like ammonia, and then she'd sit back covered in a tent and get it washed out, looking weird that way, freaky, like a little animal come up from the creek.

And then, stage two, rolled in curlers, blue prickly ones in neat rows with little yellow ones around the edges, and she'd get stuck under the loud dryer for hours. Not once did she get a manicure. Not once. She kept her nails undone, no polish, and wore an old ring with a dome of diamonds.

And only a smear of lipstick, "Shocking Pink" as it was called, bright, bright neon pink against her leathery, tanned skin and the tiger-striped, shiny helmet that emerged from Mr. Roberto's, gleaming, teased and high, but not too much. Smelling like Diorissimo, wearing Lilly Pulitzer summer dresses with aplomb, with white leather thongs, and those bony legs, her terrier, Jeremiah, would jump with joy when she got out of the car, leaving faint white marks on her shins, against the tan, from his claws. She'd scratch his tiny, furry skull and he'd settle down. Carrie would brush her cheek, admire her hair, approach the bar, pour with a little aluminum jigger the proper amount of bourbon. C.R.'d have a Coke.

There may have been those smoky, powdery almonds they loved.

They clicked on the news. They were news junkies.

They lay on the white bed, in their clothes, both sets of eyes magnified like bugs with their tortoiseshell glasses, and stare as Nixon spoke, occasional clink of ice as they drank, and C.R. lay on the floor, the Belouche carpet making the bottoms of his elbows marred and bumpy.

A family lasts a lifetime, and then it changes and all that goes, it goes, it goes. It goes, man. Don't let this good moment, this long summer afternoon, this iced tea, this talking to your mother about fried chicken for dinner, this hammock, the voice of the adults downstairs while you lie in your bed in the dark, don't let this fool you for a moment. Here it is. Take of it.

3.

It got unseasonably cold, then, and summer ended. Snow came down, and his head spun and he felt very cold but then quickly that sensation disappeared and he felt simply comfortable and all sorts of thoughts collided in his head, and he was confused but most of all was the sensation of lying in his mother's lap as he often did, he was a *mama's boy* as they used to say but he cared not, he would lie there as she watched the TV and he would approve of her subtle breath rocking him, a contrast to her later years in her sixties when he still lived in the ancestral home (you can call him a loser for that, but it wasn't untypical in his region, a child settling in the family, never marrying, and never setting up his own home, after all, the home would only go to C.R. anyway, the man wasn't a pot-smoking 7-Eleven clerk, he was a well-respected physician with a phone down there hooked to the main hospital drive), the days when he was studying for his boards and she'd attend doctors' offices all day for no reason, imagined moles that were cancerous or gangrenous or tumors, at dinner, just the three of them, him and his aged parents, she'd regale him with stories, *Imagine this, C.R., that wart, you know, that wart you said was nothing? Just a nothing you said? I think you need to, to recheck that that education I'm paying for because it's not up to snuff, son. I went to Dr. Morris and and I'm waiting there and a fella comes in and he says look at this toe now I've a small something, and you know what? You know what?*

What, Mother?

That doctor said straight up, Well, now we are moving you up to the hospital right across the way and we're taking off that toe right now. Right this instant. Imagine that! Muriel, you remember?

Muriel, in her fifties, smiled, oh, yes. Oh, yes.

So did the doctor say *your* wart was a problem?

And that reminds me, there are all, all kinds of things, you know, and other things and that thing, that thing—

Here's your coffee, Mother—

That thing. Yes.

Mother, your coffee—

You don't know when a person will just take off, when the good Lord will just take them off. Do you, C.R.?

Pardon, Mother?

You don't know when a person can just take off, when the good Lord means it. Do you, C.R.? Do they give you signs in that school?

Well, we know the failings, the failings of the system, so to speak—

And now would begin her crazed moments, her eyes reddened and straining—

Did you know it was Bertha's time, when she fell over? Could you see some glow? Did you, son, is there some scientific thing you can see? You see it in me, don't you? don't you?

Mother—

Tell me please, son—

And there would be tears or curses, Muriel would wearily wrap her in a shawl and bring her a glass of hot toddy (there's the toddy again: the toddy and its role in stress and bereavement in the Ash family).

Next came a moment, after many moments like this and worse, Mother walking naked down to breakfast, or peeing in the parlor on the sofa or cursing for hours or more and more horrific stories of imagined disease, next came the **Kraft macaroni and cheese moment,** one day, while C.R. had made a lunch of the stuff, his father came into the kitchen, ignored the fact that C.R. ate from a pan directly, stood in the doorway, sighed, and proceeded to tell his son, not ask, but tell him that his mother had dementia and would be better put in a place that could handle her, like Citadel Manor in the next town, and C.R. merely grunted, wolfing down the macaroni and cheese, *if you think that's best,* that meant him and the old man alone now, he agreed and it was done, all her clothes packed, signed and shut up by Muriel, after that the Kraft macaroni and cheese not a big favorite, all the eggy neon orange a bloated reminder of the loss of his mother, the bad taste of fake cheese, no, he'll pass on that now, preferring anything to that, his mother, macaroni and cheese, that part of his life, that part gone.

And just a few years later, after dinner at Carriage House (a new restaurant offering traditional favorites like Steak and Kidney Pie and Leg of Lamb Under a Salt Crust) with a date, Marjorie Streiss-White, to be exact, a small blond in accounting, and he'd had a great Mixed Grill, that fabulous English deal with the chop, with the kidney, and the broiled tomato, he'd even had creamed spinach, how simply divine was a place where he could get a decent creamed spinach like in the old steakhouses of yore, he'd had that and Marjorie offered some promise, he liked her, she had an intelligent way of speaking without much inflection and he liked her small, round glasses, they'd come in the front of Ashland, laughter cut short, to the sight of his father strewn on the floor, twisted in his mallard green robe, white leg purplish in the half hall light, a monstrous meaty site, dead for a few hours, Djinn whining from the staircase quietly, no more Carriage House for C.R. (mentioned in speech by acquaintances, *have you tried that Carriage House? It's real good, C.R.,* accompanied by C.R.'s senses flooded with father dead, father gone, green robe, splayed body, *thank you I'll have to pass, kind of busy tonight*). And, also, a permanent good-bye to screeching Marjorie Streiss-White, with her *oh, Jesus* over and over in the rolling vermilion ambulance light, she may have fared better had this not been the first date, but her face flashes red *dead daddy* now, no use to change it, her phone calls unanswered, his polite greetings in the hall, *he couldn't deal,* she says, how right you are, how right you are.

Walking down the hall, chowder in hand, he sees his calender there on the kitchen wall and remembers the party at the hospital, it's there scratched in his tight capitals, and he stops, sees the snow pouring down, but stops, after all, a Christmas party is hard to resist, he means to go down to his basement pad, but he stops, he stops, he stops, he goes for the stairs, past the parlor, past the rose bedrooms, to the big white bedroom, dusty and forlorn, fox prints and all, there in a closet can he find his father's evening clothes, the old Brooks Brothers, the dinner coat of silk, a cummerbund, even, wrapped by Muriel in tissue years before, and C.R. lies on their great white bed, though it's dusty and covered in a musty layer of age, he still remembers them and this being their room, lying there, he wishes his father would come back, someone, his mother or Muriel, anyone at this point.

Even Tuffy, he'd take him now. He'd take that boy. Feed him, fill him out. He'd take him crying in the long, sad halls of Ashland now, any day, over this shit. This bachelor life.

stave two

the town.

Map of Ashland

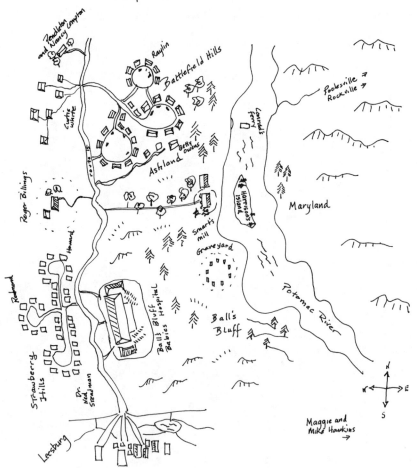

Curtis White

Being a shutin and all I course don't get out much but me and C.R. used to be real tight. We was friends in high school, such, though we don't really hang much now but you get stuck in your habits and don't see people like you used to except those who do visit like yourself and he's a busy man besides. When my leg got hurt once from a chain saw he come over to my room and talked to the doctor and got me all fixed up and made sure my room was good and got me food and stuff brought in, and in my opinion the man is decent.

I can tell you from my window I seen C.R. coming and going all hours but being a doctor and all that made sense and babies will be born when they want to, my mother always said. C.R. said he deals with those real little ones, them premies. Used to be when I was in my thirties I'd drop by for a sip with the man, say hello to his Mama, though she pretty near out of it then, but hell we'd drink some juice and shit and talk, he had a pool table down in his basement, down in his *lair*, he called it, lot of fox stuff everywhere cause his *Daddy* led the hunt for awhile back, before the accident, but hell, yeah, he's OK, but now, since the accident I pretty much stay in. I prefer to hang here and settle in and get cozy and have no need to get about. Much. You'd be surprised by the wildlife I can view from this here window like nothing you ever seen, especially the deers.

Used to hang in the Bluff and drink and stuff with girls. Shit though that's a creepy place to go you know what I mean.

These days, I like to make stews, you know deer meat usually, as how you don't have to pay for it, I'm lucky that Ray Raylin and all will give me some when they have surplus which is often so, in fact, I got some stew on the range and you will find to your good surprise it's tasty, *boy*. I'm going to fix you up a bowl. I use near a good bottle of burgundy in it.

I like to hang with him again we being friends and such, I enjoy his company. His mother was a real nice lady.

Yeah, I like Free Bird. It rocks. I don't really listen to music much though, because account of the TV is on, though when I was a teenager, that song was when we slow danced at the Prom. I had a date named Diane. I remember dancing with her to that song, that was, that was, OK, about four years before we broke up, Diane and me. Nowadays, these last years, I pretty much stay to myself.

Diane has a kid, two actually. She married that weird "mayor" guy. She caters, they say. I might call her up, see if she has any call for deer stew which is I'm saying nice eating I'm saying you could bring it to your fine gourmets and they would even like it too is what I'm saying.

Oh, that boy lives on down the road, off Ball's Bluff. Known him his whole life, yessir. He's a stuck up little bastard, too. I been to their Christmas shindigs. I'm a wires guy. Electricity's my gig, see. I do general upkeep, maintenance, general repair, set up, HVAC, AV basic for the shows. Little of this, little that. Electricity R Us, you could say. Do most of the rich people's houses around here. And that little son-of-a-bitch was all over my little baby girl, Marsha, too, when he was younger, but I said, get back, Jack. Get back unless you want the whole loaf, you know what I mean. Don't play in this playground, son. Cause it'll cost you, buddy. And he never settled down that one. Now, she got two of her own now and they live over in Purcellville. She's a single mom. I help her out and she works over at The Commonwealth. Hey. You want a cold one? Because. OK.

Now, I do stuff at the hospital too, set up their exhibits and general, what have you. Make myself handy. Make myself useful, what have you. I enjoy people.

I went over to C.R.'s recently. Short in the basement. Right in the laundry room, right over the vent. That house kind of old. That man need to replace the whole gig with new wiring I told him. That thing's dinosaur. Could sell it, get a nice new place in Battlefield Hills. Use their land, sell it and could make a good deal, include the Ashland house, make it a golf club or something. They could give him, set him up with a big old house, big columns and garages and stuff. We like our Colonial, nice kitchen, three bedroom, 2½ bath.

Free Bird? Ain't that by that band that burned up in a plane. I don't listen to that crap. I like soft country, myself. Johnny Cash, Glen Campbell. Yeah, I like ol' Glen.

Best Regards,

[signature]

I'll tell you, the place is changing. The zoning problem has gotten huge. Strip malls ever present. In my field, it's a problem. Take Fairfax. For example. Zoo. Traffic. God*awful*. Lost the grace. Every day, every day there's a new one coming in here, begging us to, you know, special *except*. People will just out and out lie. Say they want to, oh, change the zoning to put in a house for Grandma, next thing you know they've sliced the land into 1½ acre McMansion chunks. Oh, terrible, terrible. Where's the sense of, you *know*.

I belong to all, the, the right groups. We bid against. Petitions. Ah. Constant diligence. Mrs. Ash was *huge, huge* in the movement against. The Ashs were good people. Then, then they had to, Jesus, sell out. Sell the land. I guess, you know, it gets tough. But. I stopped by frequently. The old man, Mr. Carrie and I would discuss bird hunting. We often went out for doves in the fall. His dog was good, that was a good dog. What happened to that dog? Djinn, I believe they called him? Fine dog. I would treasure that dog, though I don't hunt much these days. Mr. Carrie passed away a while back and the Mrs. was ill, sent off somewhere. They were good neighbors. The boy's a doctor. Let me. Let me add more ice to that. *Shut up*, Baxter. Dog yaps. Get on! Get on, dog! Oh, he gets my shoes. Can you get a good loafer anywhere? Tell me. Do you, do you, do you dove hunt?

I'd like to get out more. My brother's up in Maine. I used to summer in New York.

Free Bird, you say? Hunh. These days I'm favoring Jazz, actually, Dixieland Jazz, not one. Not one for, uh, *rock.* Working on some stuff. That's right. *Sure!* Hate to bore you! The piano's in here.

Betty Owens

Yes, Dr. Ash's house lays right in plain view of my living room bay window. I've been in his service for these last sixteen years. I mean, I do notice it, the house, occasionally, sometimes there is smoke coming from the chimney. Which alarms me, once I called the fire department and told them their house was on fire, but I was wrong, but you can never be too sure, I have worked for Dr. Ash these last sixteen years and I wouldn't want anything to happen to him, he's a, he's a fine contribution to our county and civil well being and. Am I rambling on. I am, I apologize. That there is Mariah, my cat. One of many! I do favor cats. And Charlie, and, and, the little one there. So precious. That's Dunny. After my brother.

The felines are your friend for life, I can testify to that. I have seen them do amazing things, I have. Dr. Ash is fond of, fond of dogs, I believe, which is fine, I think, I think, as long as you have some animal feeling you'll do OK in this world.

Have a nut.

I don't believe I know that song Free Bird. Was it swing? Or later? No, don't recall that. I've, I've been always fond of the music of Mr. Herb Alpert, myself.

Best Regards,
Pendleton Compton

All The Best!
Nancy Compton

Dr: Oh, we've lived in this house for light years—
Nancy: I had to paint it all up when I moved in and wallpaper—
Dr: Nancy's got a real touch—
Nancy: I like to have a little fun with it—
Dr: Boy, can she cook!—
Nancy: His favorite is my French toast, oh, they love it, I'll give you
    the recipe—
Dr: It'll harden your arteries just looking at it, Boy!! And put on the
    pounds!! before you can say, Jack Robinson! And I'm a cardiolo-
    gist! though, pediatric that is. We don't see hardening of the
    arteries that young. Thankfully. Other issues, other issues.—
Nancy: I have a traditional Brisket they all love—
Dr: I just put it away, can't get enough—
Nancy: And my caviar pie. That's a Christmas favorite—
Dr: She's got a gift—

Dr: Yes. I know that song. I used to like that band, Lynard Skynard. Ho
    boy. I used to jam to that one, that's right—
Nancy: I like Fleetwood Mac, myself, don't you, Pendleton?

Sincerely,
Verona Howard

We have lived in this house for one year now and I just love it here, the kids have the cul-de-sac. To ride bikes and George and I have barbeques, I was raised around here and. Yes, I know the Ashs. Of course. My mother, her mother worked for them for years. And we were real poor and we had to struggle and I married George, who's from St. Louis, and he's done OK with himself, and we're doing OK, we're doing OK, Ashland is over by Ball's Bluff. I spent some time there when I was younger. I know C.R., we all do. Hon, bring out a Coke. I said, a Coke!!

I have started catering with Diane Redmond, a neighbor in my block, if you're interested we have an outfit called Thymes of the Essence and we do all types of functions and events and occasions and if you have something coming up, we'd be happy to customize a menu with your budget and concerns in mind. We do it all.

Free Bird is one of those redneck songs. One of those songs those white trash in trucks listen to, so no I don't care for it, and George and I just listen to easy music, because it mellows us out. I don't have time for music. I work.

Euphrates King

I am the partial owner of the history bookstore in town, you may know it, "The Bugle's Blast." I urge you to stop in, browse. Enjoy our selection of fine military reading material, let me ask you, do you enjoy much history, are you familiar with the Civil War, I mean _really_ familiar, because, well, I do advise you to brush up. Familiarize, uh. Uh, uh. Lost my train of thought! Ah. Oh yes, the battles, the battles are still, still important. History is always.

Go with me here. You're walking down the street. You see a log. You step around it, carefully. Why? History at work! You've learned from the past you could trip, get hurt. Men are the same, we blunder the same. Oh, the lessons! The lessons! You, my fine friend, are a virtual catalogue of history, history is the juice of our daily lives, it flows through these dusty roads and these brown-walled rivers and we breathe it every day. I bore you. I beg your forgiveness.

I enjoy docent work. I work Ball's Bluff on weekends, 11:00 and 2:00. Come on down. Come on down. Bring a picnic.

Sorry for the lack of space in here. Tend to collect things. Papers. Find a space, if you will. When I docent, I aim to transcend this era, bring people back, hear the crack of gunshot. Which is my vocation. I'm like a vessel. I bake my own hardtack, which if you know is a hard bread the soldiers ate. Tended to get rancid and wormy due to the conditions. But they ate it! Vermin and all! Vermin and all. Life was hard. Rations few. Deaths many.

Free Bird? I'm sorry. Tend to—*surprise here!*—go with the old stuff from that time. Can do "The Vacant Chair" on harmonica. Which was the big song during that time, everyone sung and cried. A boy from Mass gets killed in Ball's Bluff so they still pull his chair up to the table at Thanksgiving. Sad times. Sad times.

Muriel Hines

My mother worked for the Ash family her whole life, all her life and they were nice people and after she passed I went on up there, too. And I worked there all the while Mrs. Ash wasn't right in the head poor woman and she near fell couple times and they had to put her over at the Citadel Manor. And that was sad for Mr. Ash, he was a nice gentleman, up to his last days. I was there in the end. I was sorry to see him go. He always said, Muriel, Muriel, haha, Muriel, I'm going to leave Mrs. Ash if you keep cooking this good, and we all laugh. He love my lima beans and tomatoes and C.R. like ham like nothing in this world, as well as my squash. Those days I get up there to clean once a week though just the downstairs on account of my arthritis and I worry about that boy being all alone in the house no wife or family. I don't think he has the kind of sense his daddy had, that man was funny that's for sure. I wish that boy would marry. That place is too quiet.

Free Bird, he played that song all day long. And I started to like it a bit. I can sing it. The words aren't much.

best wishes,
Diane Redmond

Oh, yes, the Ash estate is over by Ball's Bluff and we live right here in the development and yes, I like it very much. I have a son, Todd, typical teenager, you know, testing, testing limits, and such, I. Oh! I'm sorry, I'd like to offer you some ice tea, how about. OK. Well. Is it cold in here? I feel cold. It's these computerized cooling systems I can't figure them out, do you have children? Because, because, isn't it hard, all the stages, the stages they go through. I mean its colic and toilet training and, and, and, ear infections and getting rid of the damn bottle and, and. Stuff. You know. You just try your best. You just try to be there. Are boys harder? I don't know. Candace seems rather self sufficient, with her soccer and everything. Todd is more of, a challenge. I do love him. Toddie. I do.

Free Bird is a sad song. It makes me cry. It reminds me of sad things. Like breaking up. I avoid sad songs. Lately, I haven't kept up with music. I don't know the bands. It is cold in here, I'm going to go fiddle with that control, excuse me.

forever, Kirsten Hodges

I'm, my plans are, basically, to be somebody. I want to go to a good school and then, I don't know. I guess I'm just like everyone. You're sitting on my poncho by the way, oh, you probably think I'm *so,* you know. What is this *for* anyway. I guess I really could get into modeling or maybe helping the world in some way, but how is the question. Mainly I just don't really care about anything really a lot but I'm sure as I get older I'll start to, probably. That's what my Mom says, you know.

I do not have a boyfriend. And if someone said I do, then they are lying.

Free Bird is a pretty song about a bird that was trapped and then goes to Florida. I think it's a parrot or something. I think it's classic rock. I don't know. It's not a great song you know? There are others that are better because it's just lame and old. I mean, I hope it's not your favorite or something. I think we sung that in choral, if not, I'm sure I heard it on the radio or something.

Eleanor Fitzhugh

Well, yes, I do know C.R. Ash rather well, or I thought I did, we actually dated for awhile. Yes, we did. And he's nice man but one of those those impossible types which I always seem to find, you know, the ones with no future the ones who just just fiddle with you or play you or something I don't know maybe I'm not the right girl woman whatever.

Not that I'm not happy. I'm quite happy. I'm busy. I'm successful. I would've liked children. I don't think being married is some kind of hell so pardon me. Is there something wrong with me for goodness sakes I suppose you heard that Rodge Billings and I were an item at one point. I know he's much older but he's wonderful he too claims marriage is not his bag you see. I have a knack for these types. There was James Felton, he proposed. He's the head of the Mosby league, a lawyer. But boring. Dull as dirt.

I'll never forgive C.R. He led me along. I cooked for him. His dog, that stinky old thing, oh, how I hated that dog getting on my coats and stuff. I suppose he wasn't the right one. Maybe I'm not meant to be married.

Free Bird? I don't know. Who cares who cares who cares about stuff like that. Not me.

Your friend,

June Roberts

You want my story, well, here's a story for you, a true story:

Everyday a woman I knew who lived in a small town in Virginia, would drive over route 7 to the "Ball's Bluff Babies Hospital," sign in at desk (already the panic starting), enter the elevator, press "12" for the Neonatal Intensive Care Unit and set forth to visit her dear baby who was born at a mere two pounds and as as each floor ascended, the panic grew and grew until, as the elevator's doors sealed shut, this woman's heart would be racing—terrible scenes involuntarily skitting through her head, scenes of nurses pulling her aside, doctor's rushing up to tell her, There was an emergency! I'm sorry! Terrible bad scenes involving her tiny fragile baby who suddenly had spiraled downward and had died in a mere fifteen seconds (Because she took the back road and didn't get there fast enough! Because she wasn't there all night! Because she's really bad or evil! These thoughts spin through her mind), but it didn't happen, though now, as she walks to the NICU, searching each face that says Hi! (not as friendly, their eyes down, is something wrong?) finally, she arrives to the green smock area where she puts on the customary outfit, scrubs her hand, looks through and sees his tiny pink roll through his *isolette* (doesn't that sound like a French pastry or something?), he reminds her of a doll she still has, a tiny, frumpy-faced thing named "Polly," she comes over and opens the little catch door and holds the small hand—you know it could be a minnow its so small—she watches the oxometer, which declares the oxygen content of the blood and it becomes merrier and high, and maternal feelings are at a high, this may be a sad setting, but the amount of delirious love she feels is absurd and almost crazy, *almost*, combined with the suffocating fear he could die. Have I even told you about the indignity, the trial of *bradycardia?* Do you know what it means? It means a slowing down of the heart rate. It is common among premies. And what it means is, when you have finally relaxed for a millisecond about your child, maybe it's the first time you are allowed to feed your baby, you look down and the baby is ashen and blue and has stopped breathing. Basically, it died for a brief moment or was about to, and as you nearly stop breathing yourself, a nurse notices and comes by and quickly tickles his chin or picks him up and shakes him slightly and says with a vexed little exasperated look, *oh, these darn bradies!* and then gives him back to you! she gives him back to you and says, *just look out for those bradies.* And then you are expected to bring home a child like that and actually sleep?

Well, so, she sings him a song and then her heart does another ka-bump of a different nature as the doctor comes along, a string bean man, tall, gaunt, handsome face, L.L. Bean type clothes, he is a nice man, he passes in his rounds and as she soothes and sings to her tiny son, she tries to decipher each syllable, each utterance of the wise doctor (did that *oh, me* mean that the baby is sure to die? Is that it? I don't want to ask, because then it's sealed and signed and a done deed, there is still time for plenty of superstition and prayers and work if death is imminent in the Doctor's eyes, I'll divert it with God and will, for this woman believes life is a changeable structure of possibilities, as changing and constant as the oxometer), which incidentally has sunk to the eighties, a poor level now, this woman, feels sick and hungry, it is lunchtime, and feeling because of the doctor's *oh, me* said in that particular tone, there is work to do: she goes to the sixth floor, first to attempt her pitiful six times a day milk extrusion with Darth Vader, the huge metal breast-sucker, which she attaches for half an hour and gets an ounce, *I'm drying up! Nature's way of letting go! The baby's dying! Does everyone know but me? Is it only a matter of time?* she sobs at the one ounce of milk, yes, she is crying now, but she is every day, so what, so what

I'm trying to get to is this, the woman, who is pitiful and overwrought with fear and suffering because she finally loves something *unconditionally*, finally loves another person and *does not care* if that person is deformed or damaged or unresponsive or flawed or hideous or not meeting her needs or not stroking her ego or even just being a nice bundle of baby she can show off in a new stroller in the streets, who cares? She loves him regardless of all and everything and with this feeling, this intensity, she goes down on a daily basis back down the 12 floors, she goes to the chapel and falls down and begs God, who she now knows, to spare her son's life, and God, in all his infinite love, was listening, as he always is, and as she returns upstairs, the kind doctor is there, and then the woman sits in his desk and loves him also, but she knows it not real love, there are so many shades of love around her here, and she is suffering badly! But she loves the doctor, she loves the child, she loves God, she loves all the fat nurses in their turquoise outfits and she loves the county of Loudoun, the whole state of Virginia, then she comes back to reality, sitting in a chair by the isolette, the nurse asking her to move aside slightly, so she can draw blood from his tiny bruised arm, one more time. And there is an end to this story I suppose. And I could tell you the end. But I don't think I want to, dear. I don't know.

All I know is, I love that man C.R. so much my heart could burst. That sound you hear, that sweet little murmur, is the little sound of my daughter in her bath, talking to her blue whale. You hear that sound? That's her. The story goes on. A baby named Jake died when I was there. I can't even tell you about his mother and father. I can't even think about the shape of their bodies as they walked out of the room and the taste in my mouth and how I wanted to rip out, personally, every single joyful yellow balloon from the fabric of the room divider with a scalpel, when they were in there with Jake. Or how the father caught my eye for a minute as he came out from behind that *cheerful* divider and I looked away, I didn't want to make him feel bad, I didn't want to catch the contagion of his grief. To be completely honest here. But I am sorry for that feeling.

*   *   *

I'm superstitious and I don't want to tell you my baby's name or what happened, I just wanted to tell you this story and tell you that Dr. Ash is an angel from Heaven, in my book.

I don't care about your music or gossip or what have you, Free Bird, or any fool songs. I'm talking about *life*, people, I'm talking about, that man is some kind of saint and you just *sitting* here.

stave three

the children.

todd + kirsten, 1

I.

For a while Kirsten had been a light, airy child with long blond hair, dancing through the house, wearing impossibly small leggings and little sweatshirts, all in shades of rose and lavender, and when she was ten, seemingly overnight, there came the time Kirsten's breasts were growing and felt hot and itchy under her sweaters, and there was the fact her hair became so greasy all of a sudden it looked freshly washed. The little leggings were all packed up and her legs were twice as long and now the young Kirsten wore skintight jeans and chunky boots and a little bra that barely held anything, maybe two small walnuts at the most. The boys (though much shorter and still smooth-skinned while the girls dotted on Clearasil and wore deodorant) flurried around Kirsten as she turned twelve, her body now a vaguely curvaceous imprint of an adult woman, and the parties in the basements began. Parties where boys desperately tried to be with Kirsten, to kiss, wet and slobbery (depending who she was *going with*, who she chose to sit with on the bus to field trips or pass notes with), before her mother came down with more Ruffles.

Then, around sixteen came her three adventures that summer, one quickly after another, all as fast and frantic as the boys surrounding her, imagine now suddenly you're sixteen and you wake up and feel pretty shitty and your skirt doesn't fit, it doesn't fit! Shit, shit, shit! It's a size four, for God's sake, and it takes a safety pin to wear so you go to the bathroom and

get your mother's Epsom salts and dissolve them in a glass because a girl
said you can lose weight this way and Kirsten plans to skip breakfast because, gosh, she feels sick anyway, she also plans to get some chocolate
Ex-Lax later today and going downstairs she feels dizzy and all this makes
her feel fragile and odd, driving to school she parks in her lucky spot near
the gym and Angie and Jill meet her outside, she gags as she smokes a cig
in Smoker's Court.

Her body doing weird stuff was becoming usual, first the occurrence of
her period a few years back which she had waited for desperately, but, when
it arrived unspectacularly while she was ice-skating with friends and wearing a short skirt, it stained her underwear and she had no supplies and had
to use toilet paper bunched up, oh, the horror of how unatttractive and
meaty it all was, what a nuisance, the clotty alarm of it all. So when for a
few months as she dieted it seemed to disappear she felt relieved. Maybe
she had a secret she didn't wish to advertise because mothers and doctors
would ruin it, which she thought of as *period-deprivation studies*, which was,
eat little and get rid of your period. It was exciting. Perhaps the Epsom
salts had done the trick.

Imagine, as she is five months pregnant but it only shows as a slight bulge
on her tiny frame, and Todd Redmond, the father, and her barely talk, he
does in the beginning try to engage her, to ask her if she wants to go, like,
to the park, you know, and she cuts him off, finds him lame and boring,
the fumble in the car was just sick and stupid and horrifying, she pretends,
she desperately hopes it doesn't mean *she's done it*, she's fixated on older
men now like the doctors at the hospital, especially Dr. Ash, who is some
kind of heartthrob with his crinkly blue eyes, although he's old and stuff,
she likes him, he's debonair, he wouldn't, say, stumble and be so uncool in
the car, he would be romantic and kind and sweet, she was told by someone that older men are *better*, this was her thinking those days, she was
getting tired, too tired for sports and it was just weird.

Some nights she lies there on her pink pillow with her bear Brownie
and tries to remember, to remember someone, some *feeling* she had for a
boy. Only a few monthes ago it seems she longed for them, she watched
their tight, silky muscles playing basketball and her body responded, there

was an intense buzzing of attraction in her body, she *wanted* boys, but now. Just a few months before there was this craze she felt, this insanity, and now it all dropped off and she was content to be alone. She had become some island, walking in the hall her backpack pulled tight in front of her. Maybe a doctor would understand. Maybe she was losing her mind.

Many nights she ignored the parties, the phone ringing for her and she said, *I'm too tired tell them I'm out*. She sat in the study and ate chips, watching reruns. She fell asleep early and her mother would gently wake her, with her little pointy hand, *Kirsten, honey*. On some level her mother knew something was wrong with her daughter. On some level one always knows. But many more levels of consciousness deleted those thoughts and added excuses, she's a growing girl, high school is hard work, etc.

Her mother would fall asleep on this same couch, early in the evening, when she was pregnant with Kirsten. Some fiber of her remembered that, but she avoided that dangerous route. *Growing is hard business*.

Then, Kirsten had a cramp all one morning. Weirder still was going to the bathroom in the hospital while candy-striping, having to take a shit badly and her stomach was hurting bad, and blood and goo comes out, yellow liquid, and sitting down on her sweatshirt, she must be so damn sick, Oh, help me, she moans, help me, between her legs comes out this clump, this lump, it's moving. Sick. It's moving, and making tiny noises, *Mommy! Mommy! I want my mommy!* She screams and bangs on the toilet stall door, and someone comes running in, the door swings open, she holds out the bloody bundle, and that's all she remembers, that and rushing air, maybe cold steel, she passed out and it was worse than *Scream*, worse than *Halloween*, worse than Freddy Krueger, worse than any fucking nightmare, that moment of horror, this sick moment that she had to go through. When she wakes up, they tell her she's something's Mom.

Imagine that.

2.

Todd Redmond heard some rumor, something really weird from his sister, Candace, about Kirsten. Candy and her friends were talking in the back of the massive Expedition as they drove to school, his mother had lent it to him and the girls sat in the third seat, but there were unmistakable words about *pregnant* and *baby* and stuff, and he kept saying what? What? And they laughed and said shut *up*, Candace knew he had some sort of crush on Kirsten, she hadn't seen them together, though she couldn't have imagined (and he is turning red now thinking about it, turning left on Philomont Road, thinking about the lame moment he flubbed everything and how he hit his ass against the glove handle and how close he'd been, does that count? He thinks it counts, he was in there, after all, but that wouldn't, that couldn't, like, do *it* to her, I mean you have to shoot your load, and he didn't then, back home, yes, but not in Kirsten so he couldn't have gotten her—), *what the fuck are you guys saying, shit!* he yells back there, *tell me that shit,* and there is a bunch of laughing and giggling, his sister Candace says, *I just heard some gross thing, like Kirsten had a baby or something,* and then Todd Redmond starts thinking frantically, she wasn't pregnant, I just saw her a few days ago, she was like *normal*, she wasn't big and pregnant, which slips into a feeling of being pissed off, oh, yeah? oh, yeah? OH YEAH? reviewing who it could've been, one of his friends who was hanging around her these days, she's dissed him so there's got to be someone, he feels some liquidy surge of pure rage fill him, *goddammit*, and tries to say in a superflat, calm voice, *so what's she gonna do, hunh?* but which comes out feathery and painful, then taking his attention away for a minute to check out an articulated dump truck propped on the side of the road, a full-fledged Braun, then a begrudging memory of Kirsten and her beautiful breasts (*Fucking Mike Tovel. Asshole. It's him I bet*), then he catches some gigglish mumble from Kirsten's friend Jackie, *hunh, what,* he says and she says, *I said, the baby died, she had it in the bathroom or something. It's all so totally foul.* And Todd Redmond feels an overwhelming need to pummel Mike Tovel, his good friend's head in, because he was the one who said at lunch back a few weeks ago, *I'd do her,* in response to Kirsten blowing by in some jeans, *hell, if you don't want her, I'll do her,* and Todd Redmond had laughed and said, *heh, help yourself,* acting like he had dropped her but, really, he wished she would talk to him, he drove into school and looked at her space where she always parked her little Jeep but it was filled by a Camaro and he felt a strange deflating.

hermie carson +
todd redmond +
synjyne, 1

I.

Todd Redmond began to change:

It was his mom's fault, he would say. She had her tennis, her catering. She stood downstairs in her yellow daffodil tennis skirt at the sink, wash- ing lettuce. She said, *Hi hon!* She was gone in tournaments or meets or *occasions* or *functions* most of the day, coming in at six or seven to make dinner. She was the DINNER MAKER. She gave up washing and spin- ning lettuce. Too time-consuming. She now bought salad called Tuscan Blend in neat plastic bags. She then progressed to the salad kits, complete with dressing in a pouch and croutons or shredded cheese. This saved her at least fifteen minutes. She decided cooking meat took too much time and thus she often bought the premade meat loaf or the Perdue barbeque chicken breasts. She spent more time with the microwave than with Todd. She had pared down. She had lost weight by cutting out fat and her face had gained a rhino toughness in return.

She stayed away from that place called Todd's room, having walked in one day to his embarrassed, red face as he threw a quilt over himself, *uh, Mom,* he said, though it came out coarse in his desperation for casual- ness, *can you, uh, knock,* but she had gone into robotic denial, sizing up the situation in a microsecond, and diverted it with mock irritation, I've been looking for your damn socks! Oh, here they are.

She avoided his eyes, which sent a blue, crumbled look in her direction.
There was something in his gaze that terrified her, and she longed to fold up
his body in her arms, but their life together now seemed a series of small
rejections. He scared her on many levels, one he had grown and stretched
tall so quickly she felt meek and powerless around him, his knuckles were
large and bony and she was used to the tiny, soft hands of a preschooler, the
ones that gripped her skirt as she plied them away at the day-care center
(Time for Tots!). Two, his voice was low and suddenly he was a man, and
actually quite handsome and that disturbed her, she wanted closeness with
him, but in her experience, her past, she had sought out closeness with men
with flirtation, and she didn't know how to get close with him, all avenues
seemed blocked and disastrous, she couldn't buy his attention anymore with
a candy bar or a trip to Chuck E. Cheese, she didn't know his musical tastes
or clothes or interests, and she became shy and quiet around him. She cleaned
frantically when he was in the room, trying to restore order. She would look
up to his face eagerly as he bolted in the door at six, *Hi hon!* and she grew
sad to see the pimples, the sullen face wolfing down pizza, *hey.* He was half
boy, half man, a strange hybrid, like a fragile, brute thing, half velvety flower,
half burlap sack. She longed to hold him again. He shrugged her off like an
annoyance. Fact of the matter is, deep down, lodged in his memory was how
she brushed him off, daily, when he'd needed her, how he'd spent long days
at Time for Tots! playing Legos by the door waiting for her silver minivan
to pull in, how the sun quietly sunk beneath the horizon and the sky turned
a cold blue before she drove in, headlights scoring a line through the road,
this memory defined itself in subtle, not obvious, ways. The light clinking
sound of her keys being pulled by her manicured hands from the key rack
(*Home is where the heart is,* painted in country blue), the sound of her car
crunching on gravel, the untruthful way she said *I'll see ya later,* the back of
her neck, walking through a doorway on her way out, they all brought with
them a similar dissatisfaction, a slow-burning sad pit in his guts, an off-hue.
He wouldn't have attributed it to all the days she had no time for him. He
didn't think it through. Instead these feeling-memories became knives in
their relationship, deleting her, on some levels, cutting out parts, yet allow-
ing her to remain on the periphery.

2.

It was Kirsten's fault, he would say.

She came back to school, her face paler, translucent and she ignored him, you see, he had already called Love-line one frantic, sweaty night when he couldn't stand it any longer, called them hidden down in the edge of his bed under the tartan covers, Go ahead, "Bobby" from Virginia, they had said, tell us your beef. Well, I, uh,—Go ahead, Bobby we're listening, said Dr. Drew, they could be mean and harsh sometimes, impatient with the shyness of the callers, Todd was stuttering and his voice was hushed, I was w-w-wondering, wondering if, if you do it with a girl, like for only a second, but you don't you know uh-jaculate, does, can, can she get preg-preg-preg—can she get preggers, you mean, cut in the other guy, Adam, sure, sure, right, Dr. Drew? Oh, absolutely, Bobby, dude, absolutely, you see, Bobby, you release a small amount of sperm before ejaculation, you see. But Todd had already hung up (I guess Bobby got his answer, OK, next—), hung up and ran to the toilet where his clammy head spun and he gagged a few times, and then lay on the bed and clutched his pillow to his stomach, *Todd! Toddie!* yelled his mother, Diane, *Toddie, dinner!*

3.

There was this guy that lived across the street, Hermie Carson.

Hermie had gone to preschool with Todd, they'd had playdates. They'd seen *Sesame Street Live!* at Constitution Hall, they'd eaten Goldfish crackers out back and drunk Kool-Aid and wrestled and rode trikes out front and gone to kindergarten together, their mothers' flashes burning their eyes, wearing little overalls with designs (Hermie's had a fire truck, Todd's had a bulldozer). Hermie was his little buddy until Hermie's dad shot himself in the shed in their backyard in fifth grade. (It was real cold that day, Todd remembers, the ambulance and cars all parked out front, steaming with exhaust.) Hermie was out of school for a while and when he returned he sort of stood by himself by the reading lab and pulled the threads out of his pant cuffs. His mother had a pinched look and she'd always push him by the shoulders, Go, go, play with your friends, Hermie, but Hermie would only sit by the computer in the back. He designed a computer game by down-loading instructions and called it Killer Bee Hell and he brought it to school on disc until Mrs. Trancastine discovered it, found a clump of boys going *bzzz bzzz* and *aww, got him! aww, gotcha!* and her large form loomed over them, watching each pixilated bee explode into a bloody splat.

Summer of ninth grade, Todd barely knew Hermie, but saw him occa-sionally, his dyed black hair and his gloomy, sacklike clothes, hanging out with tenth graders, the weird set, druggies by the old parking lot. He'd occa-sionally catch Hermie's eyes by the lunch Coke machine, *hey, Hermie,* he'd say and Hermie's hand was kind of dirty, he noticed, with black nail polish appearing fungal, and he'd whisper, *hey, Todd-ulus,* and that would be that. Todd would say, *how you doing,* quietly. They were cordial yet distant. At this night, though, the night Todd has called in to the radio, he holds his pillow to his chest as his mother calls up, *Toddie! Dinner!* Todd looks out the window and sees Hermie, sitting in his car across the street in the dark, just sitting there. Exhaust coming out the back, steaming and billowing.

Getting up to put on some music (a bootleg neopunk CD a guy named Ollie at school gave him) means nothing, *I'm not hungry Mom!!* which comes out warbled and honking in his effort not to cry, *Toddie! Are you OK?* I said, more honkishness, *I'm! Not! Hungry!* CD makes the air sound flatter than it already did. Look at this pitiful room, this room sucks, he bellows into the pillow which smells sour from all the extrusions of his body, from his underarms to his feet to his penis to his hair, a smorgasbord of all the scents of Todd in Distress, a cologne of angst. His hands grab his hair, Don't fucking cry all the time, Jesus. What's your problem man you're such a dumb baby is what you are just grow up for christsake. His hair feels alien and annoying and he wants to, to rip it all out. Expose his raw scalp. All his fucking blond hair. Wants to scratch his skin off. This churned-up anguish, this lack of control on his situation makes him feel so restless. How How How How How How How How How How, it becomes mantralike in between his ears, his voice following, How How How, he thinks, Oh God! How How? Let me be dead or something. Let me just go. He wants

Kirsten. He feels lost, invaded, abandoned, majorly deceived. His own baby, his actual own baby?

Born on a bathroom floor?

4.

Two A.M.

He awoke crunched in a ball and the CD still played and the light was still on. His face was wet with drool on one side.

He got up, ran to the bathroom, then ripped at his hair with scissors. Each clip and jab on his head corresponded to the surge of guitar, the pounding of drum, this rage so heavy and thick under his eyes and in his throat, and his face in the mirror looked red and wet, pimples purplish and throbbing, his eyes bloodshot, his mouth tight and pulled back, his skin he noticed was loose and pink like gum and at this moment he is disgusting, he can't even play with his dick, his body so putrid and betrayful, they, they they they ought to lock him up he's so foul so goddammit loserly, he vomits again, just bile. From the bathroom window—*what the?*—Hermie still out there in his car, steam heaving out the back.

Their eyes meet.

5.

Todd Redmond:

Silvery blond hair, arctic blue eyes. Old Navy T-shirts and cargo pants. Skateboards. Vanns sneakers. Sure deodorant. Jockey underwear. Old Brut cologne. Crest Extra Whitening Power. Sunny Delight and Hot Pockets after school. Sunday school at Crestview Presbyterian seven years in a row. Fond of construction vehicles, to an absurd level. Would translate this as a future in mechanical engineering. Aspires to Virginia Tech. Go Hokies. Kirsten was his first time, despite the story of the twenty-four-year-old flight attendant who stayed at The Ramada and he met at Kmart. Despite that.

It's *cold as a bitch* outside as he stumbles out to Hermie's car, his hands rammed in his VA TECH sweatshirt.

What the fuck happened to your hair, asked Hermie.

Uh, cut it.

Looks. I don't know, *righteous*.

All right. How you doing, Hermie?

Not bad. Yourself, my friend, Todd?

OK. What you doing out here.

Todd's breath pours out of his mouth in puffs as he leans in over the car window,

Enjoying the fine night air, my good Todd.

All this time?

Yeah. Is there an issue with that. Hey, get in. It's cold, shit.

Yeah.

Todd hesitates for a moment, but he is freezing, so he gets in.

What you doing up, Todd, pulled a groin muscle?

Ha. Just up. I don't know. Can't sleep.

Ah, yes. Neither can we. Sleep's a big waste anyway. Well. I can offer you some fine peppermint schnapps of my mother's, mixed with Kool-Aid in a toast to Reverend Jones, in *La Paper Cup*, or we could go to my pharmaceutical stash and *pro*-cure something else.

Oh, no, no. Drink's good.

Very fine.

They drink. Hermie puts in a tape which he hurtles into high-decibel tones, *Kill Switch . . . Click*, to be exact, but Todd hears it as something good. Something that feels like a really good remedy. It is at this time he notices a girl, looks like Samantha Raylin (that's **Synjyne,** Hermie says), sprawled out in the back, her black hair cascaded over the seat, her lips smeared, totally out.

She got, um, a bit, well, out of it.

Yeah. They're yelling over the music.

We can wake her up and go to my quarters. Study the classics and chit-chat. Debate the higher essential duality of nature, if you will. Toddulus.

The classics?

Fine reading material.

Yeah. Is your mom there?

Noooo, I'm talking about my *private* quarters. Not my privates, though. The shed there.

Ohh.

Yes, you know where my dad blew his brains out. I know you remember, who could forget. Still has some blood specks there. Join me. Join us.

Ohhh.

Oh, it's awesome, says Synjyne, popping up from the back, her hair mashed on one side, her white face painted sporting a crumpled edge, Hermie's fixed it up so cool. The Temple of Doom, we call it.

Its the al-*tar* of my despair, Todd.

Todd laughs.

Check out Todd's hair, Synjyne.

Whoa, you chopped it up cool.

It's still too blond, though, sweet and blond like *a leetle beety cheerleaduh guhl.*

Synjyne laughs, strokes his head, as Hermie continues,

Like a *cootie-pie angel pie*, she passes him a joint she's relit, a stinky little stub.

You like, got some point here, Hermie?

And even Hermie, so mind-altered that the trails from a car's headlights two blocks away burn rainbowed scars in his watery retinas, can feel some dead anguish in Todd, sees his eyes cindered and heavy and flat,

Hell, I'm just pulling your chain. We used to be, you know, *buds*, right?

6.

Todd's father—not dead like Hermie's dad, the plumber who took his shotgun, used for the occasional deer hunt, out to the shed one day years ago and took his own head off in one bold shot, right after dinner with his wife, Millie, Hermie, and his daughter, Janine, during a dinner of corned beef hash, along with a Rolling Rock, discussing the odd bits of daily life, like going to the play at Janine's school because Randy would be in it, a guy she had a crush on. Pass the, uh, salt, there, Hermie (*Is there a way to prevent too much mess I could spray oven cleaner on the walls first*, which is what he did, also spreading a painter's drop sheet on the floor). Yes, good dinner, Mil (he pushes the food around, leaving his stomach empty, more considerate plans about *mess*). They were eating dessert, pumpkin pie leftovers, when Todd's father said, I got to check something. Check what? said Millie. Just something. A few minutes after he slammed the back door, they heard the shot. What the heck was that? said Millie, when, suddenly, she knew. Hermie can remember, if anything, the tight, tendony angle of her neck as she paused and thought, lulling over the sound and the way her eyes grew round and rolled around the room, her voice, squeaky and soft, Go, get me, get me a phone, or something, then a hand clutching the corner of her eyebrow in a weird decorative way, her mouth whispering, Upstairs everyone! What? Mom, I didn't finish my dess—but then his mother rolled to the floor like a pile of potatoes, moaning. The children said nothing and filed upstairs and sat on Hermie's bed, all together. They heard the back door slam. Then they heard a deep, pitchy shriek from outside, the watery yell that came up from their mother, and they stayed on the bed, only their eyes flashing to each other in confusion, an ambulance sound getting closer and louder, and finally, in the street they saw the hastily parked police and ambulance, columns of exhaust filing from the backs of the cars.

Hermie's stance became: It was fun to be without the fucker, he said to his friends. That man would smack my head. I *enjoyed, no, treasured* eating out of other people's clear glass casserole dishes for months. Especially fond of the green bean casserole with the crunchy onions. I enjoyed watching the cleanup crew in orange coveralls, an old guy and his son, Roberts Sanitation, use a wet-vac on my father's remains. I did, he said. By the way, bit of interesting info: They prefer Pine-Sol to Mr. Clean. Mr. Roberts himself said that. Said it has more phosphates. I was pleased to notice they left a trace of splattered blood on an edge and I will often take the time to talk to that bit of my old man. You are majorly, majorly askew, said Synjyne to him one day in Smoker's Court, I know, I know, isn't it fucking beautiful, grinding his cigarette under his sneaker, I even amaze myself.

(I never seen anything like that boy, going on about soaps and all and shit and his father dying like that, that's some sad sad shit what that is. I feel bad for him I do, I try Lord knows I try ask my son here help out and all, but what you supposed to do when someone ain't right in the head call a doctor I suppose, I try best I can, don't want to burden the wife anymore but I tell you. That boy hurt my heart you know what I'm saying. Mr. Roberts said, standing by his truck, his face darkened under his cap in the shadow, I got children too. How a man get up and leave his family beyond me. But I don't judge people.)

But Todd's father, Bob "The Mayor" Redmond, hadn't shot himself or left or any such thing, he was a meek man, lacking in sinew, who sat in his velour chair in the heart pine den reading about heirloom roses (he favored a certain pale peach, *Mrs. Truman*), he was gone frequently on golf jaunts for business, though "The Mayor" disliked golf, he despised the waste of time, but his boss at the bank insisted he take clients, so he would go, trying to swing well and drum up humorous banter, but instead the golf sessions were silent and flat, accompanied by the sound of the clanking golf clubs, the conversation having gone dead in the first few minutes, after his peppy, *so how are things down at the shop?* had petered away and *you up with the 'Skins these days?* produced a sentence or two and then they were left walking, even the rustle of their khakis audible or the slow drone of a lawn mower in the distance. *Can I interest you in the rare, petaled beauty of an heirloom rose,* he longed to say, or *I'm rereading* Martin Chuzzlewit, *what a fine tale* but he knew these would've fallen flat on the grass, so he remained tongue-tied. At times like this his inner monologue honed around the key phrase *social misfit,* repetitively. He wondered why he was one. He was mortified by the frantic searching for subject matter the client always did, the feverish look he would give to the other groups of players, laughing and jabbering in the sun, and Bob "The Mayor" felt singed in his heart, confident the fellows at work gave him the nickname "The Mayor" not because of popularity or any such thing, but out of mockery.

Todd heard snippets of *I'll have to kiss, you know, Telford's ass on the greens* from his dad to his mother (Bob the Mayor tried to sound like a fat cat, he assumed the position, but he longed for gardening, for simple days, for digging in dirt and watching a plant grow. Goddammit, I hate golf! he flung to his bathroom mirror.) Posted to the fridge, Todd saw the locations of golf his dad frequented, *Bermuda Waters Resort Club, cabin 404,* saw the occasional Grape-Nuts bowl, wet with milk, by the sink, saw his dad half naked in a towel through a gap in the bedroom door, Hey, Todd, have a good day, son. His dad would stand there, watch him, his eyebrows an expectant raised lift.

Whoa! Am I on a Roller Coaster or What! How Hormones Play Foul with Your Feelings. His mom, Diane, had this book *Am I an Alien or Is This Normal?* in her hands and she read this chapter closely before sleep, in her peach silk ensemble with her reading glasses perched on her nose. It explained that hormones in the young man are turbulent and unpredictable and every now and then she'd stop to think how he grunted hello and how he smelled different when she forced an occasional hug and thought about his hair, his golden, wavy locks which he had hacked into some odd beige- carpeted scalp, *what the heck happened to you,* said his dad in his jogging suit, *holy cow! You want me to set you up an appointment with Smitty to fix that?*

No, Dad.

Well, what then, son.

I like it, OK.

You going punk on us now, bud? You can seriously affect your athletic rep being too weird you know.

Todd thought of Smitty, and apparently that was where he had received his first haircut, as evidenced by the framed photo hanging on the staircase wall, the one with his small red face crying above the circle of a barber's smock next to the crinkled hand of Smitty, the place where his dad always sat next to him and asked for a little off around the ears and the back, where Smitty puffed up the back of Todd's hair with that smelly powder (There you go, young man) and for hours sharp, transparent edges of hair would trickle down his back. *I think I'll pass on Smitty these days, Dad.*

She read the book and she lent it to Bob "The Mayor" and he read it, It's a phase, she said, we need to let him express his, well, his individuality, let him kind of stray and that's, that's what it says, if you love something set it free, you know. And if it comes back, it's yours. Bob The Mayor gulped at the tired poem allusion, then agreed with her and they became quiet.

Todd slunk around and flopped in front of the TV and ate popcorn instead of meals and thought frantically as he lay in his bed listening to music shaking the bed, Would I have been a good dad? Where is my kid now? If I had known I could've made him eat right and stuff. I could've taken care of him myself (for in his mind the baby was always a he, always a miniature blond version of Todd, a tiny smiling tyke). My mom would love him. I would teach him football. I would sleep with him. I could build a little bed for him and paint it and all and he could sleep next to me and when I go to school he'd play and then afterward I'd come home and he'd be all happy to see me. I'd hug him.

How can a baby have a funeral without its Dad? How can it lie somewhere and I can't put flowers on its grave? At this point he went to wash his face and he saw them, Synjyne, Hermie, in the clouded car. He went outside and got in their car. Synjyne handed him a tiny shred of paper and said *eat it, eat this* and it made his mouth feel like watery iron. The corners of his eyes shone, as if frosted liquid were careening through the membranes of his eyes. Lying back against the headrest, his head had its own motion, its own rhythm and for the first time in a while he didn't worry about the idea of the baby, he felt like the baby was there, stroking his face, the baby's tiny hand, but it was Synjyne, she pulled him in the back and he went, she folded him in her arms and rocked him in the back and he thought *she* was the baby, then he felt *he* was the baby and that made him feel sadness and she kissed him and he kissed her and he could feel her understanding, Todd yelled something, something of joy, but you couldn't hear above the Raggedy Aneurysm punching through the speakers, in some world he could see himself on his Pornstar skateboard doing air in a 360 above the edge of the skatepark he frequented, in one sense he could feel his lungs full of hot air as he ran down the length of a football field, the blur of the crowd of waving flags and cheers, in some sense her mouth felt inflamed and mind-altering and in another sense a crushed old view of himself and his fatherhood stabbed through his heart, his old heart, and he didn't care anymore who saw what a wimp he was, if he cried in front of the world, he didn't care if Hermie was watching or his friends, Donny, all those jock assholes, he drank their beer that night, he let them bring him to the black-painted shed, *Charnel House* painted in red in scratchy letters on the wall, he let them take off his clothes and paint his body, he lay naked all night curled in a fetal ball and the rhizotomy of music and acid and bourbon and beer and Synjyne's cool mouth left him as dry and as hollow as amyl nitrate, *I like the candelabras,* he said, *they're from an estate sale,* the one phrase he remembered, they painted his hair black, his dreams, were they dreams? Were goat-footed fuckers running around and his friends laughing and this baby he pulled around by its hand though it wasn't living, a tiny, limp sack, he remembers talking about the baby and crying and he remembers Hermie telling him to shut up and when he woke up, when he woke that next day in the painted shed, red burned-down candles everywhere, a smoky soot on everyone's face, a sweaty tinge in the air, rancid, wet, druggish, old cigarettes, the wolfish scent of unwashed bodies, hair, Synjyne and Hermie sleeping, he saw his craggy face in a mirror, his eyes so blue with the black hair they crackled like sun-shot jewels against fresh asphalt, he smelled girl on his hands, then, finally, he liked what he saw.

lamb of god, 1

1.

It's funny, but it's easy to eliminate feelings.

2.

Toddulus has discovered this is so. By careful application of pharmaceutical agents, kindly supplied by Hermie, his inimitable companion,
his compadre, you could say, on a daily basis, he can remain in a state of,
well, suspended emotional stasis I believe would be the best way to describe
it, assisted by thorough and practical detachment, in a neuro-Buddhist
sense, as in the experience of morphine after surgery (*click, click, click,*
CLICK, CLICK, *Is this broken, nurse??!!* Some of you will know what I
mean), and this *young buck* Todd found that he relished a certain *time-
less-ness,* a renewal, if you will, of his life afforded him by the deep and
meaningful relationship he found in that amazing young chap, his neighbor of BRILLIANCE, the Prince of the Cortege, yours truuuuuuuuuuuly,
hahahahahahahahahahahahahahahaha.

OK, in all serious, nonmocking diatribes please allow me to introduce
myself, Hermie, and tell of our friendship:

1) Todd rejected me in sixth grade AND UP, because I undoubtedly
got too weird for his ass, which means, quite honestly, he got dull as shit. I
mean, Yawn. Skateboards and that sparkly California stuff. And I was going

through a stage, as kids tend to do. I was changing and Toddulus was not. I think I was, well, evolutionarily advanced. Toddulus may have now caught up. Call it trial by death. It's a necessary stage, I would say.

yeah, and I just want to add that Todd also dissed me for the, that dumb, kirsten and ignored me when i asked him something once, about the parking lot.

He claims, Synjyne, he did not recognize you in your canopic disguise, the black hair, et al.

Can't you just say et ceddera like the rest of us, stuck-up?

As I was explaining, for years my partner in the sub-urbane environs, Toddulus, as I prefer to call him instead of the perky "Todd," ignored my ass. Not that I really cared because playing with Tonkas can only go so far, that right, Toddulus.

Unnhhh.

And, you heard him, he agrees, Tonkas are over, right? Well, Toddulus still rather likes them I have to say, ANYWHO, since REdiscovering our friendship Mr. Toddles has become enamored of my fine accommodations at Casa Cortege, fond of my beers on the bier, so to speak, chuckle, chuckle, and I, **Father,** have grown fond of him, you will recall how we played as youngsters back here in the dirt. I believe you enjoyed the company of Diane and Bob "The Mayor," his delicious parents. What is that mayor shit, anyway. Is that a joke? Because no offense, Toddini, but that man has no mayoral qualities, he's nice and all, but. I mean, maybe if he was the mayor of some freaky wimpland, maybe. I know he's your **dad,** but those yellow shorts he wears and his roses and his voice. He kind of nauseates me. He kind of does. Anyway, we are now, rightly, friends again. And, **Dad,** we are oddly linked by means of the *otherworld*, your specialty. His is from some dead baby he says he sired, though I seriously doubt it—

Unnhh.

And of course my connection is you and the good remains of you, here in front of me, the speck of you I must say I, I must say, I adore. More than in life even, here at the Moribund Legion, I fall before your grace. OK, Synjyne, **Dad,** here's a something. I'm going to go get a beer, and if I re-

trieve a Bud with my eyes averted, then the afterlife is hellish and foul
and if I get a Mich—for I think we have equal amounts, Syn?

I bought two cases at the Safeway, or maybe two of Mich and one
Bud, I don't—

Whatever, it'll *still work*, OK, OK, here's the deal—if I pull a Mich then
the afterlife is beautiful and lovely and everything we want, OK, **DAD**?
Ready? Here I go! God, it's cold in here, OK. Taaadaaa! Hey. Look. It's a
Mich, **Dad**. What do you know. You having a good time there, eh? Are you
surrounded by virgins? Are there fountains of molten gold? Are you happy?

3.

Now that the morning light has broke through, **Dad,** and illuminated
Toddulus and he awoke, yea, a full different brethren than before, he walks
before us naked and golden and proud, his hair black now in contrast to
the golden pubes he sports.

Who you talking to? A news reporter? The wall?

My **dad,** you idiot. **Dad,** you remember Toddulus?

Your **dad**? On the wall?

Exactly, my highly intelligent chum. Listen most carefully: If all matter is energy and all is ceaseless around us, if God is Love, if time is circular, if nothing is finite, if *heaven* exists, if now only exists yet it purports
the past and present, than my **dad** is as alive as ever, as represented by this
tiny crumb of his person. He is as alive as ever, in here. Do you read me?

Uh, no.

OK, then I'm beyond you.

Uh, I'd say that. Hey do you have a phone?

A phone? What for?

I have to call my mother.

You'll have to go in the house, hell, just go across the *street*, dude. You
live just across the street.

Do you want me to go with you, Todd? I'm kind of hungry. Are you,
Herm?

As a matter of fact, I am. It's Monday, isn't it. Isn't there school? Shall we
attend if only for the fact that it's pizza day? Do I make myself clear here?

Yeah, pizza.

I wouldn't mind it, some pizza.

4.

I'd like to know if you feel I have wrongly influenced Toddulus, **Dad.**

I merely seek to show the young man the real world. I feel the boy has erroneously taken a stance of paternal interest in a case where he is not responsible. Perhaps you can illuminate me further on this problem. **Dad,** I am going to toss two beer caps in the air, **DAD,** can you hear me above the raucous chant of DEADBODIESEVERYWHERE, my favorite new band? Can you hear me through the necrous fiber which separates us? Can you give me a fucking sign, just a little something to go by. Have a bird hit the window or something. Some goddamn thing. I'm not asking for much, motherfucker! I'm your son, dickwad. Pardon me, my disrespect. I grow weary of the one-way communication, though I tell myself, remind myself, this is how it always was, if you recall. Me, trying to talk to you, and you, answering in grunts, silence, or clicks of the remote control. Was I that much of a bore?

OK, enough of my pathos. Let's get back to business: So here's what I was saying, if, if, if, they both land upright, shiny sides up, sporting BUD insignia, than Todd is not the **father** of that infant, but if they land upside down then he is, then he is. And I pertain that you, **DAD** of the Underground, know all, am I right? Am I right?

Is he talking over there?

I'm not sure, I think he mumbles something all the time to that wall.

Is he majorly fucked up or something? Is something wrong?

I think he's in touch with different spheres or something.

Or crazy.

Well, OK, or crazy, or, something.

What's your story?

Story?

Why are you here, where's your home?

I don't got a home.

No home?

I mean, none I'm welcome at. My mom's hard to live with, and she said, you know, it's better if I'm, you know, on my own, and she's like cool with me being here most of the time, she calls it getting-my-shit-together time, my mom calls it tough love, whatever, you know. But my grandpa's cool. He'll give me money and stuff.

What happened to Samantha? Why Synjyne?

That was Hermie's idea, he like said she was this philosopher once, she got killed by being cut up by seashells for her beliefs or something.

Oh. So does your grandpa like Hermie?

He says he wishes I'd be with normal people. He says I ought to live with them and get myself together. But he's cool. You know him, Ray Raylin?

Raylin? Oh, yeah. He's an electrician, *Raylin's Electric*. I know that guy. My **dad** knows him.

Everybody knows him. He's a character. So, are you going to school?

I guess.

5.

Aha. My **dad** has spoken! He has bestowed wisdom in the guise of a beer can top. He has sent a sign and it indicates that you are not the **father,** Toddulus. You are free to resume your previous carefree existence.

Oh, really.

Yeah, and didn't Kirsten sleep around?

I don't think so.

Are you sure?

Yeah.

So why don't you just ask the ho.

I said, she's not a ho.

Regardless, ask her.

Like, she'll even speak to me.

Listen, let me inform you of current theory on your situ, my friend. One, even if you *sired* this infant, some would contend it is technically Kirsten's choice with its fate. It was technically, technically, though viable I have to admit, a *piece of her,* and therefore, being her body in the first place, and maybe some could argue merely a tissue growth and not human yet—though that would be hard considering the baby was born and lived—it was hers to deal with or whatever, not yours.

You are so fucked. So fucked. You think you're some kind of, genius or expert or. You're just a fool, a creepy fool. I am the **Dad.**

Of what?

Of a baby, dumbhead, a baby, even if it is small it wasn't tissue, it was alive. They buried it.

Steady, boy. Listen to my words. It's her *thing*, dude, her body, see. Though it's easy to see both sides of the argument. Nevertheless, nevertheless, *I* have to side with Kirsten here—

Oh, no. No. This is mine, too. I have rights. *I'm the father.* She gave birth, man! On a floor!

So, she needed your permission, permission from the **Da—**

Fucking A I'm the **Dad!** Here's what you are not understanding here, my friend. I would've taken the baby! What if I don't get another chance eh fuckwad what if that was my one shot my one chance my only one time to be a **Dad—**

Cool it, Toddini—

No, you cool it you fucking frigging intellectual piece of shit all your words are bullshit and your goddamn **dad** is dead he's dead dead dead dead you jerkface the truth you have no **Dad** a dead **Dad** a dead **Dad—**

I had to swing at him, **Dad,** unfortunately I hit his head and Todd swung and clipped my eye and we rolled on the ground, I bit his ear—FUCK!—and Todd pounded on my chest—God!—and blood had covered our faces, Synjyne ran over, SHIT, STOP IT, she screamed, she sat on Todd and pounded his shoulder and we both rolled to the side, breathing hard.

I-I-I'm sorry, man, I said, out of breath, I'm out of line with you.

Fucking A, said Todd, you don't know shit! Stupid fuck! YOU DON'T KNOW SHIT!

I say we go now. Let's get some pizza. It's nine. Stop crying, Jesus.

Dad, I know they think I'm nuts. But I'm really in touch with a whole different sphere of things than they are. I see a side of you I didn't know when you were alive, you know, I find you listen to me quietly and under-stand everything I do, implicitly, like when I beat up Toddulus, I wasn't trying to hurt, I'm trying to beat some shit into him, some sense, some goddamn sense, I hate to see a brother go down, I hate, **Dad,** to see an-other suffer, Jesus, **Dad,** do something over there, but give Toddulus a break and tell that baby there what's up. I was only trying to get him off the emotional hook. Find that baby over there, will you. Find that little bucka-roo and tell him his **father** is thinking about him.

lamb of god, 2

I.

Dad, on our way to school we encounter a hideous sight, something which made me bilious and faint. Toddulus' mother, to our horror, blocking the entrance to the car:

I want want to try and understand you, she said, her face wet and teary, *just give me a chance or something,* said Todd's mother, catching us kids getting into my car to go to school. She's wearing a flannel red bathrobe pulled tight around her trim waist and her hands look dry and bony, Oh, Mom, says Todd, I'm OK—

All night I wonder where you are, all night, I cry and cry, I'm thinking call the police but it says, she shakes the book in front of us, give them space, but you could be dead—

Mom—

Then I see out the window, when I'm brushing my teeth, Herman and his sorry friends, as I say to myself, But the one, the one, the one—

Hey—

—this one with *the hair* is my. Todd. Oh. God. Please. And then she grabs his arm, let me help youuuuuu—

I'm just going to school—

Is it drugs? Is that it?

He got in and slammed the door, wow, *that is heavy shit,* just go, goddammit, said Todd, rather rudely I might add and we left her, standing there, the mailman walking around the corner, Mrs. B. walking her shih tzu, some birds singing in an elm tree.

His mother walked to her house, opened the door. Went in. Maybe poured coffee. And then she might have cried some more or probably, probably cooked something, because you know what, **Dad**? She's into catering now. That's right. Since you've departed, Mrs. R. started a catering biz. I hear she's pretty good.

2.

Eating pizza at school, **Dad,** which is reminiscent of the most flavorless cardboard manufactured in western Manaus, Donny T. comes up to Todd.

What the fuck happened to you? Some rabid raccoon bite your hair off? and then, and then, *shit* all over it? Dang. And someone beat you up, too. Bad.

Drop dead.

Ooooh. Mack **Daddy.**

Get *off*.

Are you a freeeeak now?

Get out of my face.

Yeah, yeah, he says walking away. Yeah, yeah.

He finished eating the cardboard pizza with Synjyne and Herman, his eyes dark and brooding, we were strangely silent, but I could tell some fucking thing was brewing in his brain, **Dad,** I have that gift, you know, in fact, **Dad,** the day you took off, I rather knew something was up, Mom said you had been depressed but I thought you seemed oddly happy that particular day, in a weird way. **Dad,** you don't whistle, for God's sake, and yet, you were whistling that day, I recall. Don't *ever, ever, ever* whistle if you're going to do yourself in again in a new life or whatever because that is just a fucked-up, creepy thing to do, isn't it? I think so. I think it fucking cruel. In my mind, I had done something to make you happy maybe that day, for a change and you were whistling, and that about basically fucked with me in a most heinous way, my friend, a most heinous way.

Todd says to me then:

What's your **dad** on that wall, anyway? No more than tissue. What's that?

It's like a proton of himself, I said, but now he was screwing with me and I was getting, uh, *perturbed,* **Dad.**

Yeah, so there you go. That baby's my proton.

It was then he sees Kirsten, walking by the Coke machine, thinner, in a blue coat. She waves.

I can't help it, he says. I love that baby.

3.

Synjyne says, Go on. Go say hi.

Oh, I can't. She won't speak to me.

Try. Go on.

Oh, let him wallow, Synjyne, I said with admirable nonchalance. Let him stay the existential moper. It's fun. What's the option? Falling in love? Puhhhhlease.

Todd gets up slowly. His hand opened and closed nervously. I whispered, So you are a pussy! I thought so!

Kirsten was at the milk machine. As he approached, she spilled some on the stainless steel counter.

Shit. Todd. What's *happened* to you?

At this point, **Dad,** I wasn't present. Synjyne sat by me as I whispered, *Pussy. Pussy. Pussy.* Until she told me to shut up, and obediently, slave that I am, I obeyed.

(Todd stood by her, fumbling with the row of waxed cups, his hands shaking.

I, I guess, I cut my hair, you know.

I meant, your eye, it's bleeding—

—Oh, that, *Kirsten—he reaches for her hand—*can I, um, talk, talk to you sometime, just—

—What about? Her face, though, is red and downward.

—You know.

—Yeah.

Is it.

Toddie boy!! someone yells, he flicks his eyes up in recognition, *hey.*

Is it.

Hey, can I get some milk, says a fat tenth grader who pushes by his back, causing Todd to fall against her, his mouth comes close to her ear, *help me here, Kirst. Is it. Is it.*

Yeah, she says softly, it is. Her eyes red and watery, it's—

Can I. Can I talk to you later, somewhere? After school?

Come to my car, after last class, then.

OK.

OK.)

When he returned, **Dad,** there was a certain dark jubilance to his eyes.

So what did she say?

Yeah, tell us, tell us, I said running beside him, my jeans flapping raggedly around his ankles in the parking lot by the smoking region, we deign to know, oh, master.

She said, We could. You know. *Talk.* That's all. She just said that, We could talk.

Make more babies! Make lots! Like salmon!

Shut up. I'm just talking to her.

Make more babies! I danced around, my eyes flashing. Oh boy. Oh boy.

You hurt me, Herman. You cut me to the quick.

Say what?

You hurt me.

I'm just playing. I'm actually jealous to see young love bloom. I like to, I prefer to, dash it down, have it wreck unceremoniously, eeeeehwew, smash, crash. In the natural law of things.

What about me, then. Hunh.

You and I have a celestial connection. It's so beyond high school. Soooo beyond. We're like two trans-celestial beings that have met briefly on the mortal plane, yet are destined. You know. For eternity. My love.

Get, off me!

I need you, Synjyne!

You've slobbering! Ugh.

She's there, oh shit. OK.

Hunh?

Shhh.

Hey, Kirsten! he said, running forward.

Stop. It.

Kirsten stands by her car, holding books, and the sun shines down on her head, lighting the top whitely.

Hi, Todd, I was. Waiting for you.

She was waiting for you, Todd.

Can you guys. You know?

Oh. Herman.

Sure. We can go. Come on, Synjyne. We'll be in the car.

Listen, Todd.

Yeah?

I'm supposed to go to the doctor's now. But I want to, you know, talk and stuff. Can you pick me up tonight? I mean, just drive and we can talk. It's no big deal, you know. It's just not.

Yeah. Your house, OK? Eight?

That's good. Be cool, Todd.

Yeah.

4.

At his house, his mother stood in the doorway, her face still puffy and drained, a pot holder in her hand. **Dad,** she gives me the creeps.

Kids! Come in for plum pudding. I just made it!

Me, Todd, and Synjyne got out of the car, smoke from the bong in the back trailing out the window.

I just made it! It's yummalacious! It's *bad*, dudes! It's *phat!*

Shit, I commented. I think's she's lost it, man.

We kids trailed into the back door, the kitchen a huge glut of boxes, wrapped food, plastic boxes spilling forth with cookies, wreaths, smells of brown sugar, cinnamon, spices of Christmas.

Mom's catering the hospital party.

Whooooa. No shit.

It's a *Christmas Carol* theme, she says her face contorted, crying, staring at Todd. Boxes in arms are being led back and forth by her friend Verona, the husbands,

Like, Tiny Tim and stuff?

Todd. Oh, I love you. Todd.

Can you guys go home? said Todd, holding his mother who fell on his chest. Can you, well, leave us alone?

No problem. Tell her, Todd. Tell her you're a **Daddy.**

A **Daddy**? She looked up, her eyes, crushed and wet. A **Daddy**?

Can you kids help out, Verona says. Can you. Don't leave. We'll pay you all. We need help bad.

Me, says Hermie, and her?

All of you, all of you, I don't care. Just grab a box. Just come on.

What's he mean, a **Daddy**, says Diane, her face wet. A **Daddy**?

Can I help, Verona, says Todd.

We don't have enough, people, so come on, Todd. Come on.

Can I, Mom?

Yeah, OK, she said weakly. Yeah, sure.

I call Scrooge, I said. I'm Scrooge.

He's taken, baby. You can be Tiny Tim. Or a Cratchit.

OK, I'll be Tiny Tim! Cool! God bless us, everyone! Whee!

I'll be his mother. Plump, poor, and jolly, Ol' Mrs. Cratchit!

Todd, you're Cratchit. You're my **daddy,** Toddulus.

That's cool, Tiny Tim.

Move out of the way! Coming through, toads, I said, helping out immensely considering the fact I was a tiny crippled toddler, but hey, miracles are possible, **Dad,** you would've been proud of me, Hey, do we get outfits and all?

Yeah, they're in the van. I'll get them.

I was Tiny Tim, **Dad.** I wore raggedy little knickers they had cut up from some of Todd's old Virginia Tech sweatpants (he absurdly worships the

Hokies) and I had a tiny crutch, carved out of an old stick. I imagine Todd's mom probably got the old Mayorman to carve that stick, like at four in the morning, you know? *Honey, wake up! Carve me up a stick for Tiny Tim!* So fucking funny. I can see him in his garage workshop, late at night. *Will this do, hon?*

Regardless of my mockery, I take my role seriously.

It occurs to me there is a sudden air of naivete in our midst. Our faces have lost the hardness and we appear soft, cheerful, free.

I become Tiny Tim.

I am a method actor, **Dad.**

5.

Return to the time of innocence, prepubescent, preconception:

They enter, delicately and slow, the large hall of the Fauquier Wing where tables lay folded against the wall with large stacks of Saran-wrapped tablecloths and coffinish Sterno cabinets and their quiet voices sound velvety and operatic in the large cavernish space. Bring it all in, bellows Verona, in her acid-washed jeans, bring all boxes in the side hall here and we'll set up. I need snow! Let's start with snow!

She rips open a bag of the stuff and swishes it through the air.

Wheee! This is one time we want you to make a mess, get the stuff everywhere, and then Bob "The Mayor" says *hot dog!* and George just folds and unfolds his arms, *all right then*, and Hermie says *yeah*, and Todd dumps a bag on his head. *Heeee, snowstorm!*

Blizzard! Hermie returns the favor, with two bags split open and drenched.

Avalanche!

Whooooops! Need some four-wheel drive!

Yeeeeeehhhaaaa, Tiny Tim brings the snow! He dumps a big bag on Diane Redmond.

Oh, Herman, really.

Why, you look *lovely* snow-dappled, Diane, says Bob "The Mayor." My snow princess. My arctic angel.

Come on, children, spread it around! Spread it around! says Verona,
her hair covered in gobs of plastic shreds, her arms carrying two bolts of
brown tulle over to George rigging up a Grog Shack.

George, don't do it that way, baby. Over to the left, more up.

I thought you said—

I did not. Pull that pole *through*.

Opening folding tables in a whining, clanking orchestra, spreading
tablecloths, Bob "The Mayor" throwing handfuls of snow on the carpet,
Synjyne and Herman rigging up the Cratchit house, the waiters, the kids,
lining the walls and tables with greenery and Diane and Verona in the
back, sweating from the hot fog rolling out of the steam cabinets glowing with Sterno's eerie stygian blue light, the heat growing and sweat
fleeing in rivulets down their necks, their quick hands pulling and toss-
ing dough like limpid flesh to bake and squeezing large pastry tubes of
ointmental paste into puff-pastried crumpets, as they work fast and silently, (meanwhile C.R. talks to his daddy in his kitchen, as he says to
him, *Daddy, I'd tell you stuff if I was dead*), Verona and Diane leave the
hot confine of their closeted kitchen, the infernal world of singeing metal
and meat blood and searing flames and pass through to the archaic,
drifted, glistening world they created, and as they peruse the Dickensian
visage of their own making, Verona turns to Diane with a weary smile,

I think we did it, hon, I think so. God, my feet hurt.

The band, who drove up in a '79 Chevy brown van with golden, ara-
besque airbrushing, stands on the stage in linen flouncy shirts and black
flocked vests, mullet hairstyles pulled back into reasonable ponytails and
starts up the first fiddle jig of the evening she requested. They told her
they could play all the old-time tunes she wanted, the jigs, the bourrées,
the quadrilles, any cotillions or waltzes or rigadoons or even a Sir Roger
de Coverley. They could even do a bunch of good covers of Uriah Heep,
though she said that might not be necessary. Depended on how the evening
went. How much grog was consumed, how rowdy these doctors wished to
get. They may wish to throw out, she said, at the real hubbub of the evening,
something untraditional, to get the place hopping. Maybe a "brickhouse"
or a "Celebrate" by Kool and the Gang. I know it's not real Dickens-like

and all, she said, but we'll see. She smells the clove punch. Even the full dresses on the waitstaff, half-price old flouncy bridesmaid dresses she found at Marshalls, look OK in the flickering flames, and the top hats on the men are charming, Todd in the tailed jacket looks oddly elegant and his chopped hair looks urchinish and dirty, as it would living in the slums of smelly London as Cratchit, on the perennial edge of the poorhouse, Hermie takes to hobbling on the stick well, moving from station to station, helping Diane plate roast beef or saucing the turkey.

I'll take a bit of grog, Synjyne says to Sanji, from Indonesia, who claimed Scrooge and wears a top hat, who works at 7-Eleven normally, even though he is a chemical engineer. No problem, he says and goes to get it, she can hear Ted the bartender use the word *shag* in every sentence, somehow he's got the British idea in his head, though he's mixed up the centuries.

Oh, well.

stave four

the party.

betty + pendleton, 2

I.

What am I, some old dog?

Goddammit.

Son of a bitch.

Hell. I may be a lady, but goddammit to hell.

Betty, on her way home, has gotten stuck, again, on that embankment. *Crap on a stick.* Snow coming down like the devil. Oh, for goodness' sake, can I get a break here? She was in a state, a state that a cup of tea with honey would greatly have calmed, but good luck there! If I don't freeze to death, Father always said, carry a chain, he did, and how are my cats going to fare? They'll freeze. Or, or what if a spark, an electrical spark, catches hold and burns a curtain. Did I leave the lights on? Maybe the toaster will blow, catch on a rag, Holy Mother of God, agitatedly stroking their fur again and again in mental ways, what is wrong with me? Why am I such a bad driver? Why do I always hit this bank and get stuck? Thinking back to Pendleton and his *pretty little Italian shoes all mud-covered,* she has to laugh at that one, what, what, what, am I too old, too fat, too thin, too ugly for him? He and his bour-*bone*? And for Dr. Ash, am I just some old dogfood who gets stuck and no man to help pull out with chains like Daddy always had, goddamn but a single woman is just a, just a, *whatever.*

So how about that, that electrician, Ray Raylin, he liked me, I mean he came over when I was younger and redid the electricity in the house after the fire and drank some coffee I made and seemed so funny and kind and said I had a smile that lit up the place, he said that, though, he did, but he was a *dirty greasemonkey,* he. He asked if he could call on me he said but I was nervous. I said I was busy seeing someone else, I lied. He said that was a shame. A real shame. I couldn't be the wife of an electrician. That's not me, you see.

And there'd been a gentleman down at the bank some odd thirty years ago (Mr. Palmer. Mr. *Jerome Palmer*) who, who, was gracious and kind and brought me flowers and sat with my family at the church ice cream social, he commented that strawberry is just so much better than plain, isn't it, Miss Betty and my father said he talked a good finance story and they were to play golf at some point and that, that, that, had had some real promise (combing my hair, my mother had said, *you must find a man who'll take care of you and save yourself for that man,* her breath of sherry, mother beautiful, that was a day of a dance in high school). Except, going over by the parking lot, where he had a, ha! *book* for me, he said. Lying devil! Awful man! Pressed up against me on the car and and, and pushed down on me for a, oh, a kiss! An awful, awful kiss, oh, the embarrassment and running from him, I snagged my silk new stockings and came over to Daddy and Mother, I would not talk to that beast again ever. Ever! My mother said you're being rude to poor Mr. Palmer and when I told her of his transgressions she was shocked and horrified. Oh, I'd like to scour myself with lye in the remembrance, the man, the man. And except what would happen then, if I left them, Mother and Daddy and all the kids, I couldn't. Not that, that would've made any difference, in retrospect. The way things turned out. I'm the only one who remembers them. Like a family. I'm the only one.

Why, what is the thing about cars and men kissing me, such as Dr. Pendleton, oh, Pendleton is a real piece of work—

The car moves, lurches forward, spraying gauzy snow forth, don't, just don't really care for the human body much, you know, there's so many much more nicer, pretty things to talk about, Dr. Ash, did you know, did you know, take a memo, Doctor, but *I love sunsets and long walks, moon-light and soft music, cats and home-cooked meals* (she could also add, if truth was part of the picture, big underwear of polyester covering her whole stomach, eating cottage cheese with a fork, rodentlike, *National Enquirer*, sitting in the black silence in her chair by the window, watching the lights at Ashland flick from hall to bedroom).

And I love romance and your mission in life, Dr. C.R. Ash! I love the snow falling on Virginia like this and we can hold hands and listen to Herb Alpert! Big warm blankets to cuddle under and warm cocoa! Do not, I practically, *suffer,* a great revolt of bodies naked or body odors or emissions, dislike hugs or touches, repulsed by hair, by tongues. In general, I prefer touching cats. I do enjoy, making good quilts. I am thrifty, frugal! I darn! I save scraps of fabric and make things out of them, pincushions, cold drink holders, doilies, I crochet and make broom covers. I gave you one last year, Dr. Ash, I can make good rolls (dough made her squeamish, *yuck! yuck!* made her mind think of squishy, um, *buttocks*). *That kiss* with Pendleton almost made her heave, that kiss was so spittle-filled, so tongue-y, so ugh. Can't get the thought of a cow tongue out! of! my! mind!

But he was a man who liked her. She could capitalize on that, but she'd hope Dr. A. would fall for her one fine day and they'd have a platonic and beautiful thing, two people searching for the medical cure to man's ills, her with her nurse-practitioner background (useless when she discovered the human body was a foul thing, in reality), he and his illustrious career, they could make headlines as a husband-wife team of mercy, traveling to conferences in Geneva and South Africa, helping mankind (*Yes, well, my husband is a fine soul, and I just try to do God's will and support him in his godly mission, helping young, tiny babies survive*). And it helped that she judged that C.R. didn't want children, because she'd be dead before she let anyone do that stuff to her, much less give birth to a baby, she'd seen that *foulness* one day, the blood, the purple vividity, the rainbow spectrum of pumping, roiling flesh easing from one's groin—good Lord, but that was dreadful! *Not* for her.

She'd go with Dr. Ash, they'd live on the hill in Ashland, those large walnut doors. She *knew* it was good. She'd eyed that treed driveway of dogwood and cherry and saw her wedding procession filing down that path (*It's true! Well, everyone, looky here! Looky here!* Oh, the faces of those nurses when they see the ring Dr. Ash'll give me! And those sluts, those sluts, they'll see not everything is about showing off your fancies, is it now?). That was her plan. Thought she'd change the landscape. Way too much greenery for her taste and she'd put in fairy roses all around the house. (She had driven up to it one day and made plans, *OK, I'll put the lilies in here. Definitely, definitely hydrangeas all around the porch.*) The front appeared leggy and overgrown and in need of a woman's good gardening sense. She would do that first, planting in lots of white lilies and the aforementioned roses and maybe lots of hostas and maybe lots and lots of purple clematis and things that smelled good and when she went in the door (it was open, like all doors in the area), she noted she'd have to paint, maybe an Italian red color like in magazines and definitely redo the kitchen because of parties and, going upstairs, she felt she could redo the bedroom on the top floor with lots of buttercup chintz and two nice twin beds. All the fireplaces, all the fireplaces, all would be sealed and closed up forever and that woodstove in the kitchen she'd toss, too, no fires, no fires *ever*, no matches, no candles, nothing. Doctor would understand. She's sure he would.

She'd found his quarters quickly that day, scampering up the stairs with rodent speed, and she didn't take time to breathe in the air (though, in memory the smell of his bedroom she thought of as *quiet green wood*, slightly acrid, new wood smell with male fir-ness) or stop and look around, instead she scampered in adrenaline to the dresser and snatched a shirt and a sock, not to be a thief or anything but because, again, she needed it for focus and all for her visualization, so now driving home in her mud-splattered car, right now this day of December when she walked into her room to fret, needed tea in hand, *oh, my gracious kitties, Mommy's here, babies, babies*, the familiar altar was there, his face from the hospital brochure, his shirt, his half-empty bourbon Virginia Gentlemen, his socks, his notepad with scribbles, a candy wrapper, and a favorite, a handkerchief, starched and monogrammed, she put on the Herb Alpert song for thinking, *this man's in love with you*, and settled down on her bed.

2.

Though it could be that the doctor enjoys the flesh, that was probable. That was his everlasting weakness! No one'd talk chocolate flirtation to any old candy striper without heinous flesh involved, so Betty gets up the notion, since there's nothing to lose anyway, that Dr. A. had let her be because of her purity, of her vaginal, I mean *virginal*, good gracious, how did that smarmy word fly in her head? Oh, nastiness, cow's tongue, she felt she'd vomit. Don't ever, ever think, say, that *word*. Her correction, *virginal* quality and maybe he didn't want that, she could try a different note. The times spent pilfering his things in his house showed her the man indeed liked bodies and stuff, there was a woman's underwear she found in his bed, *that of a slut*, no less, lacy and black and god-awful crotchless, she had them right here, no use for him to keep them, and anyway she felt they tainted Ashland, so she took them. And she took a new copper pot, too, because it screamed *girlfriend* and those days are over, Dr. Ash.

She got dressed for the party. If Doctor was there, she'd ask him to dance. If he wasn't, she'd track him down, find him in his truck, with that old picture of the general, wrap her papery hands around his mouth and surprise him, maybe all this time Dr. A. has loved her too, but remained a gentleman who honored a good girl, and she would forge the way.

She wore that underwear, it was a bit large and sagged slightly on her tiny, downy hips traced by blue chiaroscuro of veinery. A hand of Dr. Ash could be welcome in these areas. She would tighten the eyes and not breathe. It could be over soon. This was the way of good women in the days of past and she debated the nightgown with only a slit in the cloth but she feared he wouldn't take to it. The man was modern, not a relic. A bra to match the panties was needed but she had only frayed cross-your-hearts and she was small anyway, tiny kidney brown nipples alert in the cool air of a Virginia wood house, she would skip a bra, she had one dress, a lace thing, cream-colored, balloon-sleeved, she wore at her prom some thirty-five years ago, but she could still wear it, it was all she had that was festive and pretty and maybe seductive, in the midst of her plaid skirts, cardigan blouse Smith College circa 1956 look, and she found that the dress fit, she was still a size six, nothing came along, no babies to swell the outlines, everything just got drier and more hanging, but the dress fit her and her tiny breasts stuck out, yet she still maintained a *virginal* (oh, oh, oh, she can see that other word, looming pink and foul in the corner of her mind! no!) attraction and she put on perfume from a sample, made her lips real red with some old rouge and pulled her hair down and fluffed it out, the woman then realized it was eight and the party was on full blast, and could she handle the snow?

She slipped her galoshes over cream satin pumps and went out in the dark.

3.

Who's there? Lord. Who's there?

There was the distinct sound of crunching snow footsteps coming up her drive, steady and plodding.

I got a gun so you better speak, or I'll, I'll, I'll blow your damn little head off, I will (*ooohhh, Daddy's gun is in the basement, unloaded, don't have no bullets, it's also rusted, fire-destroyed, what a fool I am*). And I'm not kidding around. No, I'm not. Right, honey?! Right?! Yes, bring that gun out, honey, because we, we got intruders! Yessir!

A man made his way through the path.

Who the hell are you screaming about? Who's *honey*?

Oh, Holy Jesus and Mary, Pendleton, you completely, completely *terrified* me.

Honey! That was a good one! Whoa. You, you look so lovely, Betty. Damn.

Oh, you think? Why, why, why *thanks*, Pendleton.

Thought you might wish for some accompaniment to the festivities tonight, Nancy ditched me 'cause she's come down with something, she got all dressed up and threw up on herself, poor woman, but, uh. Got stuck in that damn pit down there, *again.*

Oh, drat. Me, too. I've got to pour sand or something there.

Did you hear from your boss? How's that man doing?

No, I haven't, Pendleton. No, I haven't. I'm thinking he might be at this party, you know, and maybe we can all talk to him, set him straight, ease his mind.

Yeah, well.

Well, what?

I agree with you, I do. I really do. But what's up with that candy striper?

Oh, that poor girl? The one who had a baby?

Yes, you know, I walked in on them and they were. Well.

Oh, no! Oh, oh, were they. Were they, k-k-*kiss*ing?

Well, kind of.

Oh, shame! Shame! C-c-ow tongue—

What you talking about, cow tongue? What's that got to do, *Jesus*—

That girl's *out of control*! And I know her mother! What a dear soul, from church. Things we don't deserve. Toils that God sends us. So damn hard.

Well, what about him, then, I mean, come on.

Hunh?

I think he's got a little problem, she's a minor, see.

Did you tell?

Well,

Did you?

Not yet, but I think I *should*, don't you?

Absolutely not. It's her fault! She's a slut, obviously.

Oh, now, Betty!

If you tell on him, I'll, I'll do something. I'll tell them you're ill or whatever.

Oh, come on.

And if you don't, Pendleton, if you don't, then you can have me. You can.

What? What are you saying?

I mean it. You can have me, Pendleton. I won't like it. But you can have me, the first time. I'll close my eyes—

Whoa, whoa, this is not right, Betty, come on, come on, hush up, I ain't telling no one. Let's get in your car.

4.

In the car, they spun around the long driveway in the heavy snow, they could see the road, dark and cerulean at this winter hour, she had him drive, for safety's sake, and against the soft powder the car felt like it was falling along a cushioning path and it made her afeared but it also excited, reminding her of the bumptious rides of sleighs in her youth, ricocheting and dancing down a fluffy white path with children's screams in her ears, mainly the gurgles of her siblings, Charlie, Mariah, and Dunny, her younger siblings, all their sweet voices she could hear again as clear as day, drinking hot cider Mother would bring over, burning the tongue, clove caught in teeth, and she wondered, she wondered, Would Charlie be as handsome today? Would he still make her laugh and do those funny accents, making fun of the poor Arabic man who owned a convenience store in town? Would Mariah have written books, like the stories she wrote all day about horses and magicians and princesses, she always said, Can I read to you, Betty, can I read my new story to you? Would Dunny, the baby, would Dunny have been as chubby, as dimpled, as he was back in 1956, sledding on Ball's Bluff Hill right before Christmas, right before the fire.

You're awfully quiet. One of them cats up at the house got your tongue? Hunh?

Just thinking. About old times.

Ah, yes. Memories of the good old days.

Yessir.

You're a odd gal, Miss Betty. But I like you. I do. I always have.

Is that right. Well, Pendleton, you're a nice fellow, too.

Is it, you know, true?

Is what true?

What you said up there. You know. You never, Miss Betty?

Well, I've never married, have I. There you go.

Can't believe a pretty gal like yourself didn't get snatched up right quick by someone, because I'll tell you, I'll tell you, if Nancy'd not been around, I'd been an old hound dog around you, I'll tell you *that*.

You're sweet to me, Pendleton.

You have no idea.

Are you. Are you doing OK and all?

I never felt better, Betty. I don't have any fears. Life is good.

Do, did, do you pass out and all, a lot?

One and only time, up at your house. Probably a little TIA, you know what I'm saying, right?

Oh, sure.

Sometimes you get them if you have a few heart deals, angina, and stuff as I do. As many older people do. I watch my cholesterol. Most of the time, most of the time! Kind of hard this time of year, isn't it. I'll tell you *what*.

Yes, I suppose.

Where, what you do for Christmas. Go to your family's house or you do it over at your place?

I, uh. Well. I have no family, anymore. I prefer to, to, *skip* Christmas.

Skip Christmas? What the hell are you talking about? Then you're coming to our place this year, yes, you are.

That's real kind of you, Pendleton, but. But, I'm sorry, I like being home.

Oh, Betty. Nancy goes bananas, greens and holly and cinnamon all that shit, and French toast and marshmallows in the fire—

Oh, no, *no, no. No fires*. I can't abide fires. And I don't care for Christmas. I hate Christmas. I despise it all, the fakery, the, the, oh, but thank you kindly—

Oh, come on, no one hates Christmas!

I do. I do.

I just don't believe that.

I don't think you quite *understand.*

What's not to like about this time of year's what I don't understand. When you were young, it must've been good.

It was, but, you see, Pendleton. It's like this, the Lord took all my family, my family all, one Christmas, Pendleton, in a fire, I'm sad to say. That Christmas I was alone with no family and a house all burned up, so. So I'm saying, it's not really, it's not too fun for me. No, it's not. Though Lord I don't want to spoil it for you, but that's how it was, Pendleton, and I'm happy with my cats. I'm damn happy. Sorry. I'm sorry.

For what, oh, Betty.

Bringing you down. This time of year. Oh—

That's such a terrible thing, Betty! I'm awfully sorry—

It's. It's a long time ago, Pendleton.

All, your daddy, your mama?

I hate to be *depressing* this time of year.

You don't worry about me now, Betty, but I'll—oh, shit! Goddammit!

The car did that desperate sound cars do, that electric whirling tire spin which filled the car with the smell of rubber burned at high friction, and sure enough, Pendleton had gotten the car stuck in the same old gully that snagged him before, his car a mere few feet away, slid up by the embankment.

5.

Well, that's a smooth move, mister, a smooth move, Pendleton said to himself. Holy goddamn.

Oh, dear. Do I call Triple A?

Well, he looks out on the night, I suppose we could walk a bit, even over to the hospital. Can't be more than two miles, can it.

I'd say. About that.

Can you hang with that. Otherwise, otherwise we're sitting in here for probably an hour on a night like this. In the cold.

OK, I suppose so.

I don't mind carry you, Miss Betty. You don't weigh more than a feather, I'm sure.

Oh, Pendleton. That's not necessary.

Well, let's go.

They proceed down the hill, awkwardly he holds her arm (he notes he can feel the sharpness of her tiny bones through her dress and wool coat), at one point he starts to fall and knocks her sideways, whoa! whoa! and regains his balance just in time, and she screeches out a birdish yelp, OK, OK, Betty I think we're OK, here now. OK.

I think of those soldiers, Pendleton, her voice pipes out amongst the crunching of their feet.

Who now?

Those poor boys, our southern boys out in the field here, as they come up to Ball's Bluff, it's along here my daddy said they walked, they walked and walked.

That was a rough one.

So many died.

They shot their commanding officer, their own officer.

How you know that. That. That *can't* be true.

Read it, said in a letter. Said they tried to hide it, but it came out. Now that's screwed up.

I think they were overcome by the, the river.

It was cold. No food, I suppose.

Some, but they were low on stuff. Just cornmeal mush, probably.

Bacon?

Probably out.

Maybe sick.

Oh, no doubt. No doubt. Racked with fever.

Imagine your child out there.

Can't.

It was getting colder and the snow had started up again, Look how pretty, she pointed.

He was getting winded, and he cut back on talking. She found her mouth was too frozen to allow speech much. They held hands.

What's. She stopped and caught her breath. Nancy. Got.

Some. Flu. Or another.

He, too, had difficulty talking.

I think I see. The lights of it. Up there.

Unh-hunh. So damn cold.

Keep on. keep on.

* * *

Oh, Betty. This. Phew! Is hard.

Let's. Keep on.

No cars passed them. The road was silent and blanketed by snow, and it came in all directions, only the streetlights showed the whirling tiny flakes, the rest of the looming road appeared steely and dense.

Holy hell. This is a blizzard.

Appears that way. Do you have a cell?

I. I got to stop. One second. I left it. I left the damn thing in the car.

They stopped. Stood for a while. Both covered in white.

I ain't sure what to do here. Go back. Or. Or. Plod forward. God. I'm *sorry*, Betty. I'm such a damn fool. OK, let's see. There's Ball's Bluff, for certain sure.

Yes, yes, that's it, all right.

Can't see the road for shit. Big blur. That way's north, ain't it?

I'm confused, Pendleton.

Hunh.

This, this is frightening.

We'll be fine.

Where's the road.

The road? The road. The road.

Oh, shoot, Pendleton. Where's the damn road?

6.

Pendleton was carrying Betty. Carrying her in his arms like a bundle of wood. The woman had panicked, grabbed for him in the blur and twisted her small twig ankle under the rubber galosh and gave out a shriek of pain and Pendleton caught her.

Betty! Shit, you OK?

Ow, oh, oh, Doctor, I've hurt. My darn. Foot!

I can't see *nothing*.

Are we close. Are we even close.

It's dark, Betty! Hold on to me.

I can't walk!

He lifted her up, You are light, God, woman, you are *light*!

I don't. I don't eat much, ohhh, it hurts.

Hold on to me. You smell good, Betty. You smell damn good. God, I love a good-smelling woman.

Pendleton, that's my hair—

I don't even care about this snow.

I see a, a *shape*, I see lights.

I *believe*.

Is it?

I don't think I can handle much, much.

I can walk!

No, Betty, you've hurt—

I'll walk.

It's not that far! Oh, we're here! I see lights. Oh, I'm going to have a drink so damn fast. So fast. We gone *dance*. I don't care about that foot. I'll twirl you! I'll spin you! God, I'm happy! Oh, Betty, woman.

Did you ever *see* such a snow—

I want to kiss you decent.

Pendleton sets her down and she stands feebly. He stands and his face is white and mottled and he brushes off her cheeks.

God, but you are a beautiful. A beautiful woman.

Pendleton kisses her, she parts her lips as does he and cow-tongues her, the texture brings a twisted sensation in her gut and she almost falls, she pulls on his hat and his tongue goes crazy on her and the sensation moves all over her. Betty stands there. Betty feels a heat sidling through her.

Oh, God, woman.

His hands pour over her, cupping her hard cold breasts and she shudders and he pulls her to the ground, *Betty*, his voice is just some old burlap lying on a shed floor, dusty, *I got to do something*. She lies on his black wool coat, wet with snow, Pendleton fumbles with her strange underwear, she lifts up her quail hips and he slides it down, and with a rapacious fumble, the belts and snaps and clips and stuff, he's out, feels cold air on his member and is massaging her hair, shuffling it, with his great cow-tongue hands, cow-tongue lips, a meatish slice of him enters her, though she is tiny and older and unused, he feels hot and warm and Betty is afraid to admit that

it is not unpleasant, she lies there silently while Pendleton—WHUUH!—
waddles around on her and *in*, hefting and raising himself as his large belly
slams, GOD, whuuh! and he pecks her face, so damn good, woman. So.
Damn. Gooooooood. Whuuh. And now Pendleton, his face an inch away,
hard to see, but resembles a purplish globe swaying in and out of view, she
feels tenderness and kisses his eyes, what with snow they are cold and wet,
Gosh, what if we are seen?! She enjoys kissing his eyes, his face. She enjoys Pendleton. What is done feels good, it is not unpleasant, the rhythm
of him inside her, the woman lets out a rapturous peep and that is all
Pendleton can endure—My Bett—aaayyy! Oh, my Betty! He lets out odd
groans, rhinoed grunts, elephantine bellows, the man snorts, he guffaws
and shudders, amidst these, she is pleased. His head resting on her chest,
the woman is rather happy.

He doesn't move. He has fallen asleep. She says, Pendleton. He doesn't
answer, and at her glance down, she sees his mouth working, his eyes flipped
up to his back, all shown by a phosphoric twinkle of movement in this
snow night, it just doesn't look right—

Pendleton! Pendleton!

I know a sleigh in the snow when I feel one and I'm on one now,
hoodoggy. How fast by my head, by my ears and, I, Pendleton, *enjoy*.
Goddammity damn. Bour-*bone*, my brother. Bring it on. Pouring down my
gullet. God but this is pure joy. I am speed, he thinks. I am missiline, pure
aero-nautic fastness, I hear the sound, the sound of rushing in my ear and
I don't want, I don't want, *stop*. Don't slow me down, brother! Don't hold
me back! I be *coming* in my *brain*, that's what. Top that. Top that, will
you. I tell my mother alongside me that, this fun! I am having pure, fucking
fun. My mother holds on to me. There are other people. I could fly, quite
easily if I so chose. I do not choose. My feet are asleep. They are removed
from my body and they are tingling. I can feel the nerves in them quite
distinctly. They don't fucking hurt, though, because nothing hurts. I just
feel good.

We always say in our family, our mother died gently in the nice arms of
her children, though I remember no *nice*, no *gentle* being there. I was there,

after all, as a participant. My mother was all for us, watched her die of pneumonia on her eightieth birthday. Watched her eyes turn to glass knobs. I sneezed. My sister cried. Outside the window, saw an ice cream truck driving by. You could hear the bell ringing out some tune, cranking and lovely. Some children ran out. I still held my mother's hand and I watched those children. It was good to watch those children. They were simply getting ice cream. My mother was angry at me in the end, never knew why. She say *get him out, that Pendleton*, but there was no reason. I tried to think of a reason. I'd like to know, it's not unusual, I tell my patients the brain is fired with chemicals and reacts oddly, I say, but I think of my own mother and this won't work. To me, it is not a fine feeling, your own mother angry at you as she dies. Leaves a bad feeling.

Here now she beside me my mother and she is not angry and and that makes me happy, we're in the sleigh and this is the most damned best thing I've ever known, this and her, we flying down.

Hooooooooooooooboy. I enjoy.

lamb become sheep, 1

I.

It's me, again, **Dad.** Hermie, your diseased son. Yes, I'm still here. Yes, I miss you.

I believe I have found my venue, my metier. I am Tiny Tim and I love the sympathy. Two nurses have danced with me gratefully, I think entranced by my crippledness, which I emphasize. Doctors have paid me respect. I feel a new arena has opened.

With my makeshift crutch, **Dad,** and my brace, cleverly fashioned out of tinfoil, I make sporting good fun of the party. I enjoy festooning extra snow around the Cratchit house (two rental tables slammed together and covered with a cardboard eave, painted by Toddulus' **father** and trailed with greenery), I enjoy decorating the table properly with holly. I adjusted Synjyne's costume to show off more Dickensian cleavage. In short, I have been extremely helpful on the set of this fine Christmas mockery and, truth to tell, I am enjoying myself as I have never done. Explain that to me, **Dad.** Why am I having fun at this odd pseudo-Victorian bash as a crippled and penniless child? The years since you died I have spent in the back shed, Charnel House, playing morbid music and doing aimless drugs and sitting on a molded sofa with an existentialist cloud over my head, and suddenly at this ridiculous party, I feel happy.

Toddulus comes to me and asks me a favor. He says he must go meet
Kirsten. I suggest my salmon-spawning comment from earlier yet he, rudely,
seems to find no humor in this hilarity. He finds me, frankly, tedious. The
boy only wants Kirsten or that baby or something. Humor and Toddulus
remain distant and untouchable.

Synjyne and that waiter from Indonesia, Sanji, are enjoying themselves,
laughing over the grog as they chat by the Cratchits' cottage. Why he gets
to be Scrooge, I don't know. I don't recall there being a Hindu Scrooge. I
don't see this Scrooge bettering my Tiny Tim existence. A proper Victorian wench pops out of a bustier and serves warm grog (heated cranberry
juice and spiced rum) and despite her cap-frosted hair and tiny Christmas
ball earrings, tries to talk in a late-eighteenth-century cockney accent and
I find she likes to engage in a bit of old Dickensian banter, a proper sport,
a jilliwig of humor, portentous ha-ha, again Synjyne and this Sanji are
uncomfortably, well, flirting, **Dad,** and I am not pleased. Tiny Tim is sickly
jealous, **Dad,** and I'd like to pounce in his Balinese face. Then, I realized
I'd seen the Victorian wench before, *hey, don't you work at Safeway?* Why,
yes, I do, in the deli. *That's right!* and my arm stretched over the head of
this familiar Victorian-wench woman resting on the *snow*-covered eave
of the cottage.

I felt my Synjyne fading from me, **Dad,** in the arms of this bronzed
engineer-waiter, Sanji. I felt her smudged eyes now twinkled for him.
Meanwhile, Todd now, he had gone out the back door in his pantaloons
and his shredded waistcoat and his hopes for *whatever* with Kirsten, and
now, **Dad,** I am without a tiny piece of you or any of them. As Tiny Tim
I try to say, God bless us, everyone! as a joke to Greg the bartender with
the bad cockney accent but it falls limp in the air, the band starts up, I
see doctors, a crowd of black-jacketed *curaderos*, swinging lamely in the
streetlamp light of our small village and **Dad,** I wonder what to do. Where
I am. Oh, the hordes! Why in this muddley, ripshod, snow-covered visage must they pour through the door? Have people no lives but that of
the odd, hackneyed Christmas party? Are these people's lives so wretched
and foul they'd face this monstrous blizzard for a mere snippet of cheese
tartlet and punch?

Asking myself this incredulous question, I go to replenish a tray of the infamous Tiny Tim Tartlets, dragging my crutch for theatrical effect, when, as I maneuver through the hall to our makeshift kitchen where Verona and Mrs. Redmond slave, covered in waxy sweat and Sterno stench, and Lo! I see a movement by the hall janitorial entrance, and thinking Todd to be stealing a mop or something, I push the door open, and behold! Sweet treachery! My own! Heart, exist no more!

My own sweet Synjyne. In the arms of Sanji. Kissing. So much for the casual banter of causality, I *am* a casualty.

Is it my destiny to always be brokenhearted? Tiny Tim stands ashamed. *Mrs. Cratchit* pulls back from the heinous foreign devil, an engineer from a faraway tropical island.

She smiles, that deceitful woman.

How would Tiny Tim react, speeds through my pain-encrusted mind. As they both look up, their eyes widened, dewy with excitement, I say, in a sick-child voice:

Oh, pardon. Thought you were. Someone else. God bless us. All *that*.

c . r . , en route

I.

C.R. decides that if nothing else, he'll go to one last party at the hospital and feeling inspired by this decision, he prepares his *toilette*, as he says in his head and finds that expression amusing, his mother often used it without irony, *you boys go on ahead, Mother here's going to prepare her toilette*, and then his father would use the word and give it a hewn, throttled sound, Yeah, I got do my *twawl-et*, too, son and that would evoke a laugh, as her preparation was mythological in length, involving the easement of waters in a large cast-iron puncheon, and the various high-smelling unguents and steamrollers and comb devices of the high-paid *friseur*, not to mention then, *maquillage*, tinted creams and the ubiquitous lipstick (bright pink and wettish, it rolls up from the tube, a dog dick) and all the accoutrements, the battery of her arsenal of mechanical and ointmental items, whereas his father merely grabbed some alcoholed rub after a quick shave, a mere slap-slap and he was done, next to her at the double sink, robed and curlers in hair, outlining her mouth with the dog dick, over and over.

So C.R.'s toilette this evening consists of rummaging in the attic for proper attire. There are trunks everywhere and in one he manages to find an old cavalry suit, regimentals, in a trunk which is labeled *Collectibles* in his mother's fine writing, no doubt the very suit which hung in his father's library for years, but was then squirreled away by his mother, in cotton tissue layers and mothballs, a stiffened and woolen sheath, so foreign to the minty *scrubs* he grabs daily from a folded pile in a hospital closet. Underneath this jacket, a silken cummerbund of blue, some old riding boots of his daddy's, and a wide belt, which he plans to cinch around the jacket. He adds to this combo a fine old linen shirt of his father's and a fanciful piece of silk around his throat. The jacket feels heavy, a weighted bodice of hand-woven wool and he enjoys it, it comes down way to his knees and in the mirror if he puts on his Stetson and brushes back his hair, he finds, by squinting, by God if he doesn't resemble General Shrub in stature and handsomeness and if he could find, *if he could find,* a fine woman, a good woman, strong yet beautiful and kind, like his mother was (perhaps *that* was the problem on some level, not any Freudian bullshit he thought, I mean, I did not want, you know, to *do* her or anything, Jesus!) but then I would have gladly partook of the idea of marriage, of family, with a woman as capable as my mother, that intriguing, that in control, that much a master of all she undertook and I found I'm running up against, in her stead, some of the loveliest, yet inadequate halfway provisions I could find along the way—pretty but dumb, smart but flat, unambitious but pushy, sweet yet lumpish, practiced yet coy, cunning and vague, magazine women, nice to look at but all the same! God, the women became all the same! All, all, all, the rush to get some part of me and keep it. To keep it, son. And thing is, thing is, I rather like that little underage thing not because we're talking about young, brother, but that girl just goes direct yet not too, that girl seems have some kind of real interest in me, it seems, I don't think she cares about me as a doctor, I don't think she gives a shit! I don't think she wants money. She doesn't want me gussied up in a dinner coat for every party to drag along, to collect, to spring on a country club lawn, God sakes, what does she want?

2.

General Shrub, I recall, you married your wife, who was beloved, was she not, when she was only sixteen and you yourself were near my own age of forty-six and that wasn't unusual, it happened all the time so I don't know why, really, it would be such a scandal if I was to openly go on a date with that young woman, it's not like I'm taking her cherry after all, I'm not ravaging the girl, I merely find her pleasant, and attractive and I'd like to swerve, persevere, avoid the needy hormones of the late thirtyish woman who thinks of me as a future Daddy-walletman and get back to a simple date, I mean wouldn't it be fun just to drive around in a pickup and smoke some weed and drink bourbon with Coke which I haven't done in a shitload of time, instead now I'm branching into the tedious single malts and finer liquors, straight up, oh, cigars and foie gras, all the tired crapola of old taste buds that seek sensation, wouldn't it be fun to listen to "Free Bird" with that baby who would love the sound of it, and not have to figure out the medical protocol to save an infant, if not for one day, I could be a mechanic, say, or I could farm, that's good, I could start up the tractor, plow and plant corn and come back to the young arms of that candy striper and eat ham in the evening, brother, brother, tomatoes growing by the water pump, sweet fresh corn on the cob. Making love in a hammock. Buttermilk. Tree frogs in the old pool. Mornings. Coffee in a speckled tin cup. That girl in the big white bed of them, upstairs.

I'm talking, living, son. Let it be known.

3.

It's still there, her number, crumpled on the nightstand, Hello Kitty stationery. He looks at it, dials the number. No answer for a while, then her mother's unmistakable nasal tone,

Hello?

Well, good evening, ma'am. This here's Dr. Ash, from, ah. You'll remember, the hospital?

(C.R. thinks, Now I am talking like a goddamn teenager, Jesus Christ.)

Yes. Dr. Ash. (He hears the cloud of glumness in her voice.) Is. Is something wrong?

Oh, no, oh no, excuse me for bothering you all. I'm sorry. I know it's been a hard time for everyone there (he decides to be direct, gentlemanly). I was calling for, uh, for, (he looks down at the paper, he hasn't said her name before), for *Kirsten,* as I am heading toward the hospital if I could give her a lift to the party, and yourselves as well, I'd like you all to come as my guests, if you *would*—

Well, that's right kindly of you, Doctor, it is, it is. But she's not here, I'm afraid. She went for a drive with her friend—

Her friend? (That little fucker. That damn little fucker.)

Yes, Todd Redmond, and I don't know where, I'm concerned, though, for the snow, I'm very concerned, have you seen it out there, Doctor? All that snow coming down?

Now that you mention that, I do see, some business out the window here (his eyes do a quick scan for Tuffy, but all is clear).

It's terrible.

May want to call her.

She doesn't have a phone. Oh, oh, it's been a hard few months.

Yes. Yes, it has indeed.

Thank you, Doctor, for all you've done.

Well,

With the, the, that *situation* and all.

You're holding up well, Mrs. Hodges.

I do my best. As a mother can.

Well, I wish you good evening. Good evening, Mrs. Hodges.

Thank you.

By the way.

Yes, Dr. Ash.

I, uh, I saw Tuffy this evening.

She paused for a great, lurching fifteen seconds. He felt her voice was as citric as lemon afterward, and throttled. *Uh, oh? You went by Ball's Bluff?*

No, ma'am. I saw him on the steps. In the snow. Like an apparition.

Silence. Then he heard her sniffling and felt very ashamed.

I, oh, God, I'm sorry, Mrs. Hodges. I didn't mean—

Did. Did you hold him?

Yes, I did.

Oh, my Lord.

Good night.

Wait! Oh, Dr. Ash!

I'm sorry! I got to go!

4.

How fast he got in his car, how speedily he hightailed it out of Ashland now that he had a mission. To beat that little fucker into a pulp for denigrating that young girl, for trashing her life up with his, his *ejaculate*, and where was the boy this whole time? Ballyhooing around, sucking down soda at the corner drugstore? Realizing, no doubt, he was out of the high school scene, he tried to envision a horrific, *Enquirer* type of teenaged decadence. Was this boy the Mack Daddy of a bunch of teenage nubiles? Was he importing crack by small airplane from Honduras? Had he heard of the birth of his one child and just picked his nose and gone back to listening to whatever shitfuck music banged in his room (C.R. would've thought of a rapper's name or something but, gosh, he didn't know a damn one. He knew they all were like something Biggy Dogg Doogy Icehead, stuff like that. That's all).

The decent act of defending a girl's honor in the ways of old held a great appeal. It's how Shrub's folk did it and it worked for them. One did not permit such trespasses of human frailty in their world, no, they didn't. He began to feel that Shrub's jacket gave him a certain immortal quality, a manliness of old, sheer bravery had soaked through the fabric from the pheromones and sweat of the general and now by contact it flowed in the pale veins of C.R., he could go up to those mastodons and say, Oh yeah? So what. So freaking what. I did order that cc and yes sir, I knew what the hell I was doing. Of course I did. I ain't no retard, boys. I am a Shrub of the modern era and you fellows are my Ball's Bluff and get out the fucking *way*. I did order that cc and on one hand I'll tell you I did it to see if Tuffy had what it took, maybe on some level, to see if he could muster. Maybe that was it. Or maybe because I wasn't thinking about that and I was thinking I wanted that girl, that girl was going to pull me out of all this. Or maybe I did it to pull myself out of all this crap. Forever. So I didn't have to, to make a choice. Or maybe because I don't think death is real. I need to figure out what it is exactly because I'm confused. I'm seeing people go away and such but somehow they are still here and I can't move on, you see, and. And I'm venturing I might need to move on but I just don't get how or why even. Because they are gone, these people I loved, and maybe I just don't have the strength to keep reloving other people. I don't have the strength, the ability to go get another puppy after Djinn and start the whole rigmarole. I liked that *Djinn*, dammit. I think that dog could've hung on just a few more years, until I was ready to, to, to what? To move on, I suppose. Another thing, maybe I was trying to help. God knows how, but that child was going under anyway, my friends, and I was trying to speed it along for the sake of all. I can't tell you exactly why. I can tell you though, and I mean it, there is no *end*. Don't exist. I'd do it again. And I'm not talking morbidity, my friends. I'm talking death, blue-skinned, sheet-covered, stinking, rotting, eyeballs gone, black flies, maggots, morgue-loving death and note I add the word love in there because everything I did was and is out of love. And that's more than I can say for you, honky bastards.

In his proud raiment, the man proceeded to his car, his pickup, covered in a swath of gauzy snow. It started up just fine. God bless these old cars. God bless the things of old.

free bird, 4

I.

He never got sick of this song.

Goddamn, this was a good song. A man could be happy with this song.

Shit, *yeah*.

Unh-hunh.

Snow. Fuck snow.

Where's my hooch?

OK, then.

What if the party is canceled. There's that problem. And he'd like to track down that girl but who knows where they be. On a back road. In a motel. Do teenagers go to motels, quick think back. No, doubtful. C.R. recalls—cars, meadows, houses with parents gone. Motel's a later shift. Married people.

Huge temptation: Roll down the window and yell. Bellow. Something. Like he always did. He was always the guy in the back who did that stuff. Yell at people. Banshee call. He *lived* in his car, with his friends. His ears were shot from the loud music. Whooooa, car lurched over, caught it just in time. Do *not* lose control. Do not wish for D.U.I. on top of all other disgraces this particular night. If I were teenaged, where would I be? Where would I go?

*   *   *

Air, cold as ethyl alcohol on a cotton ball. Leans his head out:
Wheeeeeeeehaaaaaaaaaaaaaayeaaaaaaaaah
Yeeeeeeeeeeeeeeeeeeeehaaaaaaaaaaaaawhoooooooooooooooa

Pretty young women. All life is fragile.

2.

He sails through the snow in the truck, knows the curves of the road well, and the loss of traction makes him slip in the car, ricocheting along, he barely touches the wheel, bumping along the ruts, his rear lifting from the momentum.

Imaginary argument with his father:

Hell, boy. I suppose you're trying to throw good money away, cremate this car before the evening is done?

Does fine machinery mean anything to you? That one caused C.R. to smile. His father had said that one, an evening when C.R. was maybe seventeen, his father in the doorway as C.R. had peeled out into the driveway earlier. He enjoyed the way the man added a touch, ever so slight, of poetic humor to his barbs, his punishment. *Has your brain been pickled at night by a strange force of aliens?* was another favorite.

Where to, exactly, he thinks. He could truly be a fool and cruise Pizza Hut which in this night would be empty and also make him feel decrepit, so what's the point. But he was also damn hungry. He had a craving for Christmas food of that which he grew up on, which brought him back to the endless theme of ham, of which his thoughts harped on and on, because the fact of the matter was he had not had, since his father died, since Muriel was gone, a decent ham and biscuit, or even just a slice of good ham, and he would virtually give thirty-eight thousand dollars for one, everything in his checking account at this very moment for one perfect ham biscuit, was he asking too much, just one more time? A month ago, before all of his heartache began, he fancied himself the righteous heir to all of Ash genius. He had purchased the ham in the muslin sack in a Ball's Bluff Food Lion. He directly soaked it in a bathtub for two days, as he recalled his father doing similarly in a zinc tub out back, he couldn't find the zinc tub so he used a bathtub. His own, with claw feet. Then, he pulled it out and dried it. The water had clouded and had scum on top. That was unappealing. Scum always is. He dried it and did the pepper thing, and cloves. He baked it. He watched *America's Most Wanted* and fell asleep and the ham baked too long. He took it out and the air smelled of ammonia and the ham had deep maroon cracks in it. He sliced off a hot hunk, a mistake as his father cooled it down and sliced it thinly, and he ate it off a fork, a large stringy, hot, fumy slab, too salty and dried out and then knew his life was a ruinous shithole. How he could know about only one thing in his life, medicine, and nothing else. He felt a fool.

Essentially, he had been a mechanic of intricate, finely tuned machines. A little calibration here, another tweaking there. It had taken him years of schooling and experience to get him where he was today, Dr. C.R. Ash. Interesting that he had not noticed, until today, how this blind-swept all other things out of his life, and now that his doctoring was gone, how little was left. Had he done any good as a doctor? He tried to think, names and tiny pink heads swarming his vision, Garrison, Tocari, Scheinmann, Rector, Earley, so many babies he'd seen do well, he'd treated well, whose parents brought them in at the yearly "Premie Reunion" out in the hospital park, with the six-foot-long subs and moonbounce, shaking hands, hugging and kissing the children with *c-pap* mashed noses thrust in front of him, their parents gleeful and red-faced. These kids would've all died years back. Those parents would've been childless.

Coming down the road, barreling fast down the icy road, "Free Bird" blasting on the speakers, a calm overtook C.R., a happy feeling. He could see all the children whose lives he's saved beaming at him. He's done something with his life. Those children. Take away Tuffy, though.

When does love become a crime, he thought.

stave five

ball's bluff.

shrub

this season finds us weary + exhausted.

it is truly rectifying the men we have served + the wounded we have treated.

i dined in winchester before this battle we attempt today at the home of cousin conrad and there was a large joke about my namesake, the famous randolph cherry shrub, of which my fondness has earned me an appellation i carry with joy, we all toasted to ending the war soon, despite all rations being low. yankees had taken chickens from the yard + there was lacking molasses for the same reason, yet we ate well from stew. so many give up what they can to support us soldiers, many drink parched wheat in place of coffee, we are all sacrificing, the kind family gave me when i left a dozen hard boiled eggs and biscuits and ham, a gallon of fine scuppernong wine, of which the gentleman makes a good one, it lasted me a bit. though i've given it to the soldiers whose care i attend and they cry for food, water and they need it desperately. just today i am with men from gen. early's old brigade, a young man from marshall a minnie ball took off his knee cap + we had to amputate, an unfortunate + all too common incident, we layed him on a door with holes cut in it for blood to seep, he was the first of the day, there were following twenty seven more limbs to remove i can hear the screams even in my dreams, the distress so severe. i hear the men on the battle field dying, too, always the call for water or mother, helpless to lie there and do nothing for them. we are in need of boards for beds + straw for bedding + bandages, always the need for bandages of which the ladies of the area help kindly, sacrificing their bedding. general johnston, commander of our army, has pulled us back to centreville for now where we wait between winchester + consider taking some yankee victory in leesburg, something he thinks may be facile and manoeuverable, we had dispatched along the river to the side of the potomac, laying in wait. near larger than the james river and far more lovely. catfish near the size of a man's leg can be caught with some ease. a small amount of us there, about forty, recieved word to colonel evans that there had been a crossing at edwards ferry, we sent along troops when we saw the fool union, a crazy man, a colonel quoting poetry, sir walter scott, no less. *one blast upon your bugle is worth a thousand men.* the foolishness! our men proceeded to a weak spot in their positioning and skirmish broke out, fires rang out pinging through the air the leaves + branches fell from the trees, from the bullets weight, two men on my side, minnie balls took them out, i fired, our rifles but duty kept me busy also helping those i could i stuffed cloth in the wounds of those bleeding while reloading the musket. it gets worse. can it be worse, more men down, more shots pinging! the screaming. it was then our own horseman on a gray horse charged towards the union thinking it their own they charged + we took advantage of it. it was drunken wudman some say some say it was a phantom who led the battle i saw him with my own eyes and i know not who the horseman be, came to transpire. we advanced on them + oh, what a hideous sight! all quivering mass of men at the top of the cliff over the potomac in one huge faltering mass leaped + fell over into the water, man on man, each stabbing + crushing the other! the boats were filled with men + capsized, men were dashed, flung on the precipice + crushed in the mad rush by their own, we watched them swarm in the whirling water + i was stunned by shells above my head, minnie balls and the rushing sound of bullets, my own companion lt. harry buford a nice fellow and his slave bob form a v towards the back + feign off union men with our rifles, my leg is a hindrance for speed but he is fast and quick, his slave, to my sadness goes down, bob, a mighty fighter, i check him once but his eyes are gone and harry takes a minnie when i go to staunch and the man got up with his musket, here is the shock, harry is a woman, if it can be possible, i pulled open his chest to examine the minnie ball entrance and found this out, much to my surprise, i then feel more duty to protect this brave woman, a shot then like a horse's kick to my chest, i realized i have been shot then, for how long? my shoe quickly full of blood, my pants leaden with same, i dragged over the precipice as blood gushed, two holes in and out the knee and somewhere in the chest, breathing was like through water, harry the woman had brandy and i drank the brandy + had wrapped it but i knew myself it would not last, it would be the table again for myself as well, my last remaining leg, i felt dark then and nauseous and i heard the watery screams of the northern men, my brothers, dying in agony, below, those you see who kept their swords drowned from the weight of it, those in their heavy jackets drowned also, rolling in the river a huge festering ball of desperation, flinging arms and legs, boiling in the darkened river waters. you never seen such a dreadful sight or heard the like of it. at this point i fell out for loss of blood, my feelings when i awoke were mary and the children and mataoka my sister, i was talking to them in the parlor on a fine fall day i could see the children playing out back watched by shecalla, this was a fine recollection though it felt real to me in all regards, even the fabric on my wife's dress, as my hand lay next to the folds of her skirt felt soft and velvety, it was a fabric she'd gotten from france for that special occasion + i smoked a pipe. can it be that that day is gone forever, that day my children played out back now? i give all my limbs, all my life, for mary in those days despite the grimness of this war, the hardtack, the fat, the salt meals, the gangrene is nothing to what my poor wife endures. i am lying in the smoke + bullets and the woman, harry, in my face, it's her eyes, it's the man i hear, i want to say something. down by the river edge. mary, hold on to our last child. a patch of free birds cover the sky like black mourning lace. i hear the branches up towards the sky rustling and crackling with the scurry of bullets, that's an odd sound lovely and fearsome at the same time.

ball's bluff,
euphrates king

It was a dusty afternoon in September, trees starting to redden out back in Ball's Bluff, that huge frazzle of riverside forest, lying dormant, yet intrinsically part of the terrain of C.R.'s life. (His mother was walking there that morning with her dogs, arriving home burr-covered and flush-cheeked. His father planned to dove-hunt on the edges in the freshly cut cornfields and had asked C.R. to go with him at breakfast, but he declined, arguing a heavy load of schoolwork, the fact was, he hated the gunshot and the downy birds with purplish wounds and limp rolling heads.)

C.R., seventeen or so, long-legged, bony-faced, about the time he'd almost accomplished high school and was considering early admission to the university, kept excellent grades, yet partied as they said, which meant simply, sat around in a lot of cars, drank Miller beers, and smoked some pot, went up there after school with his buddies in the afternoon. This was a usual destination, pulling into the parking lot of the battlefield, while vans of tourists unloaded to take the small hike and see the spot where the Union men capsized into the slow, still water. He and his friends would smoke a bong by the bushes and then walk through, singing, laughing, mocking the foreigners, sitting at the final bench which sat perched over the edge and looking for the glint of some old Confederate's sword popping through the mud.

C.R. liked the camaraderie of Pendleton who dragged around beside him, and his other friends, ungoodlies, his mother said, those with *no futures,* said in her flat tenor, or *futures, yes, but different:* electricians, plumbers, one of them died a few years later in a car accident, one did construction, name of Curtis White, who now lived as a shut-in down toward the edge of Battlefield Hills. (C.R. would occasionally call on Curtis, though the old vivacity between them was hushed and there seemed little to be excited about, now that the hullabaloo of girls and drugs had worn away. They talked of the Redskins. Curtis talked often of deer, their meat, their ways. Deer paraded out his back window like soft, brown nymphs, freely in the broad light. *They cut off right quick if you move—hup—watch him watch him.* He had names for them, Butterleg, Brownthigh. They were his silent companions. He bought a salt lick and put it out back to attract them, to the ire of his neighbors. He would look at them, while eating his own venison stew. Pendleton also stopped by at Christmastime and brought Curtis a basket of Nancy's home-baked goods, Curtis'd give him a beer and they'd sit by the window. They'd talk of C.R., Redskins, and deer. And how good Nancy cooked applesauce cake. Then it'd darken outside and Pendleton would go.) *Don't you hit my deers now go real slow down that road.*

I wonder if that old coot got his fancy on a young Bambi, thought Pendleton, buckling himself in, unrolling the window. *I'm thinking you sweet on a deer probably. Need to get out and meet some ladies Curtis my friend.*

Those days gone. I'm too busy.

Ha, OK, I'll catch you later deerman.

You find me a date how about that. One of them nurses up at the hospital.

What you going to do. Give her some deer stew. Go make out in Ball's Bluff and smoke some weed son?

I don't go back in that haunt place since seventeen and that freak was there. I'd forgotten about that. I got to ask C.R. about that time.

That one particular day back then, these young boys, seeking a riverside to smoke something and drink some beer, went to Ball's Bluff, and spilled out of the smoky car and proceeded to the entrance when a man, in large khakis pulled up to his waist, his feet overpronating, crushing the sides of his sensible desert boots, one leg dragging with a stiffened limp, huge thick glasses over his exaggerated eyes, stood and looked at the boys. He held a clipboard in his hand. A sign over his breast said the name, *Euphrates King.*

You boys here for the two o'clock tour?

Was it the hair, the back which displayed an awkward crimp of bed-head, a sign of his no-doubt-lonely living situation or was it the fact he swallowed a couple times, in nervous anticipation, that stopped C.R.'s heart and made him nod slowly, to the irritated sighs of his companions?

Yes. Yes, we are. We're here for the tour.

Well, OK! OK, then. Have a seat here on this bench. Now that's fine. Very fine. Young fine men interested in history. Don't see that much. No, you don't.

(Goddamn, you ass*hole*, said Pendleton. Shut up, you fat fuck, whispered C.R., only take a while.)

They sat down, barely room for all of them, and the man stood. He wore something weird, C.R. noticed. A black double-breasted shirt of cotton with brass buttons. He was some kind of reenactor. He was a nut.

He swept his arm out in a broad sweep:

Wel—*come* boys, back to 1861! Back, back, *back in time.*

The man fumbled with a little scuffed-up cassette player. He dropped it, the batteries fell out and C.R. helped him pick it up, and then Euphrates King popped it on, blaring out a jaunty little battlefield banjo tune. He reached in his pocket and pulled out a wax-papered lump and passed out chunks of some homemade burned cracker to the surprised boys. Ravenous from weed, they chewed on the stuff.

We're entering a different world, sons. May I interest you in a small snack of my own delicious hardtack, yessir, 'CAUSE THAT'S ALL YOU'D GET FOR FOOD, MY FRIENDS. Be glad this don't have worms because usually it did! Talking about *teeth-dullers*, buddies. *Sheetrock crackers.* Yessir! Now *listen*, listen to the baleful tunes plucked by a brother in the next tent. It's early morn. Mist is rising. But first, first, let me tell you first who was here in Ball's Bluff—

—Yankees getting their asses kicked, said Pendleton,

Well, let's not be disrespectful, but good point! Mistakes were made for sure, what's your name, young lieutenant? OK, OK, Pendleton, but what I meant was, was this, *young boys*, that's who was here. Youngsters like yourself.

He a perv, whispered Curtis White in C.R.'s ear. A homo.

Ssshh! C.R. flared back. Goddamn these guys were fools.

You kids look pretty comfortable. High school maybe. Nothing to complain about. How'd you like to battle, I'm saying *fight*, against your brothers, your cousins, you hear me?

They were silent now. Euphrates' face reddened.

What I'm saying is, these counties here were divided into Union and Rebel and that means a good deal of families were split. To secede or not to secede, that was the question. *Chew on that*, compadres. Pardon my appropriation of Shakespeare. You all read *Hamlet*? Ohhkay, never mind.

To die, to sleep—To sleep, perchance to dream. Ay, there's the rub, said C.R.

When we have shuffled off this mortal coil, Must give us pause. Ahoy! Some here have an education! Thankfully. Do you know this, then: *Doomed for a certain term to walk the night, And for the day confined to fast in fires, Till the foul crimes done in my days of nature are burnt and purged away?*

Act One, Scene Five.

Teacher's fucking pet, whispered Pendleton.

I'm impressed, young man.

I was Hamlet last year.

Ah, I would've liked to have seen that. A fine, fine piece of theater. Onward, men.

Walking down the path, Curtis drew up to C.R, you crazy man. This dude is fucked. I'm going to get out of here go and smoke a doobie.

Suit yourself.

You staying?

Hell, give the man a break, there's no one here for his tour, man. We're the only ones, C.

Not my problem.

Whatever.

Curtis stuck his hands in his pocket, yet walked on with the group, sullenly. Kicked rocks.

Fellows, the start was this. Union fellows were sent down this road to check on the situation and suss it out. You got me, kids. Nod your heads, I like the rattling sound. OK. They crept through these woods. Look at them. Scrambly, sad land. Thorny. Cedars. Rattlers. Water mocs. They traipsed across this spot early morning and it was all dusk, mist everywhere. They went slow. Tiptoed. Down along the cowpath. Tripping sometimes on the damn roots everywhere. Yes, son you have a question?

Pardon me, sir, said Pendleton, how you know they trip on roots.

Son, being a docent involves a certain amount of *skill*, said Euphrates (while shaking his head, the frizzed-back part of his hair lifted on the breeze), a certain amount of improvisational ability to transcend the facts and realize the scene in all its beauty, its vivid true coloration, and thus bring it to life, and thus I thought of that, son. I see them tripping, cursing, yet persistent. Can't you see them son, can't you??

I'll try, sir.

Good, good. That's what we want here. Like I said, visibility was impaired. What was, well, different sources say different things, some say cornstalks, others wheat thatches, or some say these scrappy cedars that are everywhere here, what I mean is, the Union guys sent to check her out saw them and thought they were Confederate tents. Ohhhhhkay. Big mistake. Number one. Who do you send to tell news like this when you're a—

(What's a *docent*, mumbled Curtis White to C.R., that some kind of faggoty tour guide, like especially faggoty? Shut the fuck up, C.R. whispered back.)

You young men have a question you wish to address to all of us? I'm happy to hear your concerns about this terrible war.

Oh, well, my friend wanted to know what a docent is. That word.

Ahh. Aha. OK. Fair enough, fair enough. Some say it's a fancy word for a tour guide. I say, I say, I lead you on a tour you'll never forget. I show you the past. When we finish you will *know* Ball's Bluff. You will smell it. Hear it. Oh, yes, you will.

Docent.

That's the word, now eat your hardtack, lieutenant, and we'll scramble off this path down to the edge of the woods.

Aren't there snakes?

Oh, mercy. Buckets of them, boy! But are we wimps or are we soldiers here? I mean, come on.

The boys follow behind, and Curtis White trips.

Note I am right about the roots and tripping! You see! One can envision and go back in time! Men!

Yessir! C.R. and Curtis answer in unison, which made them look around oddly and Pendleton mumbled, Fucking *insane*.

Stop gnawing on the hardtack and listen to my words. At 0600 at this spot on October 21, 1863, Captain Chase Philbrick with his twenty men crept along here. They heard the loon—*coo-ooo, coo-oo*—said Pendleton.

Ah, yessir, son. That's it. The loon was sad and lonesome. They could hear the subtle decline of day. The smell of moss and rooted leaves flooded their nostrils. They probably had to pee bad. It was getting darker and their legs were sore, they'd just climbed that precipice. Fog was rolling in. And then.

They saw a *ghost*.

No, that was later. They saw, dimly in the field, just up here. See those trees. See them.

Those things?

Yessir, *those* things. Those they mistook for the Confederate tents. That's what they did. It was dark. Foggy. Late. Maybe they were tired beyond what is proper. This was Captain Chase's first combat patrol. They went back and told the commanding officer, Colonel Devens, the good news. They'd seen the Confeds and there were only a few of them. Such good luck—

Yeah, but they *fucked up*.

In essence, yes, son, but I'd urge you to watch your mouth. This is reverential ground, my friend. This is a burial site, I'll remind you. So, moving on, Colonel Devens gets on up there with his men, you know, same old stuff, he's thinking, you know, Where's the beef, ha, ha, you know like the ad on TV—

C.R. chuckled.

He gets there and he realizes the mistake. Corn thatches or cedars, they are not an enemy encampment. Whoops. Uh-oh. What you going to do, young-man-who-giggles-at-everything.

Me? said Curtis White.

No, the tree there. Of course, *you*. What do you do.

I don't know. Turn on back, I guess.

Oh, sure. Good idea. One problem. While you all were having fun checking out the Confederate camp, guess who heard you and now has you surrounded. Yup. Not looking good.

I'll get them bastards. Let them try.

The magnolia guard, Company K, saw your sorry asses coming back along trying to recoup.

I'm on the *southern* side, man.

Mississippians on my left, I got all flustered, my first time in battle—

What you talking about man, said Pendleton, you get *into* this.

I didn't know what to do. What's a man to do. I can't shoot my musket. I shot some trees, got my stead in the leg.

But that was the big mistake, am I right, sir?

We wake damn early, one in the morning. Sneak on out of there. We proceed toward the river. I am told, assist men towards the river. Go on to the river. Get the hell out. The reconnaissance was gallant, yet flawed. I hear a fast sound, adjutant yells, cavalry and sure as can be, a large mass are on us. Are *on* us. I feel a bad thing in my right side, feel I'm carrying an extra shrub load of lead in my pocket which serves to be my actual leg, proof of injury as I see the blood soak my garments.

You make this real. It's kind of creepy.

(I can't stand this. You can stay but I'm going back, get me a beer, C.R. Suit yourself, Pen. I'm staying here.

Pendleton edged off.)

* * *

Curtis White says, I didn't know it was like this.

Looky up there, boys. Looky up here on past this cliff.

He leads them to the end of the woods, over the Potomac. Looky down in that cold dark water. How you like to bleed in that thing.

I would *not* like it.

A boy was grabbing on my jacket, pulling me down. Like I said, I was hurt. The feeling like rain coming down on you, hard pounding rain. Then it's quiet. And you realize some of you are bleeding and some are dead. You have this still, quick moment. Some people actually *laugh*. And some are quiet. And then you feel your own injuries. Not at first, though. At first it felt like rain. You think, I guess I'm OK this time. All right! Then, then, you feel it. You look down and you see a red cloud bursting on your pants and when it's fast like that you know. You know how many get them legs cut off. You seen worms in the wounds of your brothers. So you know what road you're going down. So that's what I'm trying to tell you all, basically. *"The soldier's music and the rite of war speak loudly for him. Take up the bodies. Such a sight as this becomes the field, but shows much amiss!"*

They were quiet looking down in the river. Curtis White was thinking about how many catfish are in those reeds. Ought to have brought a rod. C.R. felt woozy and sick, wondered how he's going to get through medical school, at least he didn't have to do it in those days. He wouldn't want to chop legs off and hear men scream like that.

I wonder if. He turns around.

Where'd he go.

What. Curtis White turns around. Motherfuck.

Y'all! I want to get back they hear Pendleton's voice straining up from the parking lot. It's getting cold in the woods. They don't see Euphrates.

He was a freaky kind of guy, wasn't he.

I think he went off that way.

I told you he was a perv.

I felt sorry for him. Nobody else on his, on his tour.

I want get out of here. Come on.
Think he fell down had a heart attack somewhere?
I think we get *on* out of here.

They bruised the grass like cattle, getting out of the woods as the light fled.

hermie,
in the field

I.

Tiny Tim has fled to the snow. Not easy considering the infirmity that I suffer. There is a hell of a lot of flakes out here, and I'm flailing with my tiny crutch.

Dad! I call to you. **Dad!**

The night offers nothing but silence yet snow is hardly quiet, snow offers the sweeping of the cosmos, God powdering his wig, didn't they say. Out here, in the snow as I traverse the field I hear her. Synjyne. *Her—r—r—r—mie! Her—mie!!* How quickly she forgets the arms of the dark stranger! Through the flakes, I hear her less and less, a voice through flour. Muffled, a cotton dreariness. The field is vast behind the hospital, open and heavy with drifts. The river is near, the Potomac. Great shards of quartzine ice clutter the edges of the water. The night is dark, spilling frozen tears. Underneath my feet are the ground bones of soldiers as I approach the field of Ball's Bluff. Children died here. Young bloods my own age. I wonder what that was like, scrambling in the mud. It was cold. It smelled of river and intestines freshly opened. Watching people die.

Dad. Dad. I still hear Synjyne, far off yelling *Hermie, Hermie.* What does she care, obviously. I wait. Where's her island man, now brusquely discarded. I am cold. Where's my crutch. Oddly, the fake crippled leg hurts. I see her, an approaching shadow through the mist.

Am I in the presence of the ghost of Christmas yet to come? I asked.
The figure nods.

2.

Certain quarter machines in the entrance of Food Lion sell armbands and
shoelaces with the letters *W.W.J.D.?* which means, Synjyne told me, when
I appeared puzzled by this odd abbreviation, What Would Jesus Do? So I
appropriate this catchy phrase and twist it toward my own mind-set at this
particular time, to What Would Tiny Tim Do? What would he do in this
situation. As I said, **Dad,** I am a method actor, if nothing else.

It seems to me from my vast reading habits, as you know I detest movies
and TV and prefer the written word, I had read a theory as to the real cause
of Tiny Tim's illness. It was not some form of cerebral palsy or what have
you, birth-related injuries that cheesy lawyers wish to sue over, caused
usually by a premature-birth situation, because Tiny Tim was *getting worse,*
we all know that. The spirit had portended that to Ebenezer Scrooge.
Cerebral palsy is in and of itself an occasion not a continuance. This doctor
had theorized that Tiny Tim had a kidney disease that made his blood too
acidic, and, if simply treated with alkaline solutions, would decrease the
dreaded acidity and the child would recover quickly, although this was not
available in that time. I take that into consideration.

I am acidic. Sharp. Renally flawed.

As her figure approaches, I feel angrier and more betrayed. There was a
time we discussed our relationship once and I told her we were beyond
the strictures of contemporary outdated artificial hindrances which dis-
allowed the growth of spirituality that we all experience, in other words, I
was thinking that Candace, Todd's caramelized older sister, might possibly
have the hots for me, she seemed to stop for conversation on occasion and
I thought, by telling Synjyne that hocus-pocus bullshit, I could possibly
experience Candace and all her naked splendor. First, that was a joke, as
Candace had zero intention of that ever happening, much to my testosterone's disappointment, and secondly, I am the one who insisted Synjyne
experience the free love I had been espousing, I pushed her on Todd the
first night, I insisted she dabble in the outlaw love I felt was key to our

freedom and modernity, and now, I am burned. I am burned, burned, burned.

Synjyne, as she approaches, is whistling on the wind, a familiar tune. I realize it is not her.

I, Tiny Tim, am feeling nauseous.

Who whistles but my **father.**

Dad? Dad, I don't want you here.

The figure stops and I can't see its face.

I talk to you but I don't want you. I don't. Stop whistling. Stop whistling, fuckhead.

To my relief, the whistling stops.

If, if, I gave you the idea, I wanted you back, well, I did want you back at one point, at one point, I thought, OK, I need my **dad,** but now, I *so* don't want to deal with you. Or whatever. I so don't even want to know *why* you did it. You know? I don't think I want to know. Can you believe this snow. Truly incredible. This is the biggest snow we've had in frigging light years. Can you, can you, *talk?*

The figure is still, unmoving.

No? Yes? OK. No answer. Be that way. Have I, I wonder if I have, have conjured you up or something with my powers. Weird. Oh, or. Or. Am I dying or something? Have I really become Tiny Tim and I'm dying of whatever he died, would have died of? As if, I have so metamorphosed from the strength of my imagination that I've convinced my body that I indeed suffer from a kidney disorder? In that case, I should be able to feel his thoughts. And maybe I do. As Tiny Tim, I feel:

Afraid for my family. For I knew I was dying. My legs were weaker but I couldn't tell my father as he was very attached to me. I would lean on the crutch more. I felt dizzy often. And without hunger. It's only when, when Mum and Daddy get better, when they feed me the beef tea and we get more coal, that I feel strength soaring through my legs for the. No, I am Tiny Tim in a field and I am wondering where are my parents. Where is my London house. I am very cold.

* * *

Or, perhaps I am simply Hermie, in this field, freezing to death. Yes, of course. Oh, fucking hell, of course, you see visions when, when you freeze. I read that. You freak out and see visions and then, you like sleep. Well, guess what? Guess what! I don't want to die. I'm not ready. Fuck that, fuck you, fuck Synjyne. Fuck Todd. Fuck this place. Go away, **Dad.** You really don't belong. I'm sorry, I don't really feel pissed or anything, I just, I'd rather. Be. I'd just rather really let you go on your merry way and me be on mine, now. Whatever bugged you must've been really bad. It must've really sucked big time, and I'm sorry if I had anything to do with it. I'm really sorry. I don't think I did, though. I think we kids were OK. It's just too bad, it really sucks you couldn't have seen through it or whatever. I think I should move out and get out of that house. I think Todd and I should go on the road and get away from here. I'm not dying, don't even tell me I am. Because I reject that. I reject you.

I read a book once about this dude who went to some mountain like Everest I think and he started to freeze and saw shit, his ancestors he said, they came to give him some kind of advice and he realized he was dying so he sent them away and then he had some pretty foul, gnarled appendages, they were eaten away by the cold and stuff. Well, so I think you, you ought to go back, whoever you are and leave me alone, it was a mistake me talking to you all the time. I didn't realize it was real, all my bullshit. I. I. Didn't really think you were listening, this is weird. Whoever you are you, you don't belong here.

Dad? Are you sad? Over there? Can you see my future?

Can I just be Tiny Tim forever? Go on the road? Or something. How lame.

If you can see my future don't sure as hell tell me. You got to go now. I'm creeping myself out. I am one creepy freak.

Besides, I'm in the Tiny Tim mode now. I've got pudding to eat and stuff. Actually, I'm working, **Dad.** I've a job to do. There's a party down there.

Hermie! Her—mie!

That's Synjyne. You know, that girl? I got to go back there. OK, **Dad**? I have to go back. I miss you, **Dad**. I want you to know, despite everything, despite our relationship which has only really happened since you died, oddly enough, despite the pain and everything, I respect you and it was a really brave thing to come to me now. It was probably hard. I used to pretend you were on a business trip (as a plumber that conceit didn't really work well) and would be back and then by then you'd be able more to spend time with me, and then somehow along the way, in order not to grieve from that not happening, I merged over to talking to the spot on the wall, and did this because I thought I could prevent, you know. Tears.

But all my useless words have proven actually *right*.

You are here.

Good-bye.

That person, that whatever, starts to go away. It goes up by the woods, over by the water. I watch it go in there. It's not floating or anything. It's walking, he's walking. I'm unbelievably sad. I am so sad I want to kill myself. Shit. I am trying to stand back and, in the Buddhist way, view my emotions detached, but, but I can't, and I wish I could. Get my act together here. Because this is, this is out of control and I'm not making sense either. I want to let go. I think my story is over. I think it's time to let it go now. We can move on to the others, to Verona, to Toddulus and his baby, to those doctors, to everyone, because my story is over for you now, I've reached my goal, so to speak, I'm basically fucked up, yes, I will eat that, I will go with that. Listen, I've enjoyed this time with you all, sharing. It's been real. I just want to get out of this goddamn snow. I'm cold, people. Can you understand that. Can you understand cold to your very bones? Where are you anyway? On a beach? Is this a beach read? Or a rocking chair, cuddled up with tea and a blanket and stuff? A subway? What do you have to do with me? Who am I to you? Do I mean anything to you? Ask yourself that. Am I just some throwaway kid you could care less about, like those ones you see in (pick one):

a) the mall
b) walking by Safeway
c) outside the high school
d) working in the record store, arms jangling with chains as we ring
   you up.

I am actually not bad. I am as honest and sad inside me as you are. We are pretty much the same. Did your dad kill himself? Is it your business, is what I want to know? I mean, I know I invited you but I'm cold and feel really sick. There is somehow something askew with the fact that you know this chunk of my life and I am left on the outskirts of yours. Doesn't seem fair. Why can't I see in your bedroom? Why can't I look in your refrigerator? It pains me. We could love each other. We could have a Hermie-Dead Dad-and-You sandwich. At least, let it be said that I am a good person. I mean well.

Let's go, though. Because I'm cold, person. Lots of guys died here in 1861, you know. It was a mess. They fell in the river, the Potomac. In October. Here's the best thing, though. The best part of the Battle of Ball's Bluff. And this is true, people. Hell, this whole book is true. If you wish to imply that I am not true or something, then I will beg to differ. I will claim verisimilitude on you. I can assure you, I am most assuredly true, in every sense, but back to my story.

At the Battle of Ball's Bluff, there was a U.S. senator named Colonel Edward Baker, a good friend of Lincoln's and all. They called him "Ned." Lincoln's son was named after old Ned, that's how tight they were. But this guy was kind of an idiot, lots of bravado and a show-off. Like me, basically. He was sent to handle Ball's Bluff and given a bunch of power and appointed a general. He could do whatever the hell he wanted, but the guy, the guy was clueless and just liked the idea of the thing, he didn't know shit about battle. He didn't know tactics or any of that stuff. He was just bombardiering around, being a total pain in the ass, forming the men in a disastrous trapezoid shape for battle which was a mistake, basically left them weak at both ends, and thus precipitated the stampede in which they sped into the river, anyway, at the beginning of the battle the dude yelled out poetry, much to everyone's disgust, he quoted Sir Walter Scott, "One blast upon your bugle horn is worth a thousand men," then he promptly got shot through the head by a cavalry revolver. See, I always thought that was a really cool thing, this guy all caught up in the romance, the moment there. I can just see that guy, holding his sword up, saying poetry. He could've quoted Dickens, he could have cited old Tiny Tim. Everyone knew the *Christmas Carol* then, it was like the most popular book around, it came out in 1843, so it was already eighteen years old, Tiny Tim as a character lay in the heads of all these poor, sad kids! Dickens was BIG over here in the States, though when he visited with his wife they were disgusted with the amount of spittle we Americans deposited on everything. Huge spitoons everywhere filled to the brim with festering tobacco wattle. Trains, stagecoaches, people were spitting everywhere and it was landing on his and his wife's clothes and they were ready to go back to England, they couldn't stand it. Even the White House, during Dickens' official visit, he said, had floors covered with the gooberous stuff. Can you imagine what kind of barbarous scumbags we were?

But back to Ned, the poetic, bumbling general: In the end it was like hundreds of Union soldiers in a big tidal pool drowning. They all fell over this riverbank in a frenzy. They all drowned, right over there.

You who have the questionable benefit of cellular veracity at this moment which any second could deteriorate and in fact is deteriorating fast, I might add, does that give you the upper hand? What more do I need for existence? I have a heart, I assure you. I am bled through these pages with my heart. You are just dreaming. You are dreaming me, Dad and all around you. There are ghosts around you no less real than yourself or me. There is a whole world out there. It's so beautiful you can't even fathom.

So what I want to tell you is this. We're in this together, you and me. Right now, it's all you and me. That's all that's going on right now.

I see Synjyne far off at the edge of the hospital, she's sitting outside smoking a cigarette and I see just her dark shape and a glowing dot of orange going back and forth from her mouth. *Clump clump clump,* hear the awful sound of me walking in the snow. My knickers are wet. This is the snowstorm we wait centuries for. We are overcome with snow and it's quite pretty, my reading friends, it's quite pretty. I invite you to enjoy the sight of snow. I walk up to my love, my costume totally soaking wet, looking pretty horrifying, feeling oddly relieved. I could use a cigarette. I could use a drink. I could use kindness.

Your man, Tiny Tim, has returned, Synjyne.

Last comment, though I don't want to go, though I guess I have to, and that is, how I didn't want to be a fucked-up pitiful youth on the cusp obsessed with death. I was going to just try out the role. But it stuck. Everything you do counts. It all counts, it all sinks into you. That's what I mean, you don't get to do things temporarily, you are those things, they become you.

I'm working with getting another bit later on here, she said she'd think about it. If you can, put in a good word for me. I'm hoping this won't be the end.

verona

Verona drinks two Shrub Cocktails, a delicious combination of cherry li-
queur and rum, a few Tiny Tim Tartlets, a few rounds of the beef and gelee
Bob "The Mayor" made and the woman is feeling very, very well. Many
doctors, many of them, have raised their cups of grog and told her and Diane
that this is, *by far*, the best party this hospital of babies, on the edge of a
battle known for its bumbled and gruesome end, has ever, ever held. Verona
stood stiff and wet-eyed in crinoline, watching everyone around her. There
was a jig starting up, a group of paid dancers had started up a Sir Roger de
Coverley—and to her left came a small voice, may I have this dance?

She looked down, it was Bob "The Mayor."

Bob, honey, I don't see why not.

He grabbed her arm, strongly, she noted, and whisked her around the
waist. Bob "The Mayor" knew how to dance. Goodness' sakes alive, the
man could jig.

Bob! I didn't know you knew this stuff.

Ha! Well, Verona. I am a huge, then he swung her to the left, *huge,*
Dickens fan. I belong to a local, he swung her to the right, a local club of
Victoriana.

Beg your pardon.

A club of Victoriana, we, we do dances like this one and read Dickens
and discuss stuff.

Is that so.

Yes. I've met his grandson.

Whose grandson.

Dickens. His grandson does a, does a little show about him, in period dress and everything. It's kind of fun but a bit *sad*. For some reason.

Yeah. Move on, you know?

God, I love this party. I'm having the time of my life.

It turned out OK, didn't it. Despite all our *troubles*.

Fun had by all. By the way, I'm rereading *Martin Chuzzlewit. What* a tale.

Who?

Martin Chuz—Dickens—

Oh. OK. I read that Tale of. What's that. Two Cities.

Ah, *it was the best of times, it was the worst of times.*

Yessir.

May I interest you in the splendor of an heirloom rose?

What's that now, Mr. Mayor?

Heirloom roses. Do you garden some?

Never got into that, Bob.

Perhaps this spring, Verona, we can—

The jig ended abruptly.

Oh, that was fun, Mr. Bob. Thank you.

Oh, thank you, Verona.

She watched Bob go over to Diane where she stood with her spatula. What's he like naked, she wondered. Under his pants, his ass appeared, well, not there. Not a good sign. The ass is the engine. OK, he's a weird cookie, anyway. Verona saw him do a wide bow and stick his hand out for a dance. Oh, Lord. That man, she thought. That would get on her nerves, that faggy crap. Wasn't sure if she liked him or not. He could annoy, that's for sure. That's OK. That's OK.

A vague, troubling sense of teenage-style disappointment circled her insides. She had hoped to see her old friend, C.R. Ash. At her shining moment. She liked him. There was a time she liked him a lot. He went off to school. So did she. That's that.

What's that? Two gaping holes in the buffet—out of pasta, out of roast beef!!—and she moved her butt fast to retrieve some more pasta from the back, but then, at this point, the president of the hospital, a certain tanned and sleek man named Mr. Tyler (Ty) Carter Lewis, got up with his similarly tanned and shellacked wife, she in a period gown from the plantation days, they got up to the band's loudspeaker and did the old *tink-tink-tink* on a glass, which caused the loud, raucous hub-a-bub of medical staff to halt to a whisper,

I'd just like to, if I could have your attention here, for a moment, people.

Friends, he began, it's been a typically difficult year, there have been births. He paused, looked around. There have been, unfortunately for all involved, situations where we did all we could, and it wasn't meant to be. We've done a lot of good work here. Ray Raylin, and his crew, I'd like to thank for the whole auditorium setup committee in September, all the audiovisual setups Mr. Raylin donated to the hospital, which was just *faaaaa*ntastic, and which made huge, *huge* inroads for our medical research team, let's hear it for Ray Raylin (*applause!*). And the girls in Ward D, who raised the money for the new isolettes, a big, big, round of applause (*applause!*). Especially, especially Maggie Hawkins who basically commandeered the whole thing, in dear memory of her beloved baby Jake (*a hush falls over the crowd*). We thank you, Maggie, from the bottom of our hearts and so do all the babies. I got to thank, although *begrudgingly*, *begrudgingly*, all the Peds doctors that whipped my b-u-t-t out on the greens at this August's Golfing for Kids benefit. Yes, I do. Because although they may lose their jobs (*laughter*)—ahem, Dr. Pendleton Compton, I'm talking to you, buddy, wherever you are!—for beating me at golf, they did raise almost a hundred thousand dollars, and in all seriousness, folks, that is something I'm very, very proud and honored about. I can't leave this place, in good conscience, without mentioning the gallant efforts of our own board of trustees president, Mr. Roger Billings, Rodge? Rodge, come on up here, buddy. Come on. People, this kind man has donated countless hours of time and dedication working with the county administrators and the zoning commission to enable us to purchase the back lot for expansion in the next five years for our new pediatric wing. It wasn't easy, folks. That land was incredibly hard to get, with all the historical clauses, et cetera. There was a lot of competition and we are just lucky that old Rodge here had years of experience in the zoning area, et cetera. We are in a huge, huge debt to you, Rodge, thank you (*applause!*). Which brings us to another—

(Lord! This is boring. Oh my goodness. That man is dull, thought Verona. She blanked out, shut her eyes. Ate a few more Tiny Tim Tartlets.)

—another bit of thanking I need to do here. Is Eleanor here? Eleanor? Eleanor Hunt, get over here now. Folks, this beautiful lady, whom many of you know (*applause!*), not only organized the ladies of God's Love Outreach Coalition to volunteer here on a daily basis, this woman, single-handedly, devised and ran our popular Blankets-for-Babies Premie Network (*applause!*). To date, I can tell you there aren't and never will be premies without handmade blankets of love in our hospital. A big hand, folks! (*applause*).

Folks, to my great pride we continue to be a pillar in the community of reliability. You can count on us. There have been *great* advances in the fields we pursue here, by our own doctors, which brings us hope. H-O-P-E, people. Hope. What is this season, this season (he faltered as he readjusted the index cards he read from), this season, but not the heralding of hope? Each premature child we care for is because of hope. And faith. And caring. Three things I am proud, deeply proud to say here at Ball's Bluff Babies Hospital, we continue. To inspire. And produce. In this fine land. Thank you and Merry Christmas. And, Happy Hanukkah. And Kwanzaa. (*He paused to the roar of applause.*) And I'd like to thank these wonderful ladies, Verona and Diane, please stand! For this amazing party! I'm having a ball!

Whoooooo! the people yelled. Whooooooo!! Verona got up and smiled in her great purple Marshalls gown with lace. Diane waved a spatula from the other end as she unearthed tartlets on the platters, the other players, Bob, George, they beamed, they all stood there as the crowd yelled and clapped.

Whooooooooo!

Yeaaaaaaaaaah!

diane, later

In the bathroom of the Ball's Bluff Babies Hospital, she was crying over the toilet bowl. Sounds of raucous jigging kept coming in waves through the swinging doors. She'd had three grogs now and she was pretty drunk. Not used to drinking, she felt nauseous. That Shrub Punch was deceptive, sweet yet dangerous. Todd, her baby, was gone and a Daddy. Someone said he was a Daddy. What does that mean? How could Todd, her child, be a Daddy, who barely knew how to make a sandwich, for Christ's sake, she watched him bumble with it, he lined up the bread pieces on the wrong sides so there was always the part overhanging without bread full of jelly which as he brought up to his mouth would drop on her tile floor every damn time, she'd pick it up with a paper towel and say, Todd, line up the bread, sweetie, and he would say OK. Gosh, Diane would say, it's a simple thing really, making a sandwich, must I be the only one who cleans this floor, over and over? Again and again? Jelly glob after jelly glob. And then, pizza. Right out of the oven, smack dab on the Corian, and chop goes the knife, right on the Corian. Then brings it to the den and smack dab, pizza on the carpet, then the crust left on the table. Every time. This, this, this is what has made me fail him? Trying to keep a clean house? Are you looking for a reason? Must there be reason? Maybe it's a fault of genes. Maybe something screwed up. Bob has a weird cousin. Maybe from him. Bob's not perfect either. Maybe he's, like I said before, he's testing us. That's a teenager's job, right? Oh, but you don't believe that. You're looking for a reason. Go ahead, check out my house. Rape my house, look through my drawers. Go, go, go, go.

No one's home. Help yourself.

todd + kirsten, 2

I.

Kirsten calls Todd on his cell phone. She says they could meet, as she drives round through the Battlefield Hills development in the snow,

It's snowing pretty hard, though. Where are you?

I'm helping my mom with that party.

What party.

You know. Hospital. Christmas thing.

Oh, that. Is it fun?

It's OK, he says. I'm Cratchit.

You're who.

Cratchit. Tiny Tim's dad. You know.

In the car, she lights a cigarette.

I don't remember you smoking.

I just started.

Why?

All the stress, I guess.

Todd can't help but look at her body, he longs for her, despite his dishevelment and situation, he feels completely wound and absorbed by her.

Did you want to go to Pizza Hut. Get a Coke or something.

Well, his mind speeding forward, somewhere quiet maybe. The freaks are there, you know, parking lot.

Oh. Danny and them.

Right. Ball's Bluff, out there.

She looks at him. *It's snowing.*

Yeah, but this is four-wheel.

I don't know. I.

I mean, you know, just for talking. It's quiet.

Well. Maybe

Kirsten, *oh fuck, he reaches forward trembling,* Oh, Kirsten. Baby.

Todd.

To his extreme embarrassment, he finds he is crying.

I'm sorry. I'm such a. Pussy.

Hey.

I am. I like you, Kirsten.

Yeah.

If we could go to the park, by the Bluff, and just. Just hang or.

There is where *he* is.

Where who. Is.

Where he. He has a name. They called him, Tuffy.

Tuffy?

Tuffy's buried there. The, the *baby.*

In the graveyard?

Yes. He's there.

You named my baby, Tuffy?

They named him.

He's there?

There's no stone yet.

I want to go there. I wanna see him.

That's not, that's.

There's snow, snow on his grave.

It's not a good *idea.*

2.

Kirsten doesn't say much to Todd on the way over. She points in the direction to go. When Todd tries to talk about feelings and stuff, Kirsten puts on the radio and doesn't answer. Todd hangs over the wheel forcing her car through the snow on a small, tiny winding road leading up to the graveyard in Ball's Bluff Cemetery.

It's up here. Maybe we can walk the rest.

Too much snow.

I told you.

Kirsten, use my jacket.

I'm OK.

You can't dig him up or anything.

Why in hell would I do that?

I don't know.

Come on.

I feel sick.

Was there a funeral.

No.

Did you say some words.

No.

Well, then I will.

I held him.

Was he cute.

Shit.

What?

You're making me feel bad, Todd. I've been dealing with this, and and you're.

Sorry.

Churning up stuff.

Sorry.

It wasn't meant to be, I think.

He was too small?

Yeah.

What color were, his *eyes*, Kirst.

It's here.
Here?
Here.
This spot. Why this spot.
Because it was available. My mother said it was a good spot.
She hates me, I bet.
She's pretty upset.
Oh.
What are you doing.
I want to put my hand, *my hand, my hand.*
Oh, don't cry!
Ohhh.
Todd. Come on. Come *on.*
Oh, fuck, oh fuck.
Don't lie in the snow, it's cold.
My baby.
Jesus.
Oh, oh, oh, oh.
There'll be more, Oh, Todd! Please!
I have a fucking *knife* in me. Can you get that?
Don't do this shit to me, Todd!
Oh, God, oh, God.
It's weird, I never knew. Knew I was pregnant. I thought you were supposed to *know* that stuff.

I'm OK now. I'm sorry.
Stop saying you're sorry all the time.
But I am.
For what.
I don't know.
Neither do I.
I need to say a few words. For him. Will you, too?
Todd.
Come on.

Let's just go.

I think he needs a funeral or speech or something. It's the least, you know, we could do,

OK.

OK.

What was his name. I think of him as Keith.

Keith?

I like that name. To me, he was Keith.

Why Keith?

Think of it, it's a very cool name. It's sort of seventies.

Why not Brad. Or. Or *Todd,* for that matter.

Keith, Keith, we are your parents.

Tuffy, actually was his name.

That, now *that,* is weird.

The nurses picked it. They always pick weird stuff, like Cutie or Speedy or stuff. Kind of not real names but names, still. Kind of like temporary names.

So, Tuffy.

Yeah.

Tuffy, I salute you—

What?

Just. Just *let* me, will you. I've thought about this for a while. I've been constructing this in my head for a while.

OK.

Tuffy, I salute you, little man. I'm sorry I couldn't have met you. I bet you were super. I bet you were a cool little dude and even though you had a short time here, you made your presence known. Tuffy, I'll eat a piece of pizza in your honor, buddy, because you couldn't, *didn't,* get to eat any of it and you would've liked it. Oh, fuck. I'm not sure if, oh, *poor little guy, oh*—

You don't have to go on—

I'm not finished, I, I, and I'll throw a football for you. There are lots, lots of things we could've done, but I'll catch you next time, OK, bud? I love you.

That was nice.

Aren't you going to say something?
Well.
Come on.
Tuffy, I love you. Good-bye.
Good-bye, little guy.
Let's go now. I'm really cold.
Yeah.
Do you have my cigarettes.
No. Why would *I* have your cigarettes.
I don't know.
They're in the car.
That's right. They're in the glove thing.

betty + pendleton, 3

Sweet son of a *bitch*. Lord excuse my language but this, this takes all, said Betty to herself as she lay in the cold snow.

Pendleton! Lord's sake, man! Wake up! she said as his behemoth load squashed her flat to the ground, her dress growing colder and wetter, her face smeared with freezing tears, Oh, good Lord. I don't know what's worse. Being found. Or not being found. The insufferable cold.

Pendleton. Dr. Compton? You might want, you're crushing my. Oh, Lord, is he even breathing? It appeared so. She stroked his forehead. She couldn't feel her backside. The dress was soaked and the man was squishing her down and the snow was piling on her face and he must weigh near three hundred pounds she reckons and she tips the scales at all of ninety-seven so how can she handle this. It's then the thought comes in her head, how it did she hasn't a clue but it does and the adrenaline resulting makes her head throb.

Perhaps I've left an electric kettle on. I didn't unplug it.

Quickly she sees the resulting occurrence:

There is a gingham curtain about an inch from the kettle. She got the electric one for fire safety because she hates to use the stove. The stove, in fact, is covered with decorative burner covers (country blue with painted herbal sprigs) and is, actually, unplugged in the back. It's a decorative element to her, mainly. Her cupboard is stocked with instant Cup-A-Soups and noodle deals and mashed potatoes in a cup. Boiling water is the mainstay of her evening meal preparation. The kettle is darkened toward the bottom from constant use. It was due for a replacement as she goes through about two a year, as the, as the, as the—and here is where the woman spills into the red-hot electrical circuitry of pure panic—as the cord was, was, frayed terribly, Oh, oh, OH, OH, my lords!

The cats! Fire!!!

The cats. The cats. The cats. The cats.

Pendleton, she says furiously in his ear, get up, damn you, Pendleton. My cats are burning, Pendleton.

The man is distinctly breathing, she thinks. She pulls out a hand, rubs her face. Her head falls back from fatigue, from exhaustion.

It is dear Dunny she sees who comes along the hall and sees the fire, according to Betty, and, scamp that he is, advances for further inspection, whereupon a gingham curtain which was orange and ferocious with fire fell on his calico back and caused him to run to the bedroom where sleepy Charlie slept in the cat box lined with down and the velvet spread she had made them, Dunny's back aflame and he screeches and rolls with Charlie which causes the down and the velvet to take off and then it is a giant inferno in that room, Mariah comes running and the flames reach out to her now the whole house is swept up and the cats are screaming and the house is being enveloped the cats the cats the cats the cats the cats.

Pendleton, wake up, Pendleton wake up, Pendleton wake up, she's managed to heft out of his shoulder, Pendleton, Pendleton, Pendleton, the cats, the cats, the cats, cats, cats—

FIRE.

The cats the cats the cats the cats the cats.

FIRE.

FIRE! FIRE! FIRE! FIRE! FIRE! FIRE! FIRE! FIRE!

Goddamn Dr. Compton get a grip here because this is is is is a serious thing, cats are burning, my house is *burning up*, Dr. Compton!

She rolls out of his side, the whole bit of him cold and wet and heavy and Betty is covered in wet, cold mud and her cats are burning up and her house and she let this man have his way with her in the, in the road, for Pete's sake.

The snow's died down and she can see the lights of the hospital. She can get help there. She lifts up her dress and tries to run, floundering aimlessly in the snow as she does so, a crumpled kitelike form, her ankle some kind of snapped twig, her voice warbled and small on the snowy wind,

God, someone help a woman here! God help me! My cats are burning! Jesus! Fire!

Pendleton lies in the snow. Betty looks down the road to the hospital, see its grand lighted form through the muffle of falling snowflakes.

Fire!

Fire, God somebody! God somebody down there help me!! A man here might be dead! Cats are burning and all hell is loose!! Oh, Mother, Papa, my cats, Pendleton, oh, for Lord's sake, Pendleton, help me, help me, man.

She's standing there screaming crying for *cats cats my cats!* when she sees a car's lights whirling down the road, fast, CATS!! CATS!! CATS BURNING! That car comes from nowhere, looming heavy and fog-lit, squalling mud to the sides and if that's not bad enough, if cats burning aren't bad enough, or Pendleton in some state, freezing near her feet as she rises, is all a mere frippery, the truck that's coming doesn't stop, the truck hits the tip of Pendleton's car, spins and backs up against hers in one perfect metallic moment of skidding ice and snow, one heaving cannonball of blindsiding machinery, countersunk in the white dunes of powder, gears jiving, halting, crushing, then, stopping.

Steam. Sssssssssss.

Sandy hush of snow.

c.r., finally

I.

Coming down the road, barreling fast down the icy road, Free Bird blast-
ing on the speakers, a calm overtook C.R., a happy feeling. A joyfulness
for no particular reason, maybe distinctly for the reason of no reason, it still
seemed a good time to be happy, a song could still serve that purpose, just a
song, and what a song it was, he could sing every word to this song, this one
he knew, unlike the Christmas carols of his youth, how about his favorite,
Fall, fall, on your knees, and laaaaaaa, something, Oh, Chr—i—ist, is born, or
something, Whatever. Or how about, *We three kings of orient are, tried to smoke*
a rubber cigar, no matter what he did, only that version would come up, so
that was useless. Another good one, *God rest ye merry gentlemen, let nothing*
ye dismay! Remember Christ our sa—a—vior was born on Christmas da—ay,
to, to, to, save lalalalalalalala, whatever, Satan's power, when we go astray—
ay—ay, OK, that was half-assed. Stick to Free Bird. Which he did.

He decides to be a careless person who is lazy, has no ambition, and is
basically pitiful. He's going to quit being a doctor and be shiftless. He will
drink all day. And watch Sally Jessy Raphael. Too much responsibility has
scrambled his brain and made him make foolish, strange choices. He needs
to be a fool, to look a fool. Obviously, he is one, an unpardonable one,
even his—

It was during this stream of thought that he sailed, lost control, and
careened into the side of Pendleton's station wagon and Betty's red Honda

Civic, where his head got banged and pulpish on the wheel, and he lay there with it pounding, with the sound of a hissing, dying engine in his ears. A Ford truck, before air bags, was made heavy and steely and he lay in that rubble. A headache of soured bourbon and crashed metal descended on him, and C.R. longed to sleep, drowsy, sheepy eyes at half-mast focused on the edge of snow on his window, and the song, strangely, still played on, and he didn't move, or even blink, it was good to stay still for a second, not think so much, wait to see if blood would pour or bones would gash out of his flesh like tent poles, or if he'd go unconscious, but he didn't think much of anything, for about five long uninterrupted minutes, C.R. Ash had not a thought, his mind was blissfully, soundfully still. This is death, he thought. So nice, so quiet. A feeling like the limbo as you lie in bed and are about to fall off, that sweet drift, such good pleasure, orgasmic in its kindness to your body, all thoughts gone. Opiatic sleep. Medevac peace. Brain stem soporific.

2.

Until.

Betty flies at and claws at the truck door like a rabid Norwich terrier, her eyes blurred, crazed holes through the wet glass, *Dr. Dr. Dr. Dr. Dr.—Ash!*

Heaven help us!! There's a fire! Cats are gone, all gone! Then, then, then *you*, a crash. The world is ending! We have no control! Pendleton, he's gone. Police! Doctor! Someone!

C.R. in the stun of his accident hears only *cats* then *crash*, he's thinking of a long ropy Siamese cat, for some reason, thrown against a wall, not a pleasant thought, a banker he dated had one of those cats and he liked it, liked all animals, how weird and stupid he didn't even have a dog now, a dog—

God sakes, Dr. Ash, Dr. Ash, you hurt?

Hunh, he managed to say, then she opened the door and the cold got up on his side and Betty was draped over him, yelling, Lord! Help! Are you all right?

Yeah, I think so. Betty.

Oh, Doctor! My cats are gone in a fire! Pendleton's here! He's out!

C.R. so much wants to sleep, to move Betty out of his way, to lie in the snow, or in the car, her screeching, metallic voice, and his head is definitely spinning now,

Hold on. Hold on here, Betty.

It's just the cats, oh, the cats.

What? He's found the bourbon rolling on the floor and swigs a tough gulp, what cats?

My babies! Burned up!

What—

I left a—

And Pendleton, what, where's he.

Over there! Over there!

Goodness shit, Betty. Pendleton! Pen! What's going *on* here.

He's out. He's unconscious or dead. Oh, Lord. This is a nightmare!

Let's get an ambulance. Jesus. Pendleton!

I can't-can't, Betty wails, My cats, help me—me.

Let me by, he says as he swings and falls out the car, pounding himself into the snow, The ground came up so fast.

He's there. He's there. My cats.

Screw your cats, pardon me, Betty, but let's help Pendleton, he says spitting snow out, feeling the iron alarm of blood in his mouth, there's a man in jeopardy here, Pendleton!

C.R. stumbles up and goes over, falls on him, Pendleton! Pendleton! He lifts up his heavy hand, shit if he doesn't have a pulse. Goddamn, *yes,* he does. *Barely.* Fuck, help me here, *hello!* Was he taking a leak?

Betty is silent, crying.

What were you all doing out here, anyway.

We were going to the party.

Well, turn your head, Betty, because his, I'm going to roll him over, and his privates—

It's true, all right! All right! I admit it.

Admit *what,* here help me turn him—

We did. We did. We shared *carnal* knowledge.

How's that, I'm sorry? With *Pendleton*? Betty. Ha! *Here?*

It's not a funny, nothing *funny* about it—

Have to say I never realized you two—

It was a, it was a weird, weird thing, I—

Out here, in the *snow?*

You can call me a harlot, go ahead.

Betty, come on—

I feel ashamed!

Hey, come on!

Pendleton, he just.

There's something nice about it, if you ask me. Thank God someone's happy—

Oh, God, let's CPR him, oh, Pendleton!

Betty, we have to warm him, get him over to the, the hospital.

How's your head?

Help me, please.

I got his legs.

Goddamn, if he don't weigh a *shit*load, pardon my French.

He sure could stand to lose—

OK, OK.

Pendleton!

I can't, whoa!

He swings to the left and Pendleton falls again.

Damn. He's too heavy. Betty, Betty, stay with him. Talk to him. Wake him. I'm going to run over and get them. OK?

Yes, OK, Pendleton, honey, come on.

I'll be back.

C.R.! Stop!

What, what, Betty? What is it?

My cats, oh, C.R. My cats!

Let's deal with *the man*, for God's sake—

My cats!

Back, I'll get back. Wake him. Wake him *up*, Betty.

3.

C.R. ran down the road, pushing through the snow. He could hear the fiddling of eighteenth-century jig music, he could see cars slipshod-parked in the lot, he could hear voices. *Help me, someone!* he yelled. His head was crushed around the eyebrows, like a tremulous heavy piston had gouged it, he held a cold hand there and it felt better, and then he fell, got up, almost slipped, *someone's dying out here, I need help,* his voice though sounded meager, without strength, like when you're dreaming, a strangled little peep it was, God, if he could just get inside where it was warm, meanwhile Betty crouched over Pendleton, she'd taken her jacket and wrapped it around his body and she laid her face on his and puffed warm air on his nose, his mouth, and she said, *Pendleton, honey, Pendleton, honey, please wake up, come on, it's Betty, sweetheart,* and she said this over and over, she pinched his fingers, his ears, *I want to hear you say my name, I'm here, honey,* Why, Betty realized sadly, poor Nancy, his wife, had no idea Pendleton was ill, lying colder and colder in a road, half naked, oh, the despair, the guilt she felt. Nancy, who rightfully owned this man, lay miles away from him in his possible last hour and only she, Betty, got this moment, and she felt honored, *Pendleton, I am right by you now, and I want you to wake up, mister, wake up good right now, do it, come on.*

Betty looked up in the sky which was the dull fluctuated color of smoke. Pendleton's hand still felt warm. In her mind, her cats were cindered shards in her house, her life in ruins. *Every time you think you're doing OK,* she thought, *it gets taken away all over again.* Meanwhile, her cats were lazy furballs on her down comforter, Dunny stretched and licked his face, Mariah slept on the pillow in a perfect orange ball. Every time I love something or someone, they have to go. I guess that's just me. She warmed Pendleton's face. I got you, though, Pendleton. I would say what we have may be, it may be some kind of *love,* Pendleton. Do you think so, Pendleton? Can I call it that, you think? On her tongue, a singed flavor grew.

C.R. was at the double doors of the hospital, where he passed two interns with their wives who stared, *hey, hey,* he started toward one of them, and they laughed, the intern didn't know the doctor, he backed off, Hey, help me, man, but the words came out crooked and odd, half frozen and bourbonized and pain-clodden, he was making no sense, *a man is dying, God sakes!* They left, laughter trailing behind them. He was in the halls, falling side to side, hands ricocheting off each wall, side to side, from each seascape-pictured wall to another, grasping the handrail, he got closer and closer to the party, to the double doors to the Fauquier Wing, people were milling out in the corridors, grog in hands, and he held his hands up, *can you help me*, more grotesquely distorted bleats and rasps flung in the direction of anyone around, now his hands were getting desperate, *God! Help! Me!*

A thoracic surgeon he barely knew, his face mealy and rum-waggled, said, Lord, is that Ash? Jesus, I think it is! and C.R. came up to him, *help me, will you!*

Evening, Doctor! Whoa, you having a good time? Nice *getup*, C.R.

Help me, God help me! But C.R. could hear the words, it was bumbled sewage, vowels pokered and functionless, he felt hot tears streaming down his face, *I need your help.*

Dang, Ash, you may wish to, to calm down, now. I think, I think you need to sit, Doctor. Get some coffee! And he went off and C.R. fell toward the double doors, toward the pulsating twist of fiddles spiraling into Victorian dance music, screeching merriment and a hurrah of voices, he fell through.

He saw a tumult of colors and spinning things, people, smells. Oceans of smells too strong for him to fathom, like animal pelts and exotic spice, and simple things, like roasted chicken and tonic water, and lime, lots of things smelled like lime, but the colors were hot-smoky and red, and whinnying voices delighting and cacophonic, feet pummeling the floor, hands arched and twisting, heads rocking, and the smiles gleamed by his head, fast like long white trails of streamers and he stood silent in the middle, in the middle, rocks of words bubbling from his mouth, *God, help me, Pendleton, help me for Pendleton,* but no one heard, not a one.

It occurred to him that he could be very damaged from the accident. It was hard to discern, he tried to use his reasoning powers but they seemed to float astray, he would have to see his eyes, but he couldn't see, he couldn't speak. An overwhelming need for sleep was coming over him, and if indeed he was cerebrally damaged, then maybe he was *dying*. And would that be a bad thing. He was already pretty much dead and joyless. He was standing in this party, bloodied, hurt, alone and no one was paying heed. This was no unusual situation. This was his *life*. But he did love his friend, Pendleton. He loved *him*, he knew. He couldn't let him die in the snow.

He started to fall, his knees gave no assistance anymore, when he felt some pressure on his arm, let's dance! It was Verona, she smiled at him, you look pretty shot, my C.R., but let's dance.

My Verona, he said, smiling to himself at that joke, but she didn't hear.

I remember your sleek, sweet body, I do, he said to her. Her head tilted slightly in confusion because he was speaking Latin for all she knew, but she smiled. She smiled at him. Someone cared.

And then she spun his waist about until he dropped his head on her shoulder, put all his weight on her, and whispered in her ear, in his most lucid way, he lassoed the words around his tongue and gave all the muscle he had to them, he said *my friend Pendleton is dying help me I can't I'm injured*. He felt useless, as if he'd read a line of Chinese he knew not the meaning of, and prepared to sink forward into whatever oblivion life could offer, but to his surprise she pulled back, What're you saying? You need help?

He nodded to the dizzy blur of Verona.

You talking bullshit to me or is something wrong?

Yes, *wrong*, he shook hard, jolting sparks of pain in his ears.

Where is your friend? What's *happening*? Is that *blood* on your face?

He pointed to the road.

Where you mean, honey? What are you trying to say?

I'm saying, but it was a baby whisper, my *friend, Pendleton*.

He grabbed her hand and carried her to the side, the song had stopped, the whirling colors had stopped, the people had all stopped, looked at C.R., the fake snow splaying forth from his coat and his legs, Show me where, honey, and he led her to the outside door, There, he pointed to the side road, there, and Verona started running, pulling him, and C.R. found strength again, he pulled her through the snow, all was blurry around him, he spoke incomprehensible gibberish, but there was *action* finally. His lungs burned as he ran and Verona said,

I don't know what we're *doing*. I don't know *what* is going on.

4.

They got to Pendleton. Betty had him up and he was bluish but coughing. C.R. fell beside him, My man, his voice still weak, my man, are you there, he could see a flash of eye in the night and he hoisted him up, I'm going to get you on over. You're going to live, my friend.

What *happened* here, said Verona. Jesus Christ Almighty.

My cats are burned and my house is *gone*, for one, wailed Betty, Oh, help me, ma'am.

Cats?

Burned up alive!

What are you talking about, hon. What's going on out here.

I am sure, I feel sure, the cord to my, my kettle probably started a fire. It could. It really *is* old. And then the place *will*, is burned up. And my cats, my precious babies, too. All gone.

I'm sure that's not the case. I'm sure they are just fine.

Oh, you don't know. I just feel it. I lost my, my family and now I lose my cats!

C.R. had Pendleton up on his shoulders, all hefty pounds of him on his back, and he said to Verona, You go on and take Betty. Take Betty. To her. To her. Cats. Get her cats.

And he walked down the road, dragging Pendleton's legs, the rest of him across his back.

His voice was coming back. Listen, my man. You got to get right here. Come on back to me, man. I don't know what happened here, but get your ass *back*.

Get your ass back. Shit, man. I can't believe I can carry your damn ass. You *big*, boy. You got to go *cut back*. Forgo the butter, dude. When you get better, you lose this shit. Then you beat my ass in racquetball, my friend. Remember we used to play. We friends, right? I known you my whole damn life, boy. Now you the only one left. Hear what I'm saying? Everyone else gone to the other side but you and it's not time yet. Pendleton, I need your sorry ass *here*.

Damn, C.R.'s voice gets fainter, I feel shitty, too, dude, Goddamn my head hurts, fucking goddamn, and I didn't find my baby. You know, that Miss Thing in candy-striping. I intend to find her and marry that girl. Time I settle down. Don't give me no shit about her age, either. You showing me that porno in the lounge, those girls all no more than seventeen, unh-hunh. Sir. You know it. You know it. Anyway, what decent woman going to want me, I ask you. You're no good. You got Nancy, my friend, why you want anything else I ask you, you got it all my friend, this is why don't leave us here, now, because it isn't proper. You do *not*, I repeat, *not*, get to die on me. You do not. You like ham, my friend. My family made a good ham. I ate that shit and just thought it was, whatever. Now nobody makes that stuff. And I like to die I want some so bad.

I bet you Nancy makes a ham like that. That's what you got to live for. She make a ham and you don't even have me over. None of you all do. You all get married and leave me in the lurch. You all form a little clique or something and I don't get in. You just jealous. All my women. Who gives a fuck. You can have them—

—*ut up*. *Ut up*, came from C.R.'s back.

You talking? That you, you son of a bitch?

Sh-ut up.

OK! Whooooooo-weee! That's the ticket! OK, here we are. We're getting closer. Damn, you hurt my back. I don't feel so hot. This is getting hard. I'm. Damn. I'm hurting now. I got to put you down. Got to get a break. Tell you what. Can you walk? Can you? OK, maybe not. Jesus. OK. I'll try the back way. Up along Ball's Bluff. Go the back way to the ER. Can anyone HEAR ME? Don't have a voice. This wind carries. Come on. The back way. Hold on. It all boils down to just living, you know. Forget all that crap. Ham, all that stuff. Just *live*, buddy.

5.

C.R. fell out to the back field of the hospital, he could barely hear the band playing old waltz music (*Daddy'd like that stuff. Hear that, Daddy?*) back where it was cooler and dark, where the night air stood stark and black, the snow picking up again, he traipsed to the field, passed Hermie and Synjyne who kissed on the ledge there, he walked by them without seeing them, and Hermie mumbled something, *did you see that, Syn? Dragging some bag, or is it, is it a guy? A big-ass guy. What the hell is that?* C.R. got halfway up the hill of the field of Ball's Bluff when he slowed, he held his head up, his back quivered and throbbed in pain, he longed to rest, foolish though he knew it was, he couldn't resist stopping for one brief moment to rest, just rest, put Pendleton down for a quick second and gain some momentum, considering this he started to get blurry-eyed and nauseous, Pendleton was coughing, he said quickly, Sorry, man, I got to. Got to rest.

He closed his eyes for a minute, but then, he fell forward and Pendleton fell, too, and the two men collapsed on each other and lay there, C.R. closed his eyes to stop the spinning. He and Pendleton lay there, in the field of Ball's Bluff.

Hermie and Synjyne watched.

Did you see that? Did they fall?

We should, we should go check it out. That's weird.

Quite bizarre, I'd say.

6.

And C.R. thought:

I cut my head, that's what. It's hurting bad. Must've done some real damage. I see the sky out here in the field, out here in the cold as I lie here and can I tell you how good I feel, can I tell you the sky is so lovely I never seen anything like it, there are purple and alabaster clouds moving fast as trains across the horizon and maybe it's due to brain cells losing out my head but the whole thing is fast and perfect, it don't matter to die alone as they say. I think it doesn't matter. Worse is to be in the midst of a staff of five hundred and they ignore you, you can ring your buzzer beep beep and they shuffle by and bring you a cart of happy metal fixers, electronic doodads they pump you and charge you and then pins and needles and syringes and expedience and drugs, gushing buckets of them pouring through your veins and those people, though, don't give you no beauty, no last moments like this one, head to the crisp cold sky. I could use some chowder of my father's if he'd like to spare some, I wonder, where are you now, you sheepskinned son of a bitch, allow me at least the smell of that ham you used to make, why I could just be happy to smell that sucker. As it looked on a silver platter, some Christmases, some parties back. And you, Mother. Show yourself. I am deeply sorry, so sorry I put you away like that in that awful place, your hands shaking and the horrible smell of stew always in the air. I want to see your face. I wish I knew if there was some purpose to all this, everything.

This is the sky Shrub saw, same thing. Maybe not snow in his eyes. But he must've looked up here for a minute when he died. Saw these stars I see, though barely.

Pendleton. God, my voice isn't worth shit.

Pendleton, man. There, he has to hear that.

C.R.

OK, OK, now I'm happy. You hang in there. I can't talk to you. No voice. But you hang in there. Don't go. I just need a second here. To rest.

Help my Pendleton, help that man now, please God. Get him some help. Don't let him die like a dog. What happened to the dude. Did he misfunction? Why is everyone *besides themselves*? Have I dismantled the universe, the cosmic forces? Do not, do not, let my man Pendleton die here next to me, I'm a damn physician, he has a pulse. I felt a pulse. He spoke to me. I wish to move my legs, to move and help that man. We were friends. At some point, I was friends with the man. I'm going to sleep.

7.

Did I sleep? Am I waking? Goddamn, my head, perhaps, but there are children nearby, adolescents, and feeling very much high on some level as I feel my brain get foggier I can hear them talking in that teenager way, all uplifted sentences with artificial questions, unh-hunh, yes it's a girl, blocking my nice sky looking down at me with her black-kohled eyes, an angel maybe, though isn't it something, she looks so dark and battered and she's talking soft things in my face, they're all in a frenzy about me, they are real, *shit*, kids stumbling on my sorry ass in a field and I wish to say something about the situation, leave me be, I attempt to whisper it, but only a cough and sputum comes and anyway I can go back to my sky and die now nothing feels more enjoyable in all my long years, though she's saying, Hold on, man, hold on, in my ear and it's her perfume now, like fruity oranges and tea, my heart starts thumping, I hear the children and I'm being carried by them in some scurried frenzy, I think of Kirsten, Do you know Kirsten, I want to ask, all I do is cough, I cough, and cough. I want to say, There's a girl I know named Kirsten, but I cough. Can you tell Kirsten, tell her I'd like to see her now, I'm ready for her. I'm ready for her in my house, tell her that, will you, damn a cough for language, I have lost my throat, my words.

Pendleton! How's my man?

Pendleton. Oh, got a word out. I can hear their voices. They're scrambling, yelling. Screaming *help, help*.

Pendleton.

I hear a weird sound. My eyes are open, flickering. I see Pendleton get up. Do I see Pendleton get up? Is it possible? Get off me, motherfucker, lying across my chest. Ow! Fuck! Not CPR, man! Shit, uuuhhh, stop it. I can't speak, ow.

Pendleton. I open my eyes. He's there, smiling, looking green and hair messed up.

You looking shitty Pendleton.

Everybody's laughing. They must've heard that. I must be able to speak.

I want to close my eyes. I do. What I think is, my mother. I feel that I'd like to see my mother. I have a sense I could see my mother. Or the sheepskinned one. For what reason, if not to just watch the news with them, eat a smoked almond, drink a beer. I'd like to have nothing heavy, just an uneventful hour or so. Why didn't she visit me today. That I don't understand. I have the feeling I can die or not. I can sleep or not. What's worth it. But I'm tired. I'm really tired. I should ask Pendleton what he thinks. I don't like to do this without a decision involved. I don't want to just spin out. Don't take me to the hospital, I want to say. If I'm dying, let me right here. Let me right here. In this snow. In this field. Like Shrub. My ancestral duty.

Ohhhhhhh, whuh, UHH.

Damn you, Pendleton. I don't have a choice, it seems. I open my eyes to that fucker pushing my heart again. And the boy, too. She, that girl, she's whispering, *don't let go don't let go*.

Why not. Give me one good reason. Who even cares. I tend to take the easy way out.

What gives them the right here to this cold lone field late at night, to my little spot of despair, what brings them to disturb my night, my only night, girl in my face is holding my cheeks with warm hands, crying for me, I must say, I must say, it is pleasant to have her touch me, I do believe, I do believe I'm falling in love, not saying that's much for me, my shallow heart flitting like a brain-addled bird, but there is hope when I feel it, a grandiose hope that all will fit into place at last, that supreme understanding will reign between us, I know I'm a stupid romantic, I try to hide it, I try to kill it, I don't want to be this way, God knows I've tried to stay with a woman because she was good or decent or smart or right for me, *you don't know what's right for you*, Muriel said always, but I tried, Muriel! I tried and tried. I gave them this and that of me all I could but if it isn't right, it isn't right. Don't think every one of them wasn't my last hope, I wasn't on some hunt, I'd have been happy to get the right one, God only knows I'd have been. Does anyone know where Kirsten is? I'd like to tell her some stuff, get it off my chest. You, young lady, of the smoldering dark eyes, holding my face, it's amazing how close I feel to you and I don't know you. How I love you. How I do love you all.

What do you think, Pendleton? I admire you. Lucky bastard.
What you think, gorgeous girl, smoky-eyed thing?

Kirsten, my girl?

You, you boy pushing on my chest, your voice all affected, give me your two bits.

Someone tell me something.

8.

Imagine yourself, a mere inexperienced captain, a rookie, a fledgling leading man across this foggy quagmire, your first time out in battle, you're scared, trembling across this field—

Euphrates King. I'll be goddamned.

Imagine, young sir, that mist is rolling in.

Where's that, where's that, hardtack shit.

I think I have some spare. Made it yesterday.

You're a docent.

Yessir, reporting to duty.

Don't trip on the vines.

Ha! Like I said, you're leading your men. Into inevitable disaster. Keep in mind you're no more than seventeen. For such responsibility. Nod your head, I like to hear the rattling sound.

I've been wounded, Euphrates.

Yes. I see that.

Can you, help me out here?

It depends. I surely will try to the utmost of my capability. Like I said, you're inching along the cowpath. You see the cedars—

And you think they're, enemy, enemy camps. Why am I on the north side, though.

I'm a docent. And I specialize in sympathy, want you to understand as much as possible.

No man can own another, am I right, son? This is what we're fighting for, after all—uh! Sound of the loon.

Oo-hhoo-oo.

Good work, son. Every detail counts.

Am I dying?

This land here is the saddest land in Loudoun County. A phantom is said to patrol here. When your men turn around, you're surrounded by Confederates, see this was a bayonet war, not so much bullets. They're coming at you with swords on their guns and you, you haven't even seen the world. You haven't even loved a woman. You haven't even had a child. You barely started shaving. All you the same. Fuzz-faced boys against each other. Brothers on the different sides. They had a twelve year old on the field, my friend.

I'm, I'm not sure about this.

Melville wrote a poem about Ball's Bluff, I remember a section, it goes something like:

> By nights I mused, of easeful sleep bereft,
> On those brave boys (Ah War! thy theft);
> Some marching feet
> Found pause at last by cliffs Potomac cleft;
> Wakeful I mused, while in the street
> Far footfalls died away till none were left.

Ah, none were left! What I say is, imagine because of your inability to see the encampment, seven hundred of your men stampede and die in the cold Potomac River! It's so sad! Oh, I can't stand it. I hear the screams. I hear them daily.

Why you use that word *docent*. Why not just *guide*?

The men in the river didn't have to drown. Some insisted on holding on to their swords. Others, the heavy money they wouldn't let go pulled them down.

Euphrates King. Hunh. Brings me back. I like to have you meet the others here. All around me. Introduce yourself. You'll remember Pendleton. He doing OK? Is he OK?

Has a minnie ball taken him out? Is he crippled by rheumatism? Gangrenous nether regions?

What? No, *no*. Damn. You out there, Euphrates?

I see the gentleman in question.

And he seems all right.

He seems injured, but hanging on. Dispatches have been called.

And the others.

Mere children. A boy. A girl!

A pretty girl, ain't she.

She is dark and luminous. Blessed are the women that help our plight.

She is kind, too. She held my face.

Now we proceed in our battle.

I don't want any war stuff.

Imagine the boys now.

Euphrates, help me up. I want to get in, go on now. I need to get out of here.

You're not well. I offer you brandy, here.

Euphrates, help me up.

I've got your arm. Now heave-ho. Heave-ho. Yessir. Try.

If you knew, how I tried and tried, Euphrates, all along, before, in the days leading to this sky moment, I tried my best, with what little abilities of the heart I had, though, I'll tell you, those abilities felt, *tremendous and grand.*

I'm sure. I'm sure. The river is cold here.

I think being in love feels like all the power of the universe, all the juice of the world poured in you.

Adjutants were called forth.

Have you been, *you know?*

I find it hard to leave the battles. I don't know anyone.

Harrison's Island is across the Potomac, lone and wild. Gamesmen hunt there now. It belongs to an elite hunting club. We sold that land. We owned it once. When we did, my uncle showed it to Rudolf Nureyev. He took him across on a canoe and the Russian stood in a *fur coat*—

—Oh! *Prepare!*

Ohhhh, God! Uhh! Tell them, sto—uhh—stop the CPR, tell that child lay off my chest—

I can't, the minnies are flying.

These aren't gunshot, man, these are people pounding my chest. Goddamn hell, I am dying. Stop me from dying, Euphrates. I do *not* want to die. Get them off.

No way to do that. Think of any tragedy you've witnessed anywhere, the people who've survived. Their faces. Think of that. Think of what they say, despite all clichés of speech, because it makes no difference, it's always the same—why am I so lucky?

Am I lucky?

Am *I* lucky? I must relive it again and again, and again. Again, a boy from Mass lays at my feet. Again, the Magnolia dispatch lies severed and red in a heap. Again, I see a molten lava of men in the creek screaming, again and again.

I have killed. A child.

I've also. A bunch of children. These young boys.

Who are you, *Euphrates King*?

Young man, gather your senses. You spend your days in a clinical stratosphere bemoaning the lack of real life you see. Isn't that your thought pattern? That somehow you miss all the mud, the texture of life in that ethanol environment?

Well, something to that—

And that all your loves were shadows?

Unreal.

No substance?

Something just not there.

Didn't you seek to be a reenactor, like myself?

I thought I'd have fun—

Re-creating battle?

Something to that effect—

Look at you now, my son! Behold your clothes. Behold your setting! Two men dying in a battleground, on the cold damp field.

Is Pendleton dying? Am I? Let me up, man.

Colonel Pendleton has been wounded. He hovers and dispatches are coming. A young lietenant works on you, and Colonel Pendleton whispers directions, how to pound his hand across your chest—

CPR.

Something like that, they are yelling, there is much emotion.

Is Pendleton OK?

A young nurse, a battle nurse, bathes his forehead, a dark-eyed girl ministers to him, he is breathing, yet even now, one can hear the camp music of the enemy's ententment—

That's the party, damnit.

There may be hundreds of them!

Pendleton!

Save your strength, young man. Your heart is weak.

Pendleton, don't go on me. My friend. He's my oldest friend. Pendleton's the only damn thing left I have. God, my *old friend.*

Brothers lie with brothers out here, my friend, remember: *That thou so many princes at a shot, so bloodily hast struck?*

You on that *Hamlet* again.

This quarry cries on havoc. O proud death.

This is all a travesty. There is nothing *proud* about any of this. My life is in tatters. This is a moment of reckoning. Don't bother with me. Just get Pendleton, OK. He's got Nancy, children. Are those damn EMRs here yet.

I see the surgeons coming up the field. Brave people.

Get them to Pendleton. His son Scott. He's over at the university. Eighteen years.

Can't imagine what the enemy plans now. I hear their whooping and carrying on. Feasting on our misery. Perhaps this is their plan. Trick us with noise, come round the side. Be wary! Be cautious. Suspicion reigns high! Our reconnaissance rewards us with death! I shall report on my findings! Colonel! I have seen the enemy encampment glowing in the night air! I have heard their merriment! I know their location!

Colonel, prepare our men for attack!

Euphrates King, he left in the night, ran toward the woods, toward the Potomac River.

C.R. Ash watched Euphrates fade from the corner of his eye through the dark tumble of whitened blue darkness. How a man could run that *fast*, he thought. There was a brief feeling where he felt an uncertain floating sensation, and another moment where so many hands on him felt warm, all of a sudden, as if he could feel the blood coursing in everyone's body through their hands, all kind and alive and rosy on his own skin, if he did see his father right now, trudging up through the snow in his sheepskin, talking of his chowder, he would tell him off. You don't belong here, he'd say. There's no reason for you to be here. Mother knew that. She has nothing to explain, nothing to bitch about. I know what's going on. At this moment.

C.R. lay back and felt hands grow still on his chest, above him a leukocyte white sky, chunks of ragged snow etched in gray streaming down on his face, the specter of nocturnal panic around him, heard the children helping him, their voices cutting through the cold metal air, *right here! right here! right here!* Saw his friend, Pendleton, above him, the dark thatch of hair and his oiled eyes blocking the sky view. Where you want to go, C.R., he says. *I don't want to go nowhere man. Nowhere. Nowhere.* Sitting up, he left the cold ground.

acknowledgments

I'd like to thank the following people: Ann and John McCarty, Mark and Virginia Power, Nancy O'Connor, John Power, Tracey Donnelly, Nono Fisher, Russell Power-Kronick, Ivan Power-Kronick, Sunny Power-Kronick, Lois and Mark Backon, Murray and Sylvia Kronick, Harvey and Ellen Ussery, Wendy Sherman, Elisabeth Schmitz, Morgan Entrekin, and everyone at Grove/Atlantic, Inc., for their fantastic enthusiasm and kindness.

A special thank you to Dr. Karl Schulze of The Columbia Presbyterian Babies Hospital of New York, who not only helped my firstborn child survive and thrive, but also answered my medical inquiries during the writing of this book.

I'd also like to say thank you to my community here in Virginia for interest and support in my writing. I appreciate it tremendously.

Nani Power